MURDER BY GHOSTLIGHT

MURDER BY GHOSTLIGHT

CHARLES DICKENS & SUPERINTENDENT JONES INVESTIGATE

J.C. BRIGGS

The
Mystery
Press

PRAISE FOR

THE MURDER OF PATIENCE BROOKE:
CHARLES DICKENS & SUPERINTENDENT JONES INVESTIGATE

'This is a well-written and engaging novel …
The pages keep turning, and the evocation
of foggy Victorian London is excellent'

The Historical Novel Society

'[An] aspect of this novel that adds to its enjoyability
is the fact that it feels very much like a traditional
gaslight mystery, with footsteps in the fog, an unseen
person with sinister voice singing a well-known
tune … Put all these elements together and it
creates just the right amount of suspense'

★★★★★ *Crime Fiction Lover*

'From the first few pages you are captured by
this fast paced, descriptively brilliant yarn, which
sweeps its reader away into the tangible world of
dark, damp, foul-smelling Victorian London'

★★★★★ Dickens the Sleuth, Amazon

PRAISE FOR

DEATH AT HUNGERFORD STAIRS:
CHARLES DICKENS & SUPERINTENDENT JONES INVESTIGATE

'The dark side of Victorian London is
effectively portrayed in a chilling tale of child
murder, deceit and madness. Grab a cup
of coffee, put your feet up and enjoy'

The Historical Novel Society

'Briggs's real triumph is the creation of secondary
characters who could have come straight out of Oliver
Twist and whose fates will tug at readers' heartstrings'

Publisher's Weekly

'This is a cleverly crafted story with magnificent
period detail to flesh out the circumstances in large
and small ways. All the characters whether major
or minor ring true in this Dickens London'

Jennifer Palmer, promoting Crime Fiction

For Tom

First published 2016

The Mystery Press is an imprint of The History Press
The Mill, Brimscombe Port
Stroud, Gloucestershire, GL5 2QG
www.thehistorypress.co.uk

British Library Cataloguing in Publication Data.
A catalogue record for this book is available from the British Library.

ISBN 978 0 7509 6980 2

Typesetting and origination by The History Press

CONTENTS

PART I

MANCHESTER

'It was a town of red brick, or of brick that would have been red if the smoke and ashes had allowed it; but as matters stood it was a town of unnatural red and black like the painted face of a savage. It was a town of machinery and tall chimneys, out of which interminable serpents of smoke trailed themselves forever and ever, and never got uncoiled. It had a black canal in it, and a river that ran purple with ill-smelling dye, and vast piles of building full of windows where there was a rattling and a trembling all day long ...'

Charles Dickens, Hard Times

PROLOGUE

1850

The actor on stage seemed to be asleep, one long white
hand hanging from the arm of the velvet chair, and the
white of his shirt showing momentarily in the flickering
lamplight. His head was on his chest and he was quite still.

The theatre was quiet now, the stage illuminated only
weakly by the ghostlight left on for safety, and by the oil
lamp burning down. Someone had carelessly left it on one
of the side tables on the set. There were only shadows in the
wings, and silence.

The man making his way up the centre aisle was surprised
to see someone on stage; he had thought they were all gone.
He had only come back to check that all was in place for
tomorrow night's performance. Why was there someone on
stage? He went closer. Surely it was Bell – he seemed to
be asleep in the chair in which he usually sat when the
play was in progress, and he was dressed as Bell would be.
But Bell had left the stage after the curtain call, and anyway,
why was the curtain raised? It looked as though the play
were about to begin, as if the actor would wake and speak
his lines when the footlights came on. But it would not be

a comedy, thought the man. Somehow, the sleeping figure suggested that a tragedy would unfold. This lonely man would speak of some terrible sorrow or grief. The play he had been in that night was not the play in which he was the central character now.

The man stared. Should he shout out? Or would that startle Bell from his deep sleep so that he would be afraid, embarrassed, confused? No, he would climb on to the stage and wake him. He did so and went over to pick up the oil lamp which he shone on to the recumbent figure. Then he saw the blood on the white shirt. He looked at the dark, curling hair and the long, corpse-white hand. He shuddered at the sight of it. Bell was dead. He had been shot and the man saw now the black pistol lying on the stage as if that long, white hand had dropped it there. Suicide? Or —

A noise. Someone was in the auditorium. The man picked up the gun and raised the lamp so that whoever was out there should see that he was armed. He looked out into the darkened space beyond. He stood still, his eyes straining into the darkness. Someone was there. He could sense him. Somewhere at the back, out of sight, someone was watching the scene on stage, the scene that he had written and directed, watching the actors whom he had cast in their terrible roles – murderer and victim.

Then came the sound of someone clapping in the auditorium, the sound of mocking applause from someone who jeered at the actors. The living man on the stage pulled the trigger. A shot rang out. He had an impression of movement. Then he knew that the other was gone.

1

ACCUSED

Inspector Zaccheus Hardacre of the Manchester Police Force was not what might be called a humorous man. He had, however, a grim sense of irony forged in his youth by the spectacle of his father in the pulpit delivering the homily which enjoined his congregation to *suffer the little children to come unto me*, and then delivering a blow or two to his wife and any child who happened to be in his way on the Sunday afternoon in the chilly, damp parlour of the vicarage Inspector Hardacre had once called home. So, it was irony rather than amusement which brought a faint smile to his lips as he contemplated the man sitting opposite him in the police office in the Town Hall in King Street, Manchester.

A famous man, true, but famous men were composed of passions just as ordinary men – they knew jealousy, desired revenge, relished power, loved and hated, could drop poison in the glass, place their hands round the slender neck and squeeze. Could point the gun. And the suspect had been found with the murder weapon in his hand. A shot had been heard a short time before the police constable had entered the crime scene and the constable had smelt the sulphurous odour of a gun recently fired. The suspect had protested his innocence, but then suspects usually did. It was not often that a suspect immediately admitted his guilt – or hers, thought Hardacre, thinking of Betty Eccles, hanged for the murder of five of her children, protesting her innocence all the way to the gallows outside Kirkdale – nasty business that – five kiddies poisoned. Two years ago, William Adams had admitted his guilt after he had murdered Diana Thomas – but then he had shot her in front of a policeman. Handy that. The witness in this present case had called up a beat constable who had verified the fact that the accused was holding the gun in his hand. Well, he thought, let's hear the story. Facts were what he wanted, hard facts. And he said so to the suspect who remembered his words later; as a matter of fact in 1854, the year in which *Hard Times* was published.

'Now, what I want is facts,' the Inspector said. 'You'd best tell me how you came to be holding that gun over a corpse.' His voice was not unpleasant, soft with a northern accent. The tone was reasonable, as if the Inspector were quite ready to believe the chief suspect's version of events. There was even a hint of humour, a kind of rueful irony. But the eyes were wary, a little glint in them like chips of hard quartz. Appropriate name, Hardacre, the suspect thought as he looked at the face of the policeman. The faint smile was there again. He wondered what it meant; the Inspector looked formidable, a compact, strong-looking man with intense blue eyes and a face which might have been hewn from granite; not the polished stone of the tombs in Kensal Green Cemetery, but more like the rough grey rock of the moorlands above the city.

'Stick to the facts, sir, and my constable here will take it all down, and then we'll see, shall we?'

We shall, thought the other man, though I doubt whether we shall agree. What a fool he had been to fire that gun. But it had been frightening – that sense of someone watching, and that applause. Someone out there enjoying that little drama on the stage. But who? And Bell dead. How came he dead? Not by my hand, but it looks bad. And he had not liked him. That will come out. And the rest. And the play cancelled because one of the actors was dead and another in custody, accused of murder. Thank God he had had the opportunity to send a message to Sam. Sam would not believe it − surely he would not.

The young constable, who had been staring at the accused with open-mouthed fascination, heard the Inspector's words and came forward with his notebook in which he would take down in shorthand the prisoner's statement − not that his skills were as fluent as those of the man in the velvet coat who had learned shorthand in about three months − but then he was an extraordinary man.

'Well,' said the Inspector. 'Let's get on with it. Tell us what happened.'

And Charles Dickens told him.

The evening's performance was over. It had been a good house − plenty of laughter and applause. Mrs Gaskell had been there and Harrison Ainsworth, and Superintendent Sam Jones and his wife, Elizabeth, on a visit to cousins in Manchester. The Superintendent was an officer from Bow Street Station in London. Thank the Lord for that mercy, thought Dickens. He and the Superintendent were old friends, and Dickens had been of assistance to him in two previous murder cases. Now a third − the difference being that Dickens was chief suspect. Not a comfortable sensation.

The play was *Money* by Edward Bulwer-Lytton. They were to play for three nights at Manchester's Queen's Theatre in Spring Gardens to raise funds for Dickens's project, a scheme for a mutual insurance fund for writers and artists. Dickens had played Sir John Vesey, and the dead man, Clement Bell, had played Alfred Evelyn, the romantic lead.

After the performance Dickens had gone with the other members of the cast to dine at the Concert Tavern, but had then gone back to the theatre – something had bothered him. He was a perfectionist. Everything must be in its right place – when he travelled, he always rearranged the furniture to suit his habit, and that night on stage he had been sure that something was out of place on the set so he could not relax until he had satisfied himself that the stage was as he had directed. He had gone round to the front of the theatre, intending to view the stage from the auditorium. He had stood on the steps for a few moments thinking about the play and the cast. It had gone well, but there was a tension he could not quite fathom. It was something to do with Clement Bell.

Clement Bell had replaced Dudley Costello, a journalist who had acted with Dickens's amateur players when they had come to Manchester in 1847. Dickens had asked him again, but Costello had written to Dickens apologising for his inability to take part, and recommending a young journalist he knew who would be happy to take the role of Alfred Evelyn. Costello had written that Clement Bell was an accomplished actor, a gentleman, and a man for whose easy good temper he could vouch. Dickens had accepted the substitute. Clement Bell had the dark good looks that would make him just right for the melancholy, serious Alfred Evelyn; he was tall with brown eyes and curling hair. Yet Dickens had not really liked him – Bell was not ill-tempered, but there was an arrogance about him, and a carelessness about the feelings of others which repelled the other members of the cast who were all well known to each other and friends. Bell was essentially a loner, a man who kept his distance and, moreover, he had taken private lodgings in Manchester rather than with the cast. It was odd, Dickens had thought, given that Costello had recommended his easy manner and affability. Still, there had been no choice if the play was to go on. Dickens hated to give up on a project, especially one which would bring benefit to other writers and artists. He would be glad, he had thought, when it was all over and he would not need to see Clement Bell again.

Dickens told the Inspector how he had gone into the auditorium so that he could see the stage from the audience. The stage was lit by the ghost lamp, a light left burning for safety so that there was a kind of flickering darkness which lent something eerie to the scene. He had noted that there was an oil lamp, too, though why it was there he did not know. He told him how he had realised that Bell was dead, and how he had heard someone in the auditorium. He related how he had heard the mocking clapping and had fired. And then nothing – until the watchman had come with the police constable, and they had found him with the murder weapon in his hand. The watchman, Tom, he was called, had tried to say something, but the constable was only interested in arresting the man who held the gun.

'And this person you – sensed? You didn't actually see anyone.' The Inspector stressed the word 'sensed' and in his tone Dickens heard the scepticism.

'No, I did not, but I heard a noise and I could feel him there watching. It was as if he were watching a play – then he applauded. It must have been the murderer for I swear to you, Inspector, I did not kill him.'

'You didn't hear the first shot when you went into the theatre?'

'No, Inspector, it must have happened while I was in the Concert Tavern.'

'How long were you at the Tavern?'

'I don't know – a few minutes.'

'Did anyone see you leave?'

'Again, I do not know. Someone might have noticed, but the rest were going into the dining room.'

'You didn't go back to the theatre to see Mr Bell for some reason?'

'No, Inspector, as I told you, something wasn't in quite the right place on stage – a piece of furniture. It made the moves awkward. I just wanted to check.'

'Mmm.' It was hard to tell what the Inspector was thinking. His face gave nothing away – neither belief nor disbelief. Inscrutable, thought Dickens, determined to hold that level blue gaze.

The Inspector went on, 'And why did you fire the gun? A foolish thing to do – if there had been someone there then it's not much help, is it? That shot sent him scarpering.'

'I don't know why I fired it – I suppose to warn him not to come near me. My God, Inspector, I was frightened – Bell dead and someone skulking in the shadows and then that clapping. I suppose I thought he might come for me.'

'Hmm. But, you must admit, Mr Dickens, that until I've some evidence that there was another person there, and until I find the bullet you shot into the auditorium, your story is a bit, shall we say, thin?'

'But why should I kill Bell? I hardly knew him. Why would I put the play in jeopardy? I've lost one of my main characters, and I will have to cancel the last night's performance.'

'Did you like him?' A sudden and penetrating question. The intense blue eyes stared.

Dickens paused before answering. He would have to admit that he did not. No one did, and when the Inspector asked the rest of the cast they would tell him. But no one in the cast would have murdered him simply because he was arrogant and rather cold. And I would not have killed him because I … no, don't think of her. She could not have. Just answer the question. He was aware of something in the Inspector's penetrating gaze, something icy. He was taking too long to answer a simple question.

'I did not – he was rather a good actor, I thought, but none of us warmed to him – a cold man, arrogant we thought, too sure of himself. Odd, really.'

'Why?'

'Bell had been recommended by my friend Dudley Costello who assured me of his affable temperament – he was sure I would like him. Strange that Costello liked him so much.'

'Did he have any acquaintance in Manchester? Did he talk of anyone?'

This was hopeful. Inspector Hardacre was considering an alternative to Charles Dickens as the murderer. A pity Dickens could not help him.

'No, I am afraid I can tell you nothing of him except that he had taken private lodgings – I have the address written down, but I don't think any of the cast visited him there.'

'I shall ask, you can be sure. But while I am pursuing my enquiries, I'll have to keep you here – at least for tonight. I must still regard you as the chief suspect. Constable Kettle'll show you to the cells. Unless you have anything else to tell me?'

He knows, Dickens thought. I ought to tell him all. But I cannot. I cannot put her in danger.

'No, Inspector, there is nothing more.' Too late now. He had committed himself to the lie.

The Inspector stood. Constable Kettle escorted the prisoner to his cell.

The cell, a white-tiled room about eight feet square, looked grim; there was a roughly made cot with a raised wooden shape at the top for a pillow, a coarse woollen blanket and, in the corner a grimy looking metal bin with a lid. Dickens hesitated on the threshold, unwilling to enter and shuddering at the thought of the closing of the heavy wooden door. Might he come out only for the trial? That is if Inspector Hardacre could find no spent bullet, nor the man who had clapped somewhere in the dark auditorium. Surely Sam will have received his note – he must come.

He looked at Constable Kettle's unremarkable face; the young man was gazing at him anxiously. Dickens passed into the cell and sat down on the bed.

'Some water, sir?' asked Kettle. He knew who the accused man was: Charles Dickens. By 'eck, wait till 'e told mam. That story she loved – the one about Christmas. You couldn't believe the man 'oo wrote that could 'ave done a murder. That you couldn't – them kids, Ignorance and Want, they was called. Kettle remembered that – 'e'd seen a lot o' that where 'e come from. Mam wanted 'im to get on – no ignorance and want 'ere, my lad. At seventeen shillin's the week, the police is a good job.

An', he thought, yor could get twenty-five bob if yor was promoted – an' 'e would be. No, mam'd not believe it, neither would 'er friends, except, he thought with sudden concern for the man, I shalln't tell anyone. They'll find out soon enough if 'e is guilty but 'e int. I'm that sure – and he was surprised to find he was, not that Inspector Hardacre would want his opinion, but a man 'ad a right to think 'is own thoughts – they couldn't tell 'im what to think – even for twenty-five shillin's.

'No – er, thank you, constable. I want nothing – except to get out of here.'

'Sorry, sir, I'll 'ave to close the door.'

'I see that you must.' He bowed his head.

Kettle felt for him and resolved to keep watch through the night. Somehow the man had become his responsibility. Strange how small he was. He thought 'e'd be bigger, like Mr Pickwick, all smiles, and plump with it.

Constable Kettle withdrew; the heavy door closed with what Dickens felt to be a sense of finality, leaving him in the dark. He sat until his eyes became accustomed to the darkness, and he could make out the faint whiteness of the walls and that terrible metal bin in the corner. There was the smell of sweat and urine, the smell of hopelessness. He thought of those who had been here before him, some guilty, no doubt, and some innocent as he was. But they, the innocent, had been found guilty and had been led, pro-testing, to the gallows, to hang there, the object of the jeers of the bellowing crowd.

He would not sleep. He would not lie down here. Dickens had a superstitious habit of turning any bed he slept in to a north-south direction. Well, he reflected, he could hardly start shifting this bed. He could imagine the Inspector's sceptical face if he were to find his prisoner trying to move the bed – and in any case he had no idea which was north and which was south. He would have to wait in the dark. Waiting was agony; he could not bear to be in suspense. He must be up and doing.

The horror of that cold darkness brought fears. What if he were brought to trial? What if he were confined here, or in some other cell to wait for the truth to be found? The utter solitude by day and night; the many hours of darkness; the mind forever brooding on melancholy themes, and having no relief. It was insupportable. He thought of those early childhood days. He was familiar enough with prison – he remembered only too well his father's incarceration in the debtors' prison, the Marshalsea, with its forbidding wall, the spikes, the barred windows. He had not forgotten the mean, close streets, the festering poverty, the sheer misery of it all. His father's words had broken his heart. John Dickens had declared that the sun was set upon him forever. Would it be the same for him? His father's debts had been paid from the legacy of his mother, old Mrs Dickens, but was this to be his inheritance? His father once in the debtors' prison, his maternal grandfather an absconded embezzler – tainted blood, he thought. I have tried to escape it, and here I am, sliding down into the abyss.

He fell through the dream-dark into a place where there were iron manacles on his hands; his feet were fettered and he could feel the coarse cloth of the canvas suit he was wearing. The smell was overpowering, the stink of an unwashed body – oh, God, it was his own. He saw his hands and naked feet, filthy, ingrained with grime. He hated to be dirty. The walls dripped with wet and they were close, too close. It was a tomb and yet, strangely, it was large enough for the shadows that were with him. There was a man weeping and saying something indistinct about the sun. There was a boy in a paper hat, a boy with blackened nails who told him he would never get out; there was a boy in shabby clothes whose hands were black, too, with something sticky, and who was rubbing those hands over and over, trying to rid himself of the stains; a woman with fair hair and blue eyes, holding a baby in her arms, who was weeping, bidding him farewell, and a boy in an Eton collar who wept, too, as he went away with the woman, waving his white hand. And there was a white hand emerging from a dark sleeve, and blood on a white shirt, and a beautiful woman with a gun pointing at him. And there was an explosion of light and sound.

Dickens woke with a start in the white-tiled cell. The shadows fled and he was alone again. His face was wet. He was possessed by such a sense of loss that he could scarcely breathe. Catherine in the dream with the baby, Henry, in her arms, and the boy in the collar, Charley, his eldest boy whom he loved, all bidding him farewell, even the boy in the paper hat whom Dickens knew to be Bob Fagin with whom he had toiled in the blacking factory. How Dickens hated goodbyes. Charley weeping – Dickens could have wept then. Was he to lose them all? But he would not weep – he must master himself. For all he knew, Inspector Hardacre might be watching. He could imagine that glittering eye at the peephole, peering at a man weeping and knowing him guilty.

He stood up, shaking off the dream. A line from *King Lear* came to mind: *I'll not weep though my heart break into a hundred thousand flaws.* He paced up and down the cell. The woman in the dream – she was beautiful, but he could not say he recognised her. Yet he knew who she was just as he had known that the fair woman was Catherine even if, in the dream, they appeared as strangers – curious that. But dreams tell us what might be and, he believed, uncover our deepest fears. That other boy – the one with the black hands – he was Dickens's other self, the boy who at twelve years old had laboured in the blacking factory at Hungerford Stairs, and who had thought he was lost forever. And the woman pointing the gun – she was Oriel Greenwood, and she revealed his fear that it was she who had killed Clement Bell.

But it was not Oriel who had been in the darkened theatre auditorium watching. No, it was a man, he knew it. The sound of clapping was not the sound of a woman's hands. It had been harsh, mocking, too loud in the silence.

Still, he had not wanted to speak of Oriel to the Inspector. That would have meant telling him about Oriel's relationship with Bell. A cruel man – the kind of man who would have clapped sardonically in that empty auditorium. Except that he was dead. He had hated him, Dickens realised it now, and would have given that away to Hardacre if he had mentioned Oriel, and the Inspector would then have known that he had a motive. Let him find the unknown man. And, let us hope that Oriel was with the others at the Concert Tavern – Oh, God, let her not have been alone, waiting for Bell. Was that why Bell had gone back to the stage? Had they intended to meet there?

Outside, Kettle heard the pacing footsteps. He wished the night would pass; he was cold and uncomfortable on the hard bench. Poor man. I 'ope 'e 'an't done it. P'raps the Inspector 'as found the man 'oo was clappin' – you wouldn't mek that up would you? Still an' all, 'e is a writer – made things up all the time. Kettle shifted on the wooden bench. He did not dare go in. The Inspector wouldn't like it. Kettle was sometimes afraid of him – 'e could be so silent, grim, really. You didn't know what 'e was thinking 'alf the time, but 'e was clever, no doubt about that. 'E'd get the truth. Kettle shuddered. Gimlet eyes, that's what the Inspector 'ad – eyes that could see right through yor.

Dickens waited, too, his mind going round and round, remembering the white hand, the blood on the shirt, the hollow sound of someone clapping, the report of the gun, and the smell in the air as if the devil had been and gone, leaving a whiff of sulphur behind him.

2

DELIVERANCE

A grimy, grey dawn crept in through a small, barred window like a shame-faced visitor wandering forlornly through the dingy corridors. Dickens, who had not known it was possible to sleep standing up, felt the change, though the cell was only a little lighter – light enough to see that there was someone seated on the bed, a figure with his head supported by one hand. Whether he was sleeping or simply deep in melancholy, Dickens could not tell. He was too amazed to feel fear – had another prisoner been put in the cell and he had not heard? The man looked up at him with the eyes of his own father, his father as he had been when imprisoned in the Marshalsea. He had been weeping for Dickens saw the tears on his cheeks. He stepped forward to touch him on the shoulder, but there was just empty air. The vision was gone. Dickens sat down, ready to weep himself. John Dickens, alive and well in London, but here. What message had he brought? Had he wept for his son who would never come out of this terrible place?

He fumbled for his pocketwatch, but it had stopped – he had forgotten to wind it. What time was it? He could hear nothing outside. How alone he felt. He was terribly thirsty, but he knew he would not drink even if there had been water. The idea of using that metal bin was hateful to him. Where was Hardacre? Had he during that endless night found the murderer? Unlikely, thought Dickens. Someone must come soon.

He resumed his pacing. I might have been here twenty years. *It might be months, or years or days.* He murmured the words of Byron's poem, *The Prisoner of Chillon.* He remembered seeing the castle, wondering at the insupportable solitude and dreariness of the white walls, and shuddering at Bonnivard's dungeon. *It was not night – it was not day*, the prisoner had said and so it was here. Impossible to guess the time – night at odds with morning, which was which? How the mind wanders. I should recite something cheerful – though Hardacre might think he had turned mad if he found him singing his party piece, the song of the cat's meat man.

He would not have been surprised to look in a mirror and see himself aged beyond recognition. He had read somewhere that Sir Thomas More's hair had turned white during the night before his execution. Dickens had a passion for looking-glasses; there were mirrors placed in every corner of the house in Devonshire Terrace. Now, he thought he could hardly bear to see himself. Perhaps when Hardacre came he would see in the haggard-face of the white-haired prisoner unmistakeable signs of innocence or, perhaps, those glittering eyes would see only guilt because he had not found the mysterious man who had applauded, or because he had talked to the others in the cast and had found out about Clement Bell's pursuit of Oriel Greenwood – and his own fury with the man. His mind went back to Hardacre's question: 'Did you like him?' And to his own hesitation in answering.

It seemed to be lighter, grey imperceptibly lifting the black. What time did it get light in winter? Perhaps it was about eight o'clock, perhaps nearer nine. He would welcome Kettle's kindly face. Perhaps Kettle would bring him a cup of something, let him out into the fresh air.

He heard the key in the lock. Kettle? Yes, it was he, his face welcome in the gloom.

'Visitor for you, sir.'

And there was Superintendent Sam Jones, his grey eyes concerned.

'A prisoner, sir. Confined, as the lady said. But, away with melincholly, as the little boy said ven his school-missis died – velcome to the college, Mr Jones.'

Sam Jones could not forbear smiling for instead of Dickens, it was Sam Weller, that comic genius of *The Pickwick Papers* who greeted him. Yet, he was not deceived; he saw the tears in his friend's eyes.

'I got your message, but only this morning. The constable sent by Hardacre went to the wrong place – Marshall Street instead of Marshall Road. When he found the right place and the right house, he simply put the note through the letterbox where I found it at six o'clock this morning. You can imagine my consternation, but I have been abroad, visiting the great ones of this city about your case and am come to take you away.'

'Sam, you are my good genius – I thought Inspector Hardacre would keep me here forever – indeed, I feel that I have been in this cell for twenty years at least – is my hair turned white?'

'No, you are yourself – that is, when you are not Mr Weller. I've been to see the Chief Superintendent, Mr Beswick – we served together in London so I know him well. He's agreed to release you into my custody until such evidence be discovered that proves your guilt or innocence.'

Dickens sat down suddenly; the relief had made his legs buckle. Constable Kettle interrupted.

'There's bread, sir, and milk or tea, if you want – you look a bit peaky, if you don't mind me sayin'.'

'Not at all, Constable Kettle. I am most grateful for your solicitude. However, I will wait for refreshment until I get outside.' He smiled at the young policeman.

Kettle blushed with pleasure. 'E in't a murderer – a gent like 'im. Honest eyes – like a boy's. An' a superintendent from London! Wait till I tell mam! London! Kettle went out whistling the tune of *The Bells of St Clements* until he remembered where he was.

'And Inspector Hardacre?' asked Dickens. 'He will not be pleased. I am certain he believes me guilty. There's a look in his eye.'

'I have met him. Beswick asked him to join us. Inspector Hardacre is of a philosophical turn of mind – if you are guilty, he will find you out – and if you are not, then he will find the murderer. He told me about the person in the auditorium and is pursuing that line of inquiry as we speak. He'll come to the Palatine Hotel where I am to deliver you into the care of my Elizabeth in the next half hour. You're ready, I take it?'

Dickens did not move. His mood had changed suddenly – the forced joviality of a few moments before was replaced by a brooding darkness in his face.

'Oh, Sam, what a night I have had – such dreams and visions – I thought my father, Catherine and Charley were all come to bid me adieu. I thought all was over —' he broke off and Sam saw the tears pool in his eyes again. 'But I did not murder him, Sam, I did not.'

'I didn't think you had, Charles,' said Sam gently. 'Let's get out of here – you will not be back – of that I am certain.'

'I hope not – another night in here would send me mad. What about the others? Have you seen Lemon? Or Leech?' Dickens asked, referring to his fellow actors Mark Lemon, editor of *Punch*, and the artist John Leech, both of whom were regular members of what Dickens called his 'splendid strollers'. What must they think of him, suspected of murder? Incredulous, he hoped.

'Inspector Hardacre's seen them. They had waited for you at the Concert Tavern and were comcerned at your absence. They thought you were with them – and then you were gone. Mr Lemon went back to the theatre and encountered a police constable who escorted him back and they were told to wait for the Inspector.'

'I suppose that looks suspicious – the fact that I slipped out without a word. The Inspector asked if I had gone back to see Bell – he obviously thought I had the opportunity to kill him, and I told him I had not heard the first shot – and I did not – it must have happened while I was in the Concert Tavern. The watchman must have come out the back way, into Milk Street, to find a constable while I was walking along York Street towards Spring Gardens and the front of the theatre – and, before you ask, I saw no one. What a mess it is. What was I doing going back? I could have left it until morning.'

'Well, you did not, and Inspector Hardacre is a long way from proving your guilt. He questioned the others and seems satisfied that none of them is the guilty party. They gave each other alibis. They were all seated in the private room at the time the murder was committed. I saw Mr Lemon early this morning and he's gone already for the London train to see Mrs Dickens to reassure her, and to take a message to Constable Rogers at Bow Street – I want him to bring Mrs Clement Bell to identify her husband. Mr Leech is taking care of all the theatrical matters, and I've assured them all that you will be safe in my company. You need not worry about them, except …'

'Except what?'

'Miss Greenwood is missing – she didn't arrive at the dinner and is not to be found at her lodgings.'

'Oh, God!' Sam saw the colour drain from Dickens's face.

'If there is something significant in this, you had better tell me. Inspector Hardacre thought you were holding something back – something you didn't wish to reveal?' Sam looked gravely at his friend.

'I will tell you all. But may we wait until I have bathed and changed my clothes? I would like to feel human again.'

'Very well – but you must tell me everything before the Inspector comes if I am to protect you.'

'I promise, Sam, just as I promise that I did not kill Bell.'

Sam nodded. They went out of the cell to bid farewell to Constable Kettle and walked out into the solid respectability of King Street. Dickens paused on the steps of the great pillared portico of the Town Hall which resembled some great Greek temple. He wondered at its magnificence contrasted with the bleak little cell hidden in its darkened basement. He shuddered at the thought of what he had endured, and what he feared for Oriel Greenwood, suddenly missing. Sam looked at Dickens's face, transformed into something sickly. Terror? For a moment he did not know him. He turned away and Dickens followed him into the crowded street.

3

CONFESSION

Elizabeth Jones was waiting at the Palatine Hotel on Hunt's Bank just beyond Manchester Cathedral. She had engaged two bedrooms with a little sitting room between. Sam had thought it better that Dickens move from the Clarence Hotel near the theatre in Spring Gardens. He had told her that he and Dickens might well be staying for some days. Elizabeth was to return to London later that day. It was time to go back, she thought, to see how Mr Brim was.

Mr Brim owned a stationer's shop in Crown Street. He was a widower with two children, Eleanor, aged ten and Tom, aged six. Mr Brim had consumption – when he was ill, Elizabeth looked after the children and helped in the shop. Her only daughter, Edith, had died in childbirth – the baby, too, so Mr Brim's children filled that empty space where Edith should have been. Mr Brim would die of his disease, and the battle was terrible to behold. He would fight for breath when the coughing wracked his emaciated frame, he would stand at his counter, his face grey except for the hectic red in the cheeks, and he would struggle to rise from his bed for his children's sake, but it would not be long. Elizabeth worried about the children, about Eleanor Brim's too grave young face. The child concealed her tears and bathed the sick man's forehead; Elizabeth dreaded lest Eleanor should get the disease though she seemed sturdy enough. Little Tom, who knew Papa was often sick, tiptoed quietly into the room and stared at the man on the bed, frightened to go too near, and Elizabeth would take them to her own house while the nurse tended to him. He had been better when Elizabeth had departed for her few days in Manchester, but she had left Posy, her own young and eminently sensible servant, to look after them. Posy knew the nurse, Mrs Feak, and would fetch her if needed. Still, Elizabeth was anxious.

She was anxious, too, about Charles Dickens. She could hardly believe that Mr Dickens had been taken into custody. It was ridiculous, she thought, to suppose that Charles had murdered anyone. Sam had not believed it. He had hurried from her cousin's house in Marshall Road to the police headquarters at the Town Hall to find Chief Superintendent Beswick. He intended to see Charles's friends so that arrangements could be made to cancel the play. Then he would go to see Charles. He had asked Elizabeth to engage the rooms at the Palatine Hotel where she now waited. All she knew was that Clement Bell had been shot and somehow Charles had been suspected.

She busied herself with the kettle and tea things. They would want breakfast – it could be served in the little sitting room. She fiddled with the spoons, the cups, the plates. She looked at her watch. The Cathedral clock struck nine. She looked out of the window at the dismal, grey morning, and the passers-by hurrying to their offices and shops, muffled up against the raw wind. She put more coals on the fire and sat down, thinking about the play they had seen. She had enjoyed it – Bulwer-Lytton's satire, *Money*, especially Dickens's performance as Sir John Vesey, scheming to marry his daughter to a rich man. And Clement Bell, the murdered man. He was a good actor, she thought, handsome and noble in the part of Alfred Evelyn. She wondered what kind of man he was. She remembered a line from the play – Sir John Vesey's dictum on a society in which *men are valued not for what they are but for what they seem to be.* Well, perhaps Clement Bell was not what he seemed; perhaps he was not the noble, honourable man he played. But how dreadful that someone had killed him. Not Charles, not the man who had been so determined to hunt down the murderer of an innocent woman, and who had pursued the murderer of those poor children in London. No, it was not possible.

She stared into the fire – Charles Dickens. She thought of his goodness to Eleanor and Tom Brim, and to Scrap, the boy who ran errands for Mr Brim. And it was Dickens who had found Posy on the streets and had asked them to take her. He was probably the most famous man in London. So many people read his books – the judge on the bench, the boys in the street. He had told her of a charwoman who had described how on the first Monday of every month, she attended a tea held by subscription at a snuff shop, where the landlord read aloud the month's number of *Dombey and Son.* The woman could not believe that one man had written all that.

Yet, for all his fame, she thought Dickens somehow incomplete – there was a restlessness about him, a desire to be on the move which she thought might be wearing to a wife. She wondered often about Mrs Dickens, whom she had never met. Elizabeth did not think that Charles was ashamed of his intimacy with a policeman and his wife – she knew how much she valued Sam, and Sam had met Mark Lemon and John Forster, Dickens's closest friends; it was as if Dickens wanted to keep his friendship with Sam and herself and the Brims separate, something for himself. However, she could not help but be curious about Mrs Dickens who had eight children while she now had none. What kind of a wife and mother was she? Dickens spoke of his family with affection, especially the children, but, she thought, there was something missing in the relationship between husband and wife. He talked of his sister-in-law, Mary Hogarth, who had died at the age of seventeen – Charles had never got over it, he said. She had been, according to Charles, the most perfect of beings, and by her death, remained enshrined in his memory, unchanged, untouched. How, she wondered, could Mrs Dickens, changed by her eight pregnancies, equal the beautiful memory of Mary? It is not my business, she chided herself, but every man has his faults and I should not idealise Dickens.

Yest she knew that he was good with children, that he was fiercely protective of their innocence, and cared deeply about their suffering. She had read his articles on the orphanage at Tooting where so many children died of cholera; his letters protesting against public hangings. He cared about the fallen women at the Home in Shepherd's Bush. He talked brilliantly – sweeping one away with his eloquent defence of the poor and oppressed – but, she reflected, he was always elusive. He could be anyone – how Sam enjoyed him as Sam Weller or Mrs Gamp; he could be so many different selves – the Inimitable, the Sparkler of Albion, Young Gas and yet, when she thought of him, she always saw him alone, hurrying away, waving his hat, vanishing. The mystery of Charles Dickens.

She heard a sound at the door and Dickens was there with Sam behind him. She stood to greet them, looking up at Sam's face, visible above Charles's shoulder. Something anxious in Sam's eyes. Oh, God, he has doubts.

Dickens noticed the fleeting alarm in her eyes. She had looked at Sam. What had she seen in his face? Sam had been very quiet as they had walked away from the Town Hall, out of King Street, along St Anne's Street on to Deansgate, then towards the Cathedral and the Palatine Hotel, which overlooked the River Irwell and the cotton mills and iron works, smoking in the early morning air. Not that he had said much himself. He wondered what Sam was thinking. Had he doubts? He looked at Elizabeth. She was the same as always, her thick dark hair framing her rose complexion and her generous mouth smiling. A beautiful woman, he had always thought so, and true as steel. He shook off his fears and answered her question as to whether he would like tea or coffee.

'Anything liquid – I have such a thirst. My mouth tastes of prison cell.'

'Tea, then.'

They sat by the fire. Elizabeth told Dickens that his luggage had been brought to the Palatine Hotel, sent by John Leech, that fresh clothes were laid out on the bed, and that she would send for hot water when he was ready to bathe and change. The domestic details calmed him.

'What a night you must have spent in that cell. Oh, Charles, what a dreadful thing to have happened.'

'It was grim, but I cannot blame Inspector Hardacre – I had fired the gun. It must have seemed obvious to him and then I …' It was time to tell all as he had promised Sam. It would be good to have Elizabeth here and, besides, he wanted to convince them both. If they did not believe in him then it would be impossible for Sam to persuade Hardacre of his innocence.

'Would you prefer to speak to Sam alone?'

'No, my dear Elizabeth, I promised Sam to tell him everything. I have nothing to hide from you two, though I fear, Sam, that some of the things I tell you could be construed as a motive for murder. I told the Inspector that I did not like Clement Bell – that was not quite true – I loathed him and I will tell you why.'

'Something to do with Miss Greenwood?' asked Sam. He thought of the pallor of Dickens's face when he had told him that Miss Greenwood was missing.

'Oriel, yes. Oriel Greenwood is the young actress who played the part of Clara, in love with Alfred Evelyn,' Dickens explained to Elizabeth.

'Yes, I remember. A beautiful girl – something fragile about her, I thought, but very good in her role. Her love for Evelyn was very well conveyed.'

'Exactly.'

'She was in love with Clement Bell and now she has vanished you're afraid that she killed him?' said Sam.

'I am afraid for her, but I cannot believe she killed him,' replied Dickens. 'I told Inspector Hardacre that I was sure there was a man watching me when I found the body – that was why I fired the gun – to warn him off, I suppose. I was terrified for a moment. There was something so sinister, he – I know it was a man – clapped, a sort of jeering, mocking clap, slow, you know, ironic. Just the sort of thing Bell would have done if he were not dead.'

'Tell us about Bell and Oriel Greenwood,' said Sam. 'Begin at the beginning so that I can understand.'

'Clement Bell was a substitute for Dudley Costello who had acted with us before. Costello is sub-editor of *The Examiner*. Anyway, he wrote that he had sprained his ankle and could not come with us. He recommended Bell, a young journalist he knows. And, this is what I cannot understand – Costello urged Bell's easygoing temperament, said he would fit in with us – but, he wasn't like that at all. He was arrogant, the sort of man who rubs people up the wrong way. He did not like me, I can tell you – always challenging my ideas for the play. I know I like to run the show – I am not wholly unaware of my faults – well, some of the time.' He grinned at Sam, who knew in that moment that his friend had not done it – there was something rueful in the smile and something intimate: the smile of a man who had nothing to hide.

Dickens went on, 'But with him there was a kind of drawling superiority which grated. However, I was stuck with him – and he was a good actor. What made me furious was his pursuit of Oriel. It was as if he did it on purpose, to spite me —' He broke off. It was difficult to explain without revealing his own folly, but Sam would have to know.

'Why?'

'He knew I was fond of her – I suppose I was a little in love with her – I regarded her, I admit, as my especial charge – she was, as you said Elizabeth, beautiful and delicate. She reminded me of a girl I once knew and loved, a pianist, Christiana Weller. I own that I resented him; if he had been a single, young man, worthy of her, I would have regretted her falling in love, but I would have accepted him. But Bell – he was married and he didn't love her. I saw them – I was passing the dressing room; the door was open. She was in his arms – and he saw me. And there was such a look of triumph in his eyes. I felt ashamed and hurried away. I wondered later if he had left the door open on purpose – he wanted me to see. I cannot understand it, but it was as if he pursued her to get at me.'

'He resented you, perhaps, as a man whom he perceived to have so much more than himself. How successful a journalist was he?'

'I don't know; I knew nothing about him but what Costello told me – that was recommendation enough.'

'Aside from the tensions you have described, he seems to be a man who might well have had enemies. What about Oriel Greenwood – is there anyone who cared for her who might have wanted to rescue her?'

'I don't know of anyone except me. Inspector Hardacre will, no doubt, pick up on that. I am the most obvious suspect – unless he finds my mystery man.'

'He is a policeman. He examines the evidence and it points to you or Miss Greenwood.'

'Sam!' Elizabeth was shocked.

'It is true, though,' said Dickens. 'At the moment, I care only that you two believe me – I could not bear it if you —' he stopped and they saw the anguish in his eyes.

Sam regarded him with a steady look, and Dickens saw the man he esteemed so greatly, a man who looked the world in the face, who neither shirked nor bullied it, a man who would tell him only the truth.

Sam spoke. 'I believe you. I'll admit that I wondered because you had held something back. I am sorry, Charles. I suppose I was thinking like a policeman – I promised Beswick and Hardacre that I wouldn't allow my prejudice in your favour to get in the way of evidence – it was the only way I could convince them to release you into my custody.'

'I know, Sam. I'm grateful to be here and not in that cell. I hated Bell and I will have to tell all to Hardacre even if it deepens his suspicion that I am the killer. I wonder if he has found any trace of Oriel?'

'We shall know soon enough when he comes. In the meantime, I must take Elizabeth to London Road Station – she is anxious to get back to Mr Brim and the children. I shan't be long. Perhaps you can bathe and change while I am away. I'll ask for hot water to be sent up.'

Elizabeth put on her hat and coat and Sam went to take up the bag that was waiting by the door. Elizabeth looked at Dickens, and in her hazel eyes, flecked with gold and clear as water, he saw no shadow of doubt. He was glad for he esteemed her, too, and wanted her good opinion.

'All will be well,' she said. 'You and Sam, and the redoubtable Mr Hardacre, will find out the truth. I hope so, for whatever Clement Bell was, I do not think he deserved to die like that.'

'You are right,' Dickens replied, 'and I am ashamed that I have thought only of myself in this and not of the dead man.' He took her hand and raised it to his lips. 'I am glad to have your trust – and Sam's. Goodbye, Elizabeth – give my love to Eleanor and Tom, and to Scrap, of course. I hope you will find Mr Brim in reasonable health.'

'I, too. Goodbye Charles. Come back soon – both of you.'

They went out. Dickens put more coal on the fire and sat down to wait for the water. He felt better having told Sam and Elizabeth the truth. He had been fond of Oriel – a little in love with her, it was true. He had wanted to be first with her, and he had to admit, there was jealousy of Clement Bell. Bell had seen it. He saw his weakness, his folly, and he hated that.

He seemed to see the man more clearly now, his mind unclouded by his own anger and jealousy, and, he admitted, vanity. Clement Bell had a kind of power, a power of seeing into the weakness of other men. Had that power killed him?

4

THERE WAS A BOY

When Sam returned, Dickens was once more seated by the fire where a table had been set for lunch.

'Elizabeth is safely on her train?'

'She is, and I am ready for whatever lies beneath those inviting looking dishes.'

'This is an early lunch or a late breakfast, whichever you prefer: turtle soup, lamb chops, roast potatoes, apple tart – and a good bottle of claret. I shall need fortifying for Inspector Hardacre's questions.'

Sam sat down and as they ate he thought that Dickens looked a little less haggard.

'You're feeling better?'

'I am now that I have revealed what I felt about Bell. You know, when I held back from Hardacre, I felt as if the lie lodged in my throat like a stone, as if I could not swallow – it did not go down until I told you and Elizabeth. What a remarkable woman you have for a wife, Sam. I was ashamed when she reminded me so gently that a man has been murdered, and it should not be, whatever kind of man he was.'

'I have thought about him on my way back from the station – someone hated him. Is it to do with Oriel Greenwood?'

'I wonder. He had a kind of power over people – I thought how submissive Oriel was in his arms, as if she were defeated somehow. Perhaps he had seduced her. When I saw them,

I could only see her back but I saw that her dress was unfastened. His hands were on her naked shoulders – long, white hands, elegant, but it looked as though he were exerting force to hold her. It was just an impression – I hurried away. I did not want her to see me.'

'Perhaps she has run away from him – she was afraid, or she knew that the affair must end. It was to be the last night of your play this evening. What then for her? He would go back to his wife, surely?'

'Unless he promised that he would come back to her. Perhaps she was there, Sam, when he was shot – perhaps she saw it, and that is why she has run away. She might be afraid that she would be suspected.'

'It makes sense – let's hope that the murderer didn't see her. She might well be in danger.'

'Oh, God – perhaps he has taken her —'

Before Sam could reply, there was a knock at the door. Sam opened it to reveal Inspector Hardacre.

'Superintendent, Mr Dickens.' He came and sat down.

'Inspector, have you news?' asked Dickens.

'I haven't found your mystery man nor have I found Miss Greenwood. She hasn't been back to her lodgings. Do I have reason to suspect her, Mr Dickens? I am told that she had a close friendship with Mr Bell. I take it that was what you were holding back last night – very gallant, Mr Dickens, but not very wise.' The Inspector's tone was dry.

'No, indeed, and I beg your pardon. I have told Superintendent Jones of the relationship between Miss Greenwood and Clement Bell, and that it concerned me.'

'Why?'

'Bell was a married man. Miss Greenwood is a young woman – I feared that his intentions were not honourable. I thought his attentions would be disastrous for her.'

'They may well have been. Your concern for Miss Greenwood was just protectiveness?' The Inspector looked hard at Dickens, trying to discern whether he had a motive for murdering the lover of the young actress.

Dickens met the Inspector's gaze unflinchingly. 'I was fond of her, Inspector – in another life, I might have loved her, and I loathed Clement Bell. I do not think he loved her, I thought he wanted to spite me.'

'Why would that be?'

'I do not know – that is the part that puzzles me. He did not like me, I could tell.'

'The sort of man who'd use a woman to challenge your power and influence – to show you that he could better you in one way, at least.'

'I believe so, Inspector. I do believe he was using her, and I believe that because of what I knew of his character – not because I was jealous of him.'

'Were you jealous?' The Inspector was implacable. Dickens felt as if the question were the touch of a razor on his nerves. How much more would this man whose mind was as sharp as that razor want to know?

'I suppose I was, Inspector. Perhaps I was jealous of Bell's chance with a lovely young woman, but I did not kill him.'

Sam watched this exchange. He was uncomfortable, and sorry for Dickens, yet he understood how necessary it was that Hardacre should know the truth about Dickens's feelings for Bell and Oriel Greenwood. He had done it himself – probed the secret recesses of men's hearts, and that had helped him distinguish truth from falsehood so that he could pursue the murderer and not some *ignus fatus*. Sam looked at the Inspector, saw his lips fold in a line like a man who was going to return to the information later, and he thought what a contained creature he was – not to be drawn – yet.

'And Miss Greenwood?'

'I do not think she could have killed him – and what about the man I —'

'Sensed?'

'He was there, Inspector. I did not imagine it.' Dickens was firm.

Inspector Hardacre nodded, which Sam thought might have meant that he believed Dickens, but it might just as easily have meant that the Inspector was prepared to let the matter drop for the moment. His granite face was hard to read. There was a stillness about him combined with a steady watchfulness. He did not give much away, but Sam observed the glint in his eye – intelligent and shrewd, he thought.

'Could she have been at the theatre too?'

'That is what the Superintendent and I have been discussing – if she were there then she might have run away —'

'Afraid she might be suspected?'

'Yes, and if the murderer saw her, she will be in danger or, I thought, he might have taken her.'

'A lot of mights, Mr Dickens, but I could do with a handy witness.'

'There was a boy,' said Dickens, suddenly remembering.

'Ye knew him well.'

'Wordsworth?' said Dickens, unable to conceal his astonishment. A surprising man, Inspector Hardacre.

Hardacre smiled for the first time. 'Indeed, Mr Dickens – we know the poets, even in Manchester. I was brought up in the Lake District – a country lad – once. I could blow mimic hootings to the silent owls.'

There was something like regret in his tone. Dickens wondered what kind of a boy the Inspector had been, and what had brought him to this dark city with its chimneys and its mills so far away from the shining lakes of his childhood. The Inspector continued, 'Your boy, tell me about him.'

'A streetboy hanging about the theatre – you know the sort. A ragged child with something appealing about him. Jo – that was his name. I gave him a penny or two – he looked starved. He was always there when we rehearsed during the day, and at night before and after the performance. He could read the notices – learnt, I suppose, from bills posted in the streets. Anyway, my point is that he might have seen my mystery man. The boy would wait for me – hoping for money – he would have been there, I am certain.'

'Did he wait at the front of the theatre or round the back?'

'Usually I saw him in Milk Street, near the back door.'

'Your man must have gone out that way because the watchman and the constable he brought, after hearing the first shot, went in at the front to the auditorium.'

'Yet he was in the auditorium when I heard him clapping so he would have slipped out into the foyer – that was the only way…'

Inspector Hardacre looked grave.

Sam said, 'Suppose he didn't leave the theatre – surely it would have been safer to hide somewhere. Where could he have gone, Charles?'

'He could have gone up the stairs,' suggested Dickens, 'waited until all was quiet, and then left by the back way.'

'And the boy might have seen him?' It was a concession, thought Sam. Hardacre was willing to consider the possibility of a witness.

'I am sure he would have waited for me.'

'But you didn't see him anywhere when you returned to the theatre from the Concert Tavern?'

'No, though I went up York Street not into Milk Street. He might have seen me – after the watchman came out – that would prove I am innocent.'

'Then I suggest you and Superintendent Jones find him: he won't want to talk to the police. In the meantime, I've two constables looking for the bullet you fired, and I'm going to interview two of your actresses, Mrs Weston and Miss Anderton, to find out what they know about Miss Greenwood.'

Dickens had engaged the two actresses on the recommendation of his friend, the actor William Macready, who had acted with them in Manchester in Macready's 1849 farewell performance of *Hamlet*. Perhaps Oriel had taken refuge with Mrs Weston.

'Have you been to Mr Bell's lodgings yet, Inspector?' asked Sam.

'I've sent a constable to inform the landlady, Mrs Marion Ginger, that he is dead, and I'll have a search made of his room – we need to know more about Clement Bell.'

'Would you object to our visiting the landlady – with Kettle, of course?'

Dickens saw that quartz gleam in the Inspector's eyes as he looked at Sam. Sam held his gaze, and whatever the Inspector saw there persuaded him to assent.

'Aye, I'll lend you Kettle. He's downstairs. We'll meet again this evening, say five o'clock at King Street. When you've finished with the landlady, you can have a look for that boy, though if he heard anything last night – two shots from a gun maybe – he might have run off. Still, no harm in trying. Until later, then.' The Inspector stood up and went to the door.

'What about that gun, Inspector – did you have a good look at it?' Sam enquired.

'I did. American. Colt. Walker model. You were in America, Mr Dickens.'

Dickens opened his mouth to deny that he had ever owned an American gun, but the Inspector was gone.

'He still suspects me,' said Dickens ruefully.

'He is a policeman – and a good one, I'd say. I need to tread carefully with him – I outrank him, but this is his city, not mine. His last comment was a warning to me that it is my duty to keep an open mind. He was just reminding us that it is his case. He need not have agreed to let us visit Bell's lodgings – generous of him. And he's willing for us to find your boy. Take heart – he's a decent man. In any case, the Colt wasn't in production when you were in America – so it can't be yours.'

'Would the Inspector know that?'

'No idea. Come, let's not keep Kettle waiting.'

5

MRS GINGER

Dickens and Jones went out into Hunt's Bank with Constable Kettle who would take them to Kennedy Street, not far from the Queen's Theatre. They paused on the steps of the hotel from where they could look over the purple-dyed River Irwell. To their right over Hunt's Bank Bridge was Victoria Station; they could hear the grind and screech of the trains. Would that I were aboard and steaming back to London, thought Dickens, who suddenly felt alien in this roaring city.

Behind the station lay the huge Manchester Union Workhouse, and across the river were the great mills with their tall chimneys rising into the air like so many competing Towers of Babel, churning out smoke which ascended in great black swathes so that the sky seemed to press down on the city like a great dirty hand. Ironworks, print works, tanneries, foundries, furnaces – the very air seemed to throb with the unceasing sound of industry. Nothing of nature here, Dickens thought, remembering Inspector Hardacre's little sketch of a boy whistling to the owls. Nature as strongly bricked out as fumes and gases were bricked in, and he thought of the labyrinth of narrow courts and close streets where the factory workers lived their dark, unrelenting lives, prisoners of the great machine – the juggernaut called progress.

Kettle looked at Dickens and wondered what he was thinking as he gazed across the river. The Inspector 'adn't said owt when 'e come down, he'd just looked thoughtful and told 'im to take them to Kennedy Street.

'We're ready to go, Constable Kettle, if you will take us. Thank you.' Sam smiled at the young man who thought how polite the London policeman was. What a chance – to tek a Superintendent about – from London, too.

They made their way back past the Cathedral and down Victoria Street, past the vast Exchange Building into King Street again, into Tib Lane, after which a right turn brought them into Kennedy Street where they stopped at number 24, a respectable looking terraced house with steps up to the front door.

On the steps with a scrubbing brush in one hand and a clay pipe in the other sat a bedraggled heap of human-ity beside whom Mrs Gamp, even with her disreputable umbrella, might have been mistaken for a lady of quality. She resembled two large, lumpy bolsters which had been tied together with string and left perhaps for the dust cart. She had no neck, her head seeming to be an additional lump to the top bolster. There were no eyes, merely creases in the grimy fabric of her face. Surely this was not the land-lady Mrs Ginger, whom Dickens had, naturally, imagined as a spicy sort of redhead with a temper to match.

Kettle, who must have seen some sights on the Manchester streets, approached the woman cautiously. 'Mrs Ginger?'

The heap of pillows collapsed and swelled, collapsed and swelled again, and a stink as of old beds in which dried fish had slept wafted out. A sound not unlike the sound of a gaseous liquid being forced from the neck of a shaken bottle emerged from the crease that must have been the mouth. Kettle retreated, a look of consternation on his face.

The pillows swelled and collapsed again; a gurgling sound like bubbles came out. She was laughing. They waited. Kettle hovered uncertainly.

Dickens whispered to Sam, 'She should be a woman but her beard forbids me to interpret her so.' He had seen the black hairs on her chin.

Kettle repeated his question, only louder this time. 'Are you Mrs Ginger?'

The woman on the steps chuckled again, a hoarse, deep chuckle like a man's. Her mouth was open now, revealing stumps rather than teeth. 'Nay, lad, Chew's the name. Betty Chew.' She wheezed again. Sam dared not look at Dickens though he felt a quiver of suppressed laughter coming from him. He'll write her, he thought, he will not be able to resist her.

'Is Mrs Ginger in?' asked Kettle.

Mrs Chew's little button eyes opened. She gave the two men a knowing look. 'Aye – though she int in a receivin' mood. Aweepin' for 'er fancy man. Perlice bin already ter tell 'er yon's dead. Face like a dish clout. 'Er's that disappointed. Well, 'tis the Lord's doin', I dare say.'

Very interesting, thought Sam. Mr Bell had another string to his bow. Perhaps Mrs Ginger had discovered his attentions to Miss Greenwood. Quick work, though, Bell had not been in Manchester more than a week and he had two women in thrall to him.

Mrs Chew looked at the men curiously. 'Want lodgins, do thee? There's a spare room goin'. Gentlemen lodgers is allus welcome.' She gurgled again. No love lost between Mrs Ginger and her employee if that's what Mrs Chew was.

'No, Mrs Chew. We wish to ask Mrs Ginger about her lodger – just a few questions.' Sam was cautious. No need to mention murder.

'E'd not 'ave married 'er, mark me. Too 'igh for round 'ere. They 'ad words. Passionate woman, Mrs Ginger. Mind, 'e was cool as a cucumber – sarky, though. Nay, 'e wor off in a day or two I reckon, an' not like to cum back. Anyroad, it's 'oney attracts flies not vinegar.'

Dickens couldn't suppress his snort of laughter. Mrs Chew gave him an approving look. 'Reet sulker, she can be.'

The front door opened and they saw Marion Ginger, a slender woman of about thirty-five with black hair looped up above her ears, falling into ringlets behind. She was very pale, her white skin a contrast to her gleaming black hair. She wore a black dress with white collar and cuffs – altogether a neat and elegant figure though, Dickens noted, much older than Oriel Greenwood and, for that matter, probably older than Clement Bell by a few years. Intriguing. Mrs Ginger looked down at her charwoman with distaste and irritation.

'Mrs Chew, have you finished the steps? Please get on. Do you gentlemen wish to speak to me?' She looked at Kettle with the same distaste as she had looked at Mrs Chew. 'I have spoken to a constable already about Mr Bell. You surely cannot wish to speak to me again.'

Sam spoke up. 'We are sorry to disturb you, Mrs Ginger, but I am Superintendent Jones of Bow Street and we need information about Mr Bell, if you would oblige us.'

Mrs Ginger coloured slightly, and they saw her lips tighten. She had obviously thought that she was done with the police. She was not likely to admit to her affair with Bell – if Mrs Chew were right. Probably, Sam thought – Betty Chew's eyes were sharp. People always thought their secrets were concealed behind the closed door – how often they were wrong.

'You had better come in then. Mrs Chew, you may go home now. The steps will do until tomorrow.'

'Shall I tek the washin'? Won't tek me above a minnit to cum in an' get it.' Mrs Chew looked as if she wanted to get inside. No doubt she would listen at the door if she could.

Mrs Ginger's voice was ice. 'No, thank you. Come tomorrow at the usual time.' She opened the door to admit Dickens and Jones. To her chagrin, Kettle followed them up the steps. Dickens glanced down the steps. Mrs Chew looked at him and winked. He winked back. She chuckled again as she hauled herself to her feet.

They went into a room to the right of the entrance hallway. There was a staircase leading to the upper rooms and, beyond the hall, other doors which led, no doubt, to the kitchen and dining room. The parlour was comfortably furnished with a velvet sofa and chairs and a round mahogany table with a green chenille cloth on which stood a vase of green leaves. Kettle remained by the open door. Mrs Ginger did not ask them to sit, but stood facing them. She was composed enough, though her eyes flicked almost imperceptibly from time to time to the door where Kettle stood. Long, heavy-lidded eyes – secretive, Dickens thought, and sensual. Perhaps she was expecting someone – another lover? She was attractive, but there was a fierceness about her. Interesting that Clement Bell had been involved with two such opposite women – the young and fragile Oriel Greenwood and this dark woman about whom there seemed to vibrate a kind of intensity.

'I don't know what else to tell you.' Mrs Ginger was brisk. 'I told the other policeman that Mr Bell was a lodger here for a week. I hardly knew him; he was at the theatre so often. I didn't see much of him, but he was a pleasant, quiet gentleman.'

'You know that he has been shot? And that this is a murder inquiry?' Sam was brisk, too.

'The constable told me. I am sorry, of course, but I know nothing of Mr Bell that could help you.'

Sam was firm. 'There might be something here that furnishes us with a clue. Do you have other lodgers?'

'Not at the moment.'

So she was alone with him, thought Dickens. He looked at Mrs Ginger's hands, surprisingly large for a woman, bigger than his own, strong, wide at the palm and with long fingers. She could have clapped like a man; she might have killed Bell. For all her self-control, he sensed that she was, as Mrs Chew had said, a passionate woman. Capable of jealousy.

Sam was asking if Mr Bell had received any visitors during his stay in Kennedy Street. Mrs Ginger shook her head, 'No.'

'Would he be here when you were out, perhaps?' Sam queried.

'It is unlikely. He usually took his breakfast at about nine o'clock then he would go to the theatre. I would not see him again until he came back after the performance at about ten o'clock.'

'But in the afternoons when we had finished the rehearsal, perhaps he could have come back then – before the evening performance?' Dickens put the question, knowing that there were times in the afternoon when the cast of the play went about their own affairs. Of course, Bell might have been with Oriel Greenwood.

Mrs Ginger looked at Dickens and again he felt that almost imperceptible tremor in the air. The heavy white eyelids closed so that her eyes were veiled for a moment.

'I doubt it. If I go shopping then it is in the morning, not the afternoon.'

'Do you have a servant here who might have seen him come back?'

'There is a girl who is a general servant – her room is off the kitchen. She might have seen him if —' there was a slight inflection of irony in her tone – 'if he came back.'

'May we speak with her?' Sam asked.

'I am afraid not – she has gone home. As I have no lodgers at the moment, I let her go for a couple of days to see her mother and family.'

Very convenient, thought Sam. 'And her address?'

She did not answer.

'I must remind you, Mrs Ginger, that we are conducting an inquiry into murder. I need to know everything about Mr Bell, and I need to question your servant. She may have seen him with someone.'

'Very well. She lives in Salford, behind the prison where the father is, I believe, Back Saxon Street – I don't know what number. It's off Gore Street.'

'And the name of the girl?'

'Amy Sweet.'

'Age?'

'I don't know – thirteen, I should think.'

'Did Mr Bell have any acquaintances in Manchester – did he mention anyone at all?'

'I cannot say. I hardly knew him.'

Sam asked if they could see his room. She assented. 'There's nothing to see – his luggage was ready. The play ended tonight. He said he would leave tomorrow morning for the early train.' She looked at Dickens. Her gaze was hostile. She knew who he was. I'll bet she has seen the play, he thought, and she knew about Oriel.

Kettle led the way upstairs to an innocuous room on the first floor; on the single bed, there was a tweed suit and a surprisingly worn carpetbag with metal jaws and a snap-lock. Bell had obviously intended to wear the suit for his journey back to London. Sam saw that the bag was locked. No doubt Inspector Hardacre would get it open. He would be very interested to see inside. Kettle opened the wardrobe and the drawers in the chest, and looked under the bed. Nothing. Not a button, not a pin, not a speck of dust. Sam wondered when it had been cleaned so thoroughly – surely not in the time that had elapsed between the visit of Inspector Hardacre's constable and their own arrival?

Mrs Ginger spoke, 'I cleaned out the room and placed his personal belongings in the bag after the constable came to tell me that Mr Bell was dead. I assumed someone would come to take them away.' Her voice was cool. She looked levelly at Sam, holding his eyes as if daring him to think otherwise.

It seemed extraordinary that she should so calmly have set about removing all traces of his presence if she had been involved in an affair with him – unless she had determined to conceal anything which might be evidence of her relationship.

'What was he wearing when he went to the theatre last night?' Sam asked.

'His greatcoat. A suit.'

'We will take these now thank you, Mrs Ginger, and we'll leave you in peace,' said Sam, indicating to Kettle that he should take the suit while he picked up the bag.

She preceded them down the stairs to open the front door. It closed with a decisive bang after them. She had not spoken another word. Nor, thought Dickens, had she said anything about the dead man. And despite Mrs Chew's remark that Mrs Ginger had been weeping for her 'fancy man', he had not seen any trace of tears. A passionate woman? If so she conceals it well, he thought. She could have fired that gun without flinching. Rosa Dartle, that's who she reminded him of, though without the scar. He had described Rosa Dartle in *David Copperfield* as having some wasting fire within her, something eating away at her.

6

HEDLEY'S COURT

'What do you make of Mrs Ginger, Constable Kettle?' asked Sam.

Kettle could hardly speak for astonishment. Inspector Hardacre was that close he hardly ever asked what you thought. Close as a bleedin' trap, some of the other constables said. One o' them loners, Kettle always thought. Deep, that's what 'e was – yor couldn't tell what 'e were thinkin' not if yor studied 'im for years. Superintendent from London, well 'e were a different man altogether.

'She could o' done it, sir. Did yor see 'er ands? She could o' done that clappin' an', sir, I could see 'er with a gun – right fierce she wor, I thought.'

'Exactly what I thought myself, Kettle. Very observant of you.'

Kettle's face shone as if it had been polished. 'What 'ave I to tell th'Inspector, sir?'

'We shall tell him just that. We shall tell him that we think she might well be a suspect, and we should be able to find out more from Miss Amy Sweet about Mr Bell. It's not near five o'clock yet so we've time to visit the theatre again. We're looking for a boy called Jo whom Mr Dickens saw hanging about the theatre, who might have seen something last night.'

'We must find him, Kettle,' urged Dickens, 'he could prove my innocence if he saw me walk past the end of Milk Street after the watchman came out – he might have heard the first shot – fired before I went back into the theatre.'

'Aye, sir, but 'e'll not want to talk to me. Anyway the Inspector wanted me to —' he stopped, not liking to say that Hardacre had asked him to keep a close eye on the gentlemen from London.

'I understand, Kettle. It's the Inspector's case, and he's quite right to ask you to accompany us – he must be sure that the case is investigated properly. You must come with us to the theatre. We can have a look round – if we find him, Mr Dickens can question him.'

They walked along King Street to leave the carpetbag and suit belonging to Bell for the Inspector to examine when he returned, after which they walked towards Spring Gardens, past the solid bulk of the Bank of England and its equally substantial neighbours, the Manchester and Salford Savings Bank and Cunliffe's Bank into which the prosperous looking Mancunians were going, no doubt, to examine the profits from the mills and factories. No sign of a thin boy in rags.

Dickens asked the landlord of the Concert Tavern about the boy. Bob Nab had seen the boy a few times, though he couldn't say where he came from or where he went. There were mostly warehouses around these streets now, but, he told them, there were still a few tenements in Nickle Street – the boy might live there. Kettle took them up Milk Street where there were back yards to office buildings. Marble Street contained the vast warehouses for the cotton spun in Ramsbottom, Bury, Bacup and other towns beyond the city. They asked a woman who stood at the doorway of one of the houses in Nickle Street. A boy named Jo? She couldn't say – her neighbour 'ad a brood o' brats – bloody little pests – she didn't know the names. She pointed round the corner and they went into what was called Hedley's Court – a collection of tenements round a yard filled with refuse and mud where some barefoot children played and a slatternly woman sat on an upturned half barrel watching them. The place was squalid and dark; the tenements lay in the shadow cast by the huge warehouses of Phoenix Street.

'Perhaps, it would be better to come back tonight,' said Dickens. 'He might come back to the theatre or we might see him around the Concert Tavern.'

'No 'arm in askin' now we're 'ere,' said Kettle, and he walked into the courtyard to speak to the woman. 'Know a lad name o'Jo?'

'Might do. What yor want 'im for?' Her stare was hostile. She did not trust Kettle's uniform.

'Might 'ave some information.' Kettle was equally laconic. He had too much experience of the tenement dwellers to give away too much detail.

The woman looked over at Dickens and Jones standing at the entrance to the court. She saw two well-dressed men. 'What they payin' for this information?' she said loudly enough for them to hear. They stepped into the court, Sam ostentatiously putting his hand in his pocket. She watched – might be worth a tanner, she thought. 'Aw right. Jo, over 'ere!' she bawled.

A ragged boy ran over, a dirty, yellow-faced, spindly-legged child of about ten. Dickens knew immediately that this was not his Jo. He shook his head at Kettle.

'Dost tha know any other boys name o'Jo?' Kettle asked.

The boy looked at the three men. He was baffled by the question. Dickens looked at the pinched face which was like a wizened old man's, sharp, all angles, with none of the roundness of childhood. He had seen many like it in London, in Seven Dials and St Giles's. He thought, he doesn't understand. I'll bet he has never had a soft word in his life.

'Another boy?' he asked gently. 'Another boy, Jo?'

The boy shook his head. He did not know what they wanted of him. He looked at Dickens with a kind of wistfulness as if searching for the kindness he had never known. The woman shook him. 'Answer will thee – yor stupid, ar Jo. Dost tha know a kid – Jo?' She shook him again. She saw the tanner vanishing – gormless fool.

'It doesn't matter,' said Dickens. 'Perhaps you would take this with my compliments – I'm sure your Jo would have helped if he could.' He offered her a shilling. She'd probably drink it away. He saw the empty bottle by the barrel, what Cruikshank had called the instrument of all their misery – not that he agreed entirely. Poverty and hopelessness led to drink, the desire for oblivion. He wondered if there were a father of all these children.

She snatched it from him and put it in her pocket. 'Ta, mister,' and Jo was pushed away to resume his game with the others children, as dirty and shabby as he.

They were leaving Hedley's Court just as another woman came in, a woman with a wasted face, waxen from hunger, and behind her dragged two children, their faces pinched as Jo's, and their clothes as ragged – both barefooted on this raw day.

'Ignorance and Want,' murmured Kettle.

Dickens and Jones looked at him, amazed.

'Them kids – like what you described, Mr Dickens. Our mam, she read yor book, said thee must a' seen it thyself.'

'I have. Do you know, Mr Kettle, I conceived the idea of *A Christmas Carol* right here in Manchester, and I am very glad your mother approves.'

Sam remembered Elizabeth's cousin, Simon Watson, speaking about Dickens's speech at the opening of the Manchester Athenaeum in 1843. Dickens's theme was the cruelty of ignorance. Simon had recalled Dickens's observation that ignorance was the prolific parent of misery and crime, and he had told Sam how the speech was greeted with shouts and a thunderous ovation.

Dickens continued, 'Besides crime, disease and misery, ignorance is always brooding – that poor child there didn't understand a word we were saying.'

'What's to do, eh?' Kettle's young face fell and looked older for a moment, youth and hope erased by time and sorrow.

'Not much, Mr Kettle, it is true, but perhaps one day, if we all begin to think it is wrong, and there are men in Manchester who do think so, I firmly believe.'

'I 'opes so, sir – them kids, like animals they are. 'Tisn't right, our mam says.'

'And I agree with her. A wise woman, Mrs Kettle.'

Kettle was pleased. 'She's a Rechabite, sir. Don't 'old with drink. One o' the first – Tent Ebenezer Number 1. Feyther, too, afore 'e died – subscriptions paid for the funeral. Yor can see what drink does in there, right enough.'

Kettle and his mam would have taken The Pledge as members of the Order of Rechabites, which took its name from the Old Testament Tribe commanded to drink no wine. Dickens approved of the Friendly Societies springing up to educate and help the working classes, though he was not convinced that total abstinence was the way to improve the prospect of happiness. He wondered what Mrs Kettle had thought of the party at Mr Fezziwig's in *A Christmas Carol* – negus and plenty of beer, and the Christmas bowl of Smoking Bishop Scrooge was to drink with Bob Cratchit. Well, he thought, looking at Kettle's honest face, he is a young man of sound principles, no doubt thanks to his mam, and that is worth a great deal, abstinence or not.

Kettle continued, 'Believes in education, our mam. I wor a labourer afore I cum in to th'police – went to night school at the Mechanics Institute. Mr Gaskell taught us – know 'im, Mr Dickens?'

'I have not met him, but of course I know Mrs Gaskell's work.'

'*Mary Barton* – you've read it, sir?'

'Yes, I have – a great book about Manchester life.'

The three men walked back to Milk Street, passing the theatre, but there was no ragged boy to be seen. They would have to come back later, Dickens thought, provided the Inspector had not found any further evidence to deepen his suspicions of him.

Inspector Hardacre was there when they returned to the Police Station. The carpetbag and clothes were on his desk. Superintendent Jones told him about their impressions of Mrs Ginger, Kettle interrupting to say that he thought she could have done it. The Inspector's eyes glinted at this interesting suggestion.

'Did you believe your Mrs Chew was telling the truth about Mrs Ginger and Bell?'

'No need ter lie, sir – and there's a little servant, name of Amy Sweet, who's bin sent on 'oliday. Mrs Ginger gave th'address – nobbut she wor reluctant.'

'Well, we must find little Miss Sweet – mayhap she'll confirm what Mrs Chew had to tell you. If so, we might have found another suspect.' He looked at Dickens as he spoke. 'But you were sure the person in the auditorium was a man.'

'I know but Mrs Ginger's hands —'

Kettle broke in again. 'See, sir, they wor big 'ands for a woman —' he stopped, suddenly conscious that he had interrupted. Sam Jones saw the blush stain Kettle's pale workaday face, but when he looked at Hardacre, he saw that his eyes were amused.

'Aye, lad, carry on – I sent you there to find out and I am interested – for Mr Dickens's sake.' He even smiled briefly at Dickens.

'Well, that's it, sir. Summat not right there, that's all.'

'All right then, Kettle, you've done well. Now, get along and wait for the Superintendent and Mr Dickens. I want you to take them to talk to that girl. You can come back and tell me all about it.'

Kettle went out and Inspector Hardacre turned to Dickens.

'Did you find the boy?'

'No,' Dickens had to admit. He had been reassured by the Inspector's smile, a bit like seeing the sun, albeit a faint one, on a winter's day, but he wished they could have found Jo. If Jo had seen him after the first shot, then that would be a fact for Inspector Hardacre to chew on. Dickens had not forgotten the Inspector's insistence on the facts.

'We thought of going back to the theatre later,' said Sam quickly. He could read the disappointment on Charles's face. 'He might be hanging around.'

'I hope so. In the meantime, I've had a look at Mr Bell's suit and the carpetbag – I forced the lock.'

'Interesting?' asked Sam.

'Yes and no. No, because they are unremarkable – there are no clues, no threatening letters, for example, as might be a convenient means of identifying the murderer. No sums of money to give us a handy hint of blackmail. Pity, that.'

'And yes because?' asked Sam.

'Because there is nothing – nothing personal. The clothes in the bag belong to Mr Nobody. Not a laundry mark and all clean, freshly washed. Not new, no, but hardly worn. And, no handkerchief.'

'It is odd,' acquesced Sam, 'but he may have a servant at home who does the laundry – no need for a mark, and Mrs Chew will have washed his clothes at Kennedy Street.'

'True, but have a look for yourself, Superintendent, and tell me what's not there.'

Sam looked in the bag, and in the pockets of the suit. 'Nothing – there is no sense here of the man who owned these things. Did he have anything on him – I mean the body?'

'No, his pockets were empty. So, where's his money? Where's his train ticket? A man usually carries his money or tickets with him. Mr Dickens, Mr Bell would have been travelling back to London tomorrow after the last performance of your play?'

'I assumed so – it was not something we discussed.'

'Was he wearing his own clothes or his costume when you found him on stage?'

Dickens thought. He saw in his mind's eye the white shirt, the blood, the impression of dark clothes which he had assumed were Alfred Evelyn's costume.

'I think so, but I cannot say for certain. Because he was in his chair, I thought he must be wearing his costume, but he might have changed – if he did then his costume will be in the dressing room.'

'But it wasn't there last night – we looked in his dressing room. There was no suit there, so we must assume that he was still in costume when he died. The tweed suit at Mrs Ginger's was his only other outfit.'

Sam said, 'Mrs Ginger said he was wearing a greatcoat when he left for the theatre – was it in his dressing room?'

'No – odd that.' The Inspector looked puzzled.

'Perhaps the murderer took it?' Dickens offered.

'Hadn't the murderer got his own coat?' Inspector Hardacre looked at Dickens's coat.

'It is mine I assure you, Inspector. Bell's coat would have been much too long for me.'

The Inspector measured Dickens with his keen eye. 'A point in your favour, Mr Dickens.'

'Thank you, Inspector. I'm obliged.'

'Well, what we do know is that someone took his money and his train ticket, and any other personal things he might have had with him. He might have taken the coat – worth something, mebbe. For now, we must concentrate on finding Miss Greenwood, your lost boy, Miss Amy Sweet, and I must bring Mrs Ginger in to question her more closely about Mr Bell – she might be more forthcoming if she finds herself in a cell.'

She might indeed, thought Dickens. He wondered would she be a match for Inspector Hardacre, or would she wilt under his stare. He could not imagine her unbending, but then the Inspector was a formidable adversary.

'Did Mrs Weston or Miss Anderton know anything about Miss Greenwood?' Sam asked the Inspector.

'They don't know where she is. They knew about her relationship with Mr Bell – she seemed totally enthralled by him, but they couldn't understand how she'd fallen under his spell in so short a time. They wondered if she knew him before. What do you make of that, Mr Dickens?'

'I don't see how she could – but he could have been in Manchester. Why not? He was a journalist; he must have travelled out of London.'

'Perhaps he knew Mrs Ginger before – I remember thinking that it was surprising that he had two women in thrall after just a week,' Sam put in.

'Well, I daresay I'll find out more from Mrs Bell. She'll know if he came to Manchester before. I also found out that Miss Greenwood's family live in Cheshire – Whaley

Bridge – nice little country spot, so I've sent a sub-Inspector and a constable on a little jaunt. She might have gone home – had enough of him, mebbe.'

'I hope so,' said Dickens, 'although surely she would have told Mrs Weston or Miss Anderton first; it's not in her character just to leave. Something serious must have happened to make her run off without a word.'

'Aye, that's a good point, and it makes me wonder if she saw something – any road, if she's not there, someone might know where she is. Now, I'd like to see Mrs Ginger. Kettle'll take you over to Salford to see the servant girl – you should go now before it gets too late, dangerous spot near the prison. Find out what you can about Bell and any relationship he had with Marion Ginger. The girl will know something – servants always do. You can look for that lad afterwards.'

'Shall we meet later?' asked Sam. 'Might you dine with us at the Palatine Hotel at about nine o'clock?'

'I'll be there.' The Inspector's voice was mild enough, but why was it, Dickens thought, that his most innocuous words sounded like a threat?

7

SALFORD

The New Bailey Prison loomed black over the River Irwell, dwarfing even the Irwell foundry and mill, and the marble works, all of which seemed to cower in its shadow. Its massive walls had eight turrets which gave it the look of a fortress built to withstand attack. It was a vast place, over six hundred feet in length and three hundred and fifty feet at its broadest to house as many as seven hundred prisoners. The strong iron entrance gates were in Stanley Street and led to a space bounded by iron grating. As in Newgate, symbolic fetters were suspended above the entrance as if the prisoner needed this reminder of his fate. Deep within lay the condemned cell, a dungeon with no natural light where the prisoner waited, sleepless and terrified, for the day of his execution. Dickens shuddered at the thought – he might have been carted there if it were not for Sam, might still be if Amy Sweet had nothing to tell them about Clement Bell. And what if the boy, Jo, had disappeared? He didn't want to think about that.

Their way took them along New Bailey Street, an area notorious for robbery and prostitution; the alleys off it looked dark and threatening. They could see the lines of back-to-back houses huddled like broken boxes. The street was crowded now with passengers hurrying to and from the railway station, men with blackened faces, and sallow, bent women coming from the foundries and ironworks, the mills and marble works along Stanley Street. Women came and went from the shops: the butchers, ironmongers and greengrocers, and everywhere there was unceasing noise. The city seemed to move, shift, settle and resettle under the weight of industry. Dickens, remembering his ascent up Vesuvius to peer into the rumbling, fiery cone where flames tumbled night and day, thought that if a man were able to soar above Salford and Manchester, the sight would be very like looking into that flaming crater.

'Carlyle was right,' he murmured to Sam, 'when he said that Manchester was built on the infinite abyss. It seems to move beneath one like an earthquake.'

'I hope not – I should like to survive long enough to get home, if you please.'

Kettle knew the way, taking them left into Gore Street by the railway station, the brewery and The Egerton Arms, thence into a little knot of cramped streets to Back Saxon Street, unpaved, full of stagnant pools of water and refuse, reeking of coal smoke and decay. The houses skulked together in the unlit courtyard where Kettle enquired about the Sweet family, who, he was told, lived at number 4, a tiny house where the windows were mended with oilskin.

At his knock, the door opened to reveal a girl of about twelve or thirteen years – Amy Sweet, they presumed, a little thing in a brown dress and shawl, with fair hair scraped back from a thin face in which wide, grey eyes looked frightened at the sight of the policeman – they remembered that Mrs Ginger had mentioned her father being in prison. Kettle stepped back to allow Dickens to speak for them, he being the smallest and, Kettle thought, the least intimidating.

'Amy, my dear, my name is Mr Dickens. We have come to ask you some questions about Mrs Ginger and the lodger, Mr Bell. Will you let me come in?'

She opened the door wider. Dickens stepped in, but the other two stayed on the threshold – Sam had seen how small the room was and they could hear perfectly well from the doorway. There was just the one room downstairs, a scullery with a sink, a few shelves with assorted pots including a red tea caddy of Japan ware, making an incongruous bright spot in the shabby room. There were a rough deal table on which there was a tin candlestick with a yellow dip in it to send some feeble light into the gloom, a couple of chairs and an open fire for cooking and heat. There were two smaller children, about seven and five years old, sitting on a rag rug before the fire, and a woman, who was an older version of Amy, faded and worn, was stirring a pot on the fire. She looked at them, alarmed when she saw Kettle's uniform.

'Nowt to worry about, Mrs Sweet – just enquiries.' Kettle had seen her anxious frown.

'They want to know about Mrs Ginger, mam,' said Amy.

'Upstairs, you two childer – Amy needs to speak to this gentleman – up, now, quick.'

They obeyed her without a word, and scrambled like two monkeys up a fixed ladder, disappearing through an aperture in the ceiling. There was no staircase.

'What is she to tell yor, sir?' said Mrs Sweet. 'Mrs Ginger int a bad woman. She's give Amy a little 'oliday – with pay an' all – nobbut what our Amy deserves it. She's a good girl – brings home 'er wages when she can.' Mrs Sweet looked fondly at her daughter – she was proud of her.

'I am sure she is, Mrs Sweet. Amy, we would like to know about Mr Bell who stayed there,' Dickens spoke gently.

Amy looked puzzled. 'What dost want to know?'

Dickens was not sure how he should put his enquiry. Would she understand if he were too discreet? 'We wondered if he had any visitors while he was staying with Mrs Ginger?'

'Donnot think so – never saw no one. Only Mr Bell and Mrs Ginger – they wor sweet'earts. She dint think I knew but I saw them, so did Betty Chew – yor can ask 'er.'

'What did you see?'

Amy gave him a mischievous look. 'Saw 'em kissin' once an' 'e stayed in 'er room. Never slept in 'is bed but I never let on. 'E wor nice to me – give me a tanner. Said not to say.'

'Amy, love, you shouldn't talk about Mrs Ginger like that,' interrupted her mother.

''Tis true, mam, all the same. Yor said I should tell the truth and I am.'

'Had Mr Bell ever stayed with Mrs Ginger before? I mean before this last week?' asked Dickens.

'Aye, 'e cum some months ago, can't remember 'xactly – stayed a week.'

'And did he have any visitors then?'

'A donnot know. Never saw no one.'

'What was he doing in Manchester then, do you know?'

'No. Mrs Ginger just said 'e wor on business.'

'And Mrs Ginger, is she good to you?'

'Aw right – cross as two sticks sumtimes but she give me money to cum 'ome.'

'Was she ever cross with Mr Bell?'

'They fell out sometimes. 'Eard 'em afore I cum away. I think Mrs Ginger wor askin' when e'd cum back. I donnot think 'e would say.'

Mrs Sweet frowned. 'Amy, yor shouldn't be listenin' at doors.'

'They was shoutin' – I couldn't 'elp it,' protested Amy.

Dickens smiled at Mrs Sweet. 'It's very helpful to us, Mrs Sweet. Anything else, Amy?'

'Mr Bell cum out – 'e looked angry but 'e laughed when 'e saw me – a funny laugh like 'e 'ad a secret an' 'e put his finger on 'is lip an' winked. Dint see 'im no more. Mr Ginger saw me. She was angry an' said I could cum 'ome.'

It was clear that she wasn't able to tell them anything else, but at least she had verified Mrs Chew's tale and, importantly, they now knew that Clement Bell had been to Manchester before, though for what purpose they would have to hope Inspector Hardacre had found out from Mrs Ginger.

'When must you return to Mrs Ginger's?'

'She said she'd send a message when she needed me.'

Dickens wondered if the message would come; if Mrs Ginger had murdered Bell, and was confessing now to Inspector Hardacre, then there would be no summons back to work for little Amy Sweet, and no wages to bring home when she could. That would be a disaster for the family.

'I donnot know as if I want 'er to go sin' she's telled me the state of things there – it int right that my girl should see things like that.' Mrs Sweet was indignant.

'Eh, mam, we need the money – what'll we do if I canna get work? I donnot want to go to th'factory. And feyther cannot —' she stopped short.

'These gentlemen donnot need to know about feyther – we've said all that's needed. If that's all, sir.' She looked at Dickens – she wasn't going to tell them about her husband.

'Yes, thank you, Mrs Sweet, and Amy, too. Might I?' He felt in his pocket and drew out some shillings which he offered to Amy, who looked at her mother uncertainly. Mrs Sweet looked at the money. She needed it, but was it right to take it?

'Thank you, sir. I donnot like to tek it, but —' she looked up at him, her eyes moist now.

'Please do, Mrs Sweet. I cannot stress too much how important Amy's information is, for me especially.'

She looked at him. There was something in his eyes, as if they saw and understood her proud hesitation, and at the same time he seemed to know her need, everything about her. She nodded and he put the coins into her hand, smiling.

'Bless thee, sir.'

'And you, too, Mrs Sweet. Goodnight.'

And they were gone. Amy looked at her mother as she put the money in the red tea caddy. There was something like light in that usually worn face. Later, much later, when she was grown and Mrs Sweet was dead, she would see his picture in a book, and wonder that Charles Dickens had come to her house all that time ago, and why mam had never spoken of him again. And she would think about the shilling she had found in the tea caddy with her mam's wedding ring, two precious items.

The three men walked away back to New Bailey Street and the bridge which would take them back to Manchester and to the Queen's Theatre to look for Jo.

'Rowed then – 'e was leavin' when yor play ended, Mr Dickens, an' not cummin' back. She 'ad a motive.' Kettle was pleased. Summat to tell Inspector Hardacre. I was right, he thought, Mr Dickens dint do it. He thought about Mrs Ginger and her large hands. Twenty-five bob mightn't be so far away.

'So she did, Mr Kettle. And that makes her a suspect, especially as Bell had been in Manchester before. Their relationship was not new,' observed Sam.

'Perhaps he had made promises that he wasn't going to keep – and, perhaps she knew about Oriel Greenwood, *and*,' Dickens stressed, 'she sent young Amy away straight after the quarrel. Was she planning something?'

'She might well have been. I daresay Inspector Hardacre will find out a good deal more from Mrs Ginger. A woman scorned, eh?' said Sam.

'She'll tell,' said Kettle. 'They allus does – Inspector Hardacre 'as that way with 'em. 'E'll find out all 'er secrets. I donnot know 'ow – but 'e will.'

'I believe it,' said Dickens, imagining the Inspector's hard blue stare boring into Marion Ginger's very soul.

A ten-minute walk through the gas-lit streets brought them to the theatre where Dickens looked gloomily at the notices declaring that the play tonight was cancelled; there would be plenty of disappointed playgoers, and much to do to refund the ticket price. And he was disappointed, too, that the money for his proposed insurance scheme would be less than he hoped. Clement Bell had brought nothing but trouble – in death as in life. Uncharitable being that I am, he thought to himself.

There was no slight figure hunched by the door in Milk Street, but the door was open so Dickens went in to enquire of the watchman if he had seen the boy.

'Aye, Mr Dickens, sir, 'e's inside. 'E wor waitin' for yor so I let 'im come in out o' the cowd – 't'int fit for a dog out theer. 'E looked that starved, I give 'im a piece o' me bread an' cheese. Inspector let yor go then? I knowed yor 'adn't don it, sir, but yon constable as came wi' me was that keen t'arrest someone, he wouldn't listen.'

Dickens was astonished. 'Just a moment, I must ask Constable Kettle and the Superintendent to hear what you have to say.'

At his summons, Kettle and Superintendent Jones came in.

'The watchman has something to say about last night. Did you see something?'

'I 'eard Mr Bell – 'e was talkin' to someone on stage – wondered what 'e wor doin' sin' play wor finished – 'e seemed angry nobbut that I could 'ear the words —'

'Did you see the other person?' Dickens asked eagerly.

'Nay, sir – just an outline – tallish, in a dark coat or summat – anyways, I thought it want my business, an' Mr Bell 'ad a right to be there so I cum back down the corridor to me box when I 'eard the shot. Sent me right out for a policeman an' when we cum back I sawed yor wi' the gun an' yor knows the rest.'

'How could you tell that the figure was not Mr Dickens?' Sam asked.

'Don rightly know, sir – just it worn't – knew constable wor wrong, sir, when 'e took Mr Dickens away. In any case, I saw Mr Dickens go out wi' t'others, across to th'tavern. Couldn't be in two places at once, could 'e?'

'I am most obliged to you, Tom, and we shall tell Inspector Hardacre what you saw.'

'You didn't see Mr Dickens come back from the Concert Tavern? Before the first shot?' Sam knew the watchman's evidence might not be enough for Inspector Hardacre, but if the watchman said he had not seen Dickens come back from the Tavern before the first shot was fired that would be even better.

'Dint see 'im at all until me an' t'constable seen 'im on stage wi' t'gun.'

'Did you see the boy, Jo, at all?'

'Nay – I just dashed out for t'policeman, but 'e mighta been there – best ask 'im.'

Dickens went down the corridor to the backstage area where he found Jo curled up on a hamper with an old cloak wrapped round him. Perhaps Tom would let him stay the night; perhaps Tom had let him stay on other nights.

He wondered what the boy might have seen – or heard.

'Jo? It's Mr Dickens.'

'Eh, sir.' The boy woke. 'Wondered where you wor, sir. Saw the policeman take you away. Heard them shots, sir, last night.'

'Jo, the Inspector has an idea that I might have killed someone so I need you to tell me and the police what you saw and heard last night.'

'Police, sir? I donno.'

'Please, Jo, there is a constable here – you can trust him.'

'All right.'

Dickens called the two men over. Tom Watson came, too, curious to hear what Jo had to say.

'I wor by the back door, sir, just waitin'. Thought you might come out after the play, but you didn't see me – you wor with them others. Saw you go round into York Street – knew you wor going into the Concert Tavern. Thought I'd go in to see Tom – he sometimes lets me stay in the theatre – but then I heard the shot and Tom come rushin' out – didn't see me. He went into York Street. I waited a bit. Saw you, sir, walkin' past the end of Milk Street. A bit after, I heard the second shot.'

'Did you see anyone else?' asked Kettle.

'Saw the constable takin' Mr Dickens away. Then I went in. I heard someone – thought it was Tom, but then I knew it wasn't – not his walk – quicker, so I hid in Tom's box there.'

'Did you see if it was a man or a woman?'

'Too scared to look, sir.' Jo looked curiously at Sam who had asked the question. He turned to Dickens again. 'Do it help, Mr Dickens?'

'It does Jo, and I thank you. You will stay here tonight? Is that all right, Tom?'

Tom nodded. 'I'll look after 'im, sir.'

'I will come back to see you Jo, as soon as I have time.' Dickens thought he might do something for the boy. There must be somewhere he could go other than the streets, or the workhouse. Perhaps there might be a place for him at Grant Brothers. Dickens knew the Grant brothers, mill owners in Ramsbottom; he had met them in 1839, and had so admired their liberal charity and unbounded benevolence that he had immortalised them in the persons of the brothers Cheeryble in *Nicholas Nickleby*. The true story of the Grants' rise from poverty in Scotland to wealth in the Lancashire textile trade made him think that they would find him a place. The boy was intelligent, Dickens believed, and there was something about him, something in his manner of speech which had in it some suggestion of education. Well, he would find out as soon as he could.

They left Kettle to report to Inspector Hardacre while they went on to the Palatine Hotel, where they would wait for Hardacre to come to dine.

'It is enough, don't you think, Sam, even for the Inspector? Tom saw me go to the Concert Tavern, and he heard Bell talking to someone. He knew it wasn't me. Jo saw me at the end of Milk Street after the first shot, and heard someone, even if he didn't see them; whoever it was must have been the killer. Perhaps he waited, as I thought, and left after I was taken away.'

'Or she – Tom could not tell, nor Jo. Still, I do think it must be sufficient. I wonder what Mrs Ginger has had to say.'

'Summat, I 'opes,' said Dickens. And with that Lancastrian observation, they made their way to the hotel.

8

THE IVY GREEN

Inspector Hardacre came to dine, having listened to Kettle's report of the evidence from Tom, the watchman, and Jo. They ate their loin of mutton, cheese, and apple charlotte in companionable quiet, though Dickens was somewhat impatient for the Inspector ate slowly and thoughtfully – a man not to be hurried.

The remains of the wine poured, and the last of the cheese eaten, the Inspector sat back in his chair.

'A most welcome feast, Mr Dickens, Superintendent, for which I'm much obliged. I don't eat in hotels very often or enough at home, my wife says.'

Wife? Dickens could not help but wonder what kind of woman might be the partner of this enigmatic man, and he wondered had he children to whom he was an indulgent father, taking them up to the Lake Country where he had roamed the hills and fields as a boy.

Sam was answering him. 'Mine, too, Inspector – she worries much about the food I get when I'm not at home; mostly I hardly know what I've eaten.'

'True enough, Mr Jones. Well, I listened to Constable Kettle, and I'm intrigued by the glimpse Tom Watson had of the figure on the stage – it sounds as though it could have been a man or a woman, but not you, Mr Dickens, I think that's clear now – and had that fool of a constable taken a proper statement from Tom Watson at the time, you might have been spared a night in the cell – I'm sorry for that Mr Dickens.'

'I assure you, most unaffectedly and cordially, Inspector, that I accept your apology, and acknowledge truly that had I not concealed my knowledge of Mr Bell's relationship with Miss Greenwood, you would not, I think, have been so suspicious – I am sorry for that.'

'Then we're quits, Mr Dickens. Now, I'll tell you about my interview with Mrs Ginger. Not keen to talk, she wasn't. Eyes darting sparks – an angry woman, I thought.'

'Sharp as an edge-tool,' Dickens said.

'Very apt, Mr Dickens. Well, I waited, and she waited, and when she saw I was prepared to wait all night, she gave in and told me her story. I'll leave you two to draw your conclusions as to whether she has killed Mr Bell or not – I'll keep my own view out of it until the end.'

'She did not confess then?' asked Dickens.

'No, she did not. She admitted to her relationship with Mr Bell; she knew you'd gone to see Amy Sweet, and that she'd likely tell you anyway. She told me that he had lodged with her before. She believed that he'd come to live in Manchester and pressed him on the matter this time. She admitted that he was evasive and she suspected some liaison at the theatre. They had words, as Mrs Chew reported, and he told her he would be going back to London and didn't know when he would be back – she was furious because he was so cool about it all. He'd used her, she felt, but she'd not gone to the theatre – she was adamant about that.'

'Did you believe her?' Dickens wanted to know.

'Hear me out, Mr Dickens – you'll be able to judge better when you've heard it all. I asked if she was a widow, and she told me she was not.'

'And the husband?'

'Her husband is confined to an asylum in Cheshire where she comes from. After he was committed, she sold up and came to Manchester where nobody knew her or her story, and she admitted she was prepared to live with Bell.'

'Did he know about the husband?' Sam asked.

'He did and said it didn't matter – he said when he first knew her that he was prepared for them to live as man and wife, but he'd obviously changed his mind – Miss Greenwood changed it, perhaps.'

'But when did he first know her – surely not only when he came to Manchester?' Sam was not satisfied by the story that Bell had lodged only once before – it was all too quick.

'Ah, I can answer that. They met in Liverpool about a year ago. She'd left her husband who was ill by that time in the care of an old friend. Had to get away for a time, she said, so she went to Liverpool for a break. She stayed at The Adelphi Hotel and there met Bell.'

'The Adelphi, eh? Not short of money then.' Dickens had stayed at The Adelphi.

'She's not, at any rate. They met on subsequent occasions when she could prevail upon the friend to look after her husband.'

'Always at The Adelphi?' asked Sam, who was curious about who was paying for these trysts.

'The Royal Waterloo at Crosby was another favourite. Anyway, after some time she had her husband committed to the asylum in Upton-by-Chester.'

'So that she could move to Manchester and there, she thought, set up house with Bell,' deduced Dickens. 'Think how her dreams were shattered when he told her he did not know when he would come back: she had committed her husband and envisaged a new life with Bell.' Dickens thought how desperate she must have been. 'We've forgotten something important,' he added. 'Bell was married. Suppose he told her?'

'Well remembered, Mr Dickens,' said the Inspector. 'That does add something to the mix. So, what do you two think now you've heard the tale and the possibility that she found out he was married already. Superintendent?'

'She has a powerful motive – love, jealousy, revenge, a mixture of all three? And she had the opportunity. She would know when the play ended, she could have gone to his dressing room – he may have taken her to the stage, knowing it would be empty. Tom Watson heard Bell – he sounded angry. He might have told her again that he was not coming back, but …'

'But, you're not convinced.' The Inspector filled the pause.

'I can see her turning a gun on him, seizing it, say, and pointing it in the heat of anger, but to take it with her to the theatre supposes premeditation – that she went there intending to kill him. I can't see that somehow, though we only have her word that he said he didn't know when he might be back. Amy Sweet couldn't really tell whether he was saying that he wasn't coming back. However, if he had told her that their affair was at an end because he was married then I can see that she might kill him.'

'Mr Dickens?'

'Sam is, of course, right about motive, and I think she is capable of such passionate rage that she could kill, but the picture we have drawn of her does not fit with the person who clapped so mockingly in that dark auditorium. Once she had fired the shot, she would have gone, surely. It doesn't fit, Inspector.'

'I see that, Mr Dickens. I confess I'd thought she'd done it – I thought she might have killed him because she'd abandoned her husband for him, and now he was doing the same to her, but now you remind me of your invisible audience, I see it doesn't fit. Still, we'll keep her in mind.'

'And where does that leave us?'

'It leaves us with Miss Greenwood, who is not at Whaley Bridge,' said Hardacre. 'I want to know where she is. If, as we suppose for now, Mrs Ginger is innocent, then we must believe that the murderer is the tall figure Tom Watson saw, and that it was a man who might have some connection with Miss Greenwood.'

Sam thought about the missing woman. 'There must be a connection between the murder of Bell and Miss Greenwood's disappearance. It can't be a coincidence that she vanished at the time of the murder. Either she is involved with the murder, knows who the murderer is, or, as you thought earlier, Charles, he has taken her because she saw something.'

'Liverpool?' Dickens suggested. 'We know that Bell was there – could the murderer be someone he knew there? It's worth enquiring at The Adelphi, someone might remember; a waiter, a member of the staff might remember him – and Mrs Ginger – and might recall someone who was with them. Mrs Ginger might know of someone Bell knew there?'

The Inspector looked at Dickens. He had not thought much of him the previous night – he'd known that he was holding back and it had irritated him. But he's got some sense, he thought now, and brains enough to think things out. Well, he would, thinking out all those plots for his novels. Inspector Hardacre liked the books – his wife did, too. Read them to the children. But Hardacre, a man of strict common sense, didn't believe that the man who wrote them had to be a man you'd like. Kettle had taken a shine to Dickens, though, and declared that the man who wrote with such understanding about the poor could not be a murderer. Kettle was shaping up very nicely, was beginning to have ideas of his own and was not afraid to utter them. Aye, you could be wrong about folk.

'I'll send my sub-Inspector to Liverpool tomorrow and I'll see Mrs Ginger again – see what she can recall about Liverpool.'

'I've stayed at The Adelphi,' said Dickens. 'I know the landlord, Mr Radley, an excellent fellow and much respected. Do you want me to write a note for your Inspector to take? I could say I'd be obliged for his confidential help to you in the matter.'

'Aye, I'm obliged to you, Mr Dickens.' The Inspector turned to Sam. 'Superintendent, will you bring Mrs Bell and your constable to King Street tomorrow?'

'I will. I expect them in the early afternoon. Rogers will bring her on the earliest train.'

'Well, I'll say goodnight. A most instructive evening – my thanks to you both.'

'It's a rum do, Inspector,' said Dickens, 'but summat will turn up – as Mr Micawber might have said if he'd come from Lancashire.'

The Inspector smiled. 'Right you are and I'll be glad to be shut on it, as we say oop 'ere.'

Then he was gone. Dickens burst out laughing. 'A surprising man, our Inspector. I think he's changed his opinion of me – thank the Lord.'

'I think he was impressed by your suggestion about Liverpool. Yet somehow I don't think the answer lies there. Someone here, in Manchester, had cause to murder Bell – or, and this is something we have not thought of, someone from London. London is where he lived. And that is where we can assist the Inspector – by investigating Bell's life in London.'

'I tell you what, I am still puzzled about Bell – how is it that Costello thought so highly of him? How can a man make division of himself so that he is one man in

Manchester and quite another in London? And what will his wife, poor woman, tell us of him?'

With the sobering thought of Mrs Bell who must identify her dead husband and answer the Inspector's questions, they went to bed where Dickens lay awake for a while, thinking of the time he had visited his sister, Fanny, who had lived in Manchester with her husband, Henry Burnett, before her death in 1848. I ought to visit Henry, he thought, remembering the pleasant cottage in Higher Ardwick where he had stayed. He remembered the green where there was a pond with ducks where he had walked with the little lame boy, Henry, who had died just a few months after his mother. He could go tomorrow morning, perhaps, before Constable Rogers arrived with Mrs Bell. He had news for Henry about some songs he wanted to publish. Dickens had written in January to J.G. Lockhart, who had written the songs for which Henry had composed the music. Henry was an accomplished musician. Music! He sat up suddenly.

'Of all the calf-eyed, donkey-eared fools – madness! Madness! How could I have forgot?'

Dickens recalled a visit to Manchester in 1843 to stay with Fanny, when he had met some neighbours whose niece, a girl of fourteen, had been introduced to him. He had thought her a very charming girl, pretty and accomplished, possessing a very sweet voice. Her name had been Margaret Greenwood then so he had not made the connection, but Oriel had reminded him of their meeting when he had engaged her to play Clara. She had taken her second name, Oriel, for her stage career. Now he thought there was a very good chance that her aunt or cousins lived still at Higher Ardwick and might know where she was – she might even be with them. Tomorrow, he hoped, there would emerge some clue about her whereabouts. He fell asleep at last, exhausted.

Something woke him – the sound of feet tramping, the sound of iron on stone – clogs, he thought, that was it. It was still dark, but the mill hands were going to their work. Six o'clock, the Cathedral chimes said. Too early. He turned over, and slept again. In his dream, his dead sister, Fanny, was singing, a low, mournful song; he recognised the words of his own poem *The Ivy Green*:

> *Creeping where no life is seen,*
> *A rare old plant is the ivy green.*

But at the end of the song it was Oriel Greenwood who was standing in the ivy-clad archway of a ruined church. Through the archway he could see the moonlight shining down on the crumbling marble tombs. Then she was gone, but he could hear the words still, lingering in the air:

> *Creeping where grim death has been,*
> *A rare old plant is the ivy green.*

And then he woke, but the scene remained as clear as if it had been real – it was the scene etched on the front cover of the published song, the music composed by Henry Russell way back in 1838. He had not thought of it for years. The picture had shown the ruined church, the graves and stones all tumbled in the ferns and grasses, and thick ivy entwining the falling walls and clinging to the arch. There was a great round white moon in the picture as there had been in the dream. But there had been no slender fair-haired girl in the picture. A dream of Fanny and Oriel, singing of grim death in that ruined place. He felt dread for what it might mean.

9

MANCHESTER LADIES

Over breakfast the next morning Dickens told Sam about meeting Oriel Greenwood all those years ago. Sam agreed that they had time to go and see if there was any trace of her in Higher Ardwick. He noted, too, that Dickens seemed preoccupied with some other thought. The bright eyes were clouded – what was he remembering?

'And there is something else, something that troubles you – about Miss Greenwood? Have you remembered something?' he asked.

Dickens looked at his friend. Sam was perceptive, always observant and aware of others' feelings. That is why he is such a good policeman, he thought.

'I dreamt of her; she was singing *The Ivy Green*.'

'From *Pickwick*?'

'Yes. I haven't thought of it for years, but in the dream she was standing in a ruined churchyard. I wonder —'

'If it is a presentiment – you think she might be dead?'

'I fear it, Sam. You said yourself that it is too much of a coincidence that she should vanish when Bell was murdered.'

'I know – it worries me, too. Well, let us go to Ardwick and hope that she's there.'

'The Entwistles they were called, neighbours and friends of my sister Fanny and her husband, Henry Burnett.

I should call at his house, too. He might know if Oriel is at the Entwistles. What do we tell her relatives?'

'That we are looking for her. Best to tell the truth – that way we'll have a better chance of finding her.'

'You are right, as always, Sam.'

Outside, the morning was grey and wet, the air damp like a woollen blanket, a shivery sort of morning with a kniving wind carrying sleet, pinching the faces of passers-by so that they looked miserable and harried: unhealthy faces with nipped mouths held fast against the driving sting of the wind.

There was a cab waiting at the hotel steps, the driver bunched up in his greatcoat. Seeing them hesitate on the steps, he asked if they wanted a ride and agreed to take them to Higher Ardwick. Inside the cab smelt of the same damp wool of the sky, and there was straw on the floor giving off a musty odour, a smell that reminded Dickens of his lonely journey as a child from Chatham to London where, though he did not know it then, work in the blacking factory waited.

The cab took them along London Road past the railway station and on to Stockport Road into Ardwick itself, where they drove past the solid, comfortable villas and grand houses of the Manchester mill owners and businessmen who lived in this green suburb, away from the rush and clamour of the city; they saw the grounds of Ardwick Hall, a handsome Georgian house built in 1795. They were set down at Elm Terrace; Henry Burnett lived at number 3, a three-storey Georgian house with creeper growing over the front windows and door, over which there was an elegant fanlight. The last time Dickens had been here, in July 1847, Fanny was alive, though even then he knew that she would not live – Fanny, whom he had loved and who belonged to the childhood days in Chatham when they had wandered about the churchyard on a winter's night, looking at the stars; Fanny, who had helped him with his homework; Fanny, who had been elected as a pupil to the Royal Academy of Music while he went with his father to the Marshalsea Prison; Fanny, who had sung duets with him. She had not been able to sing for him then.

The maid, Mary, told them that her master was not at home – he had just gone by train from Ardwick Station. They went in so that Dickens could write a note for Burnett and leave the reply he had received about the songs from J.G. Lockhart. He asked Mary about the neighbours, the Entwistles, at whose house he had first heard Oriel Greenwood sing. There was only the old lady there, Mary told them, and a servant, but the old lady would be glad to see Mr Dickens, she was sure.

The Entwistles were mill people. George Entwistle's father had been a self-made man who had risen to prosperity through hard work and invention. He had begun as a spinner and his fortune had come from the creation of a more efficient spinning machine. He had died years before, leaving his mill to his son. The old lady of whom Mary spoke was his widow, now in her seventy-fifth year.

Dickens led the way across the road to Elm Lodge, a large Georgian house where the servant showed them into a bright parlour where an elderly lady sat reading by the fire. She was a neat woman in a white cap and black gown. Her hands in their black fingerless mittens were twisted with arthritis and her back was now bent, but the eyes in her placid, wrinkled face were serene, clear as grey water. She had heard her servant announce Mr Dickens and another gentleman, and she turned with pleasure to speak.

'Why, Mr Dickens, thou art welcome on this cheerless day. We have not seen thee for a long time. Art come to see Mr Burnett?' Her voice was low and rippling – like a soft breeze through moorland grasses.

'I am, but he is not at home so I thought to come and pay my respects to my old friends. This is my friend, Mr Jones. I hope I find you well.'

'Thou art welcome, Mr Jones – come both to the fire.'

They sat on a comfortable sofa, glad of the warmth of the flames.

'I mun tell thee how sorry I was about Mrs Burnett – she was a good woman, your sister – and a fine singer in our choir. What a pity it was, and about the little boy, a singular child; very quaint our pastor Mr Griffiths said, and I think so, too. Well, he is with God, and away from his suffering. He reminded me of little Paul, Mr Dickens – thou canst see I have been reading about Mr Dombey and his son again.'

'Thank you for your kind words, Mrs Entwistle. I miss them both, and it is true that I thought much of little Henry when I imagined Paul Dombey.'

'Thou wilt take a cup of tea and an oatcake – thou hast time to stay a while?'

'Indeed we do and we will be glad to drink tea with you.'

The servant was instructed to bring tea. Dickens asked about the family. He would be able, he hoped, to bring up the subject of Oriel Greenwood in the most natural way.

'They are gone to Sale Moor to see the new child of Lizzie's cousin – Lizzie is my daughter-in-law, Mr Jones, and she has gone with Alice, my granddaughter. I am too old to go a-jaunting as far as Sale.'

The tea was brought along with fresh, crumbly oatcakes which melted in the mouth.

'And they are all well?' asked Dickens.

'They are – fine doings we've had these last days. A dinner with Lily and Mr Gaskell, at home here, and Miss Jewsbury and her brother came – thou knowest Mrs Gaskell, o' course.'

'I do and I shall go to see her while I am here – I should like to get a story from her for my new magazine, and I have read Miss Jewsbury's work – I shall ask for a story from her, too.'

'And they all went to see your play, Mr Dickens – came back full of it. And they thought Margaret very good, as well as you.'

'Margaret?'

'Aye, I know she's using that other name, but I mind her as little Margaret. I always thought cousin Phillis a bit silly to call her Oriel.' Mrs Entwistle sighed.

'And has Mar– Miss Greenwood been to see you all?' Dickens asked smoothly.

'Nay, we have not set eyes on the lass for a while – busy with her acting. She lodges in Manchester – I am not sure I like that for a young girl, though cousin Phillis tells me her landlady is a good woman. Still, I think she would be better at home. Old-fashioned, I am, I daresay.'

'Miss Greenwood is a very talented actress …' Dickens paused, at a loss as to where he might go next. Mrs Entwistle looked at him shrewdly – she knew, he thought, the wise old woman had seen something in his face.

'Eh, lad, thou hast something on thy mind – thou mun tell it me.'

'I don't know, it —' Dickens was uncertain. Would it be right to tell the old lady something which her family might not wish her to know? Mr Entwistle perhaps ought to know first.

'Thou thinkst I am so frail as to be blown like a leaf. Not so, Mr Dickens. I am old, 'tis true, but we are made tough here, and I was working in the mill when thee was born. I lost my first boy, Thomas, when he was but a babe, and my daughter, Jane. They are buried in the cemetery across the way, a quiet, green place where I go sometimes in better weather to see my childer. There is nothing thou canst tell me that I cannot bear.'

Her grey eyes were steady and the quiet strength there steadied him. He glanced at Sam, who nodded. Sam had seen the steadfastness in this fine lady – she had seen much in her long life, hardship as well as prosperity. She might be able to help them find Miss Greenwood.

Dickens told her everything, and that they feared that Miss Greenwood might be in danger. Mrs Entwistle listened intently; her eyes registered pity and occasionally shock, but she sat quite still, her crippled hands motionless on her lap.

'A wicked tale, Mr Dickens, and I am afeared for poor Oriel – I mun call her that, I suppose. She has not gone to Whaley Bridge. Thou knowest it for certain?'

'We knew yesterday evening – Inspector Hardacre has asked them to let him know if she comes home. We cannot help wondering if someone knew about Clement Bell and quarrelled with him about Oriel, and perhaps ...'

'Killed him for her sake, not meaning to, but having words, as the watchman said —' she had taken it all in, remembering the detail – what a good witness she would make, thought Sam, sensible, intelligent and quick in her understanding. She continued, 'Angry words that led to death.'

'Is there anyone?' asked Sam.

'Anyone who loved her so much that he would kill to save her?' She looked troubled now, and Sam saw that she was torn between her instinct to tell the truth and her desire to protect whoever it might be.

'I do not want to tell thee. There is someone who loved her and grieved that she seemed changed, for changed she was, Mr Jones. Sin' about six months gone. She played at the Theatre Royal in Manchester, and that is when she become distant from us. Cousin Phillis told us she was too busy to come to see us – she had her career to make, or some such. I do think Cousin Phillis spoilt her a bit – her only child, and Mr Greenwood long dead. I sometimes think Oriel got too much of her own way, though I do not like to say it.'

'And to whom was she so changed, Mrs Entwistle?'

'I will tell thee, but first thou mun promise not to seek him before Oriel is found. Oriel mun tell thee the truth about him and then if thou mun seek him —'

'I can promise you that,' Sam replied firmly. 'We will only question him if there is no alternative. Tell us about him.'

She was reluctant. However, Mr Jones looked like a man she could trust. He was gazing at her with eyes as grey and steady as her own. She liked him – he had a calm authority, but there was kindness in his eyes, too, and honesty.

'His name is Robert Alston, son of Mr Alston who owns a mill in Ancoats – good people. O' course he loved her. Who would not? And she seemed fond of him until she got her part at the theatre. Happen he was not for her, she wanted something different. But, Mr Jones, I canst not see him killing a man – not as you describe it, nay, I cannot. He is a solid lad, steady, quiet – a good lad, true.'

'Is there anyone else whom you can think of who might know where she is?'

'Miss Jewsbury was very fond o' Oriel. She encouraged her in her acting. Miss Jewsbury is by way of wanting young women to take up writing, acting, music or teaching, not housewiving – well, I don't know about that, but Oriel might have gone to her. She lives at Carlton Terrace in Greenheys, not far from Lily – Mrs Gaskell. A twenty-minute walk from here.'

Dickens rose and went over to the old lady where he knelt and touched her hands. 'We shall go there directly. And, Mrs Entwistle, I promise we will not approach Robert Alston unless we must – we do not know enough about Oriel's disappearance yet.'

'I pray that thou wilt find her. I will tell all to George and Lizzie – they mun know the tale. God bless thee, Mr Dickens, and thee, Mr Jones. Send me word when you find her.'

They went out of the firelit room – Dickens glanced back to see Mrs Entwistle gazing into the flames. How sorry he was to have brought such ill-tidings.

Dickens looked at his watch. 'It is eleven now – about twenty minutes to Greenheys, according to Mrs Entwistle. Say fifteen minutes to be pleasant to Miss Jewsbury – I wrote to her asking her about writing for *Household Words*. I shall simply say that having been to see Henry, I thought I might call. I can mention the play which ought to lead to Oriel. She will surely say if Oriel is there. Afterwards, we can get a cab to London Road Station and be there at about midday. Some lunch, perhaps, while we wait for the train.'

'It may take longer if Miss Greenwood is there,' said Sam. 'You might have to stay a while – you'll have to persuade her to see Hardacre. In which case I will go on to the station.'

They walked on in silence. Sam thought that Dickens would be able to get the story from Miss Greenwood, if she were there, and pray heaven she was. He did not know why, but he doubted it – something to do with Charles's dream. Charles believed in the prescience of dreams, and Sam had a horrible feeling that the dream might come true. Oriel's disappearance troubled him as did Dickens' haunting sketch of the unseen hands clapping in the empty theatre. The case was like a dream which vanished in the morning light, leaving you with a sense that someone was hovering in the shadows, someone you could not see but who left a disturbing feeling of fear.

'Robert Alston,' said Dickens unexpectedly. 'We'll have to tell Hardacre about him.'

'And our promise that we would not speak with him unless we had to?' said Sam. 'Were we a bit rash there, Charles?'

'Probably, but that good woman deserved our pledge. I will have to persuade Hardacre. Somehow, I think he'll understand.'

'I hope so,' Sam murmured.

'Interesting what Mrs Entwistle said about Oriel,' Dickens continued, 'that she got too much of her own way. I did not see her like that, but I wonder what light it sheds on her relationship with Bell. I may have it all wrong, of course, perhaps she is not so innocent or submissive as I thought.'

'She is an actress, Charles – it may be that she could be whatever she thought a man wanted her to be. However, if she wanted her own way, she might have gone with him.'

The thought troubled Dickens – to think that she was so in thrall to Clement Bell that she would abandon everything – even him. It could not be. She had worked hard in the play. He had praised her and she had admired him in return. Vanity, he thought – mine.

They came at last to the house in Carlton Terrace where a maid let them in and took Dickens's card to Miss Jewsbury, who came out smiling to meet them. She was a small, dark-haired woman who looked directly at them with the confidence of a woman who had made her own way, Sam thought. He wondered what influence she might have had on Oriel Greenwood and her mother. Mrs Entwistle clearly thought that Cousin Phillis was rather too susceptible where her only daughter was concerned.

As soon as Miss Jewsbury spoke, they knew that Oriel was not there – if Oriel had taken refuge there then Geraldine Jewsbury would have known that there was something amiss, and she might not have been surprised to see Dickens.

'How very good of you to call, Mr Dickens – this is most unexpected after your kind letter. Have you been to see Mrs Gaskell?'

'Not yet – I have just been to see Mr Burnett, and Mrs Entwistle. She mentioned you had been to see the play and that prompted me to come and ask in person about your contribution to *Household Words*.'

'I should like to contribute very much. Will you come in and take some refreshment?'

'No to the refreshment, thank you. We have had tea and oatcakes with Mrs Entwistle.'

'Ah, you will be full of good things then.'

Geraldine Jewsbury led them into a drawing room where another fire burned brightly; there was a desk on which were papers, ink and a goose quill pen very like the ones which Dickens used. She saw his glance.

'I am planning a new book, Mr Dickens. It is to be called *Marian Withers*, a tale of Manchester life – and a love story, too. It is going rather slowly just now.'

'I know what you feel. How often I sit with what may be called a blank aspect, waiting for David Copperfield to come.'

Miss Jewsbury smiled at her distinguished guest and fellow author. 'That is it exactly, Mr Dickens – I am waiting for Marian who is proving somewhat elusive. But I am forgetting my manners. Do sit for a while Mr …' she looked curiously at Sam.

'Oh, forgive me,' said Dickens. 'This is my friend, Mr Jones – he has been in Manchester visiting. We are to have lunch together.'

'Were you at the play, Mr Jones? We all enjoyed it, Mr Dickens – a fine satire on London society, though it is not just in London where money is grasped for, I think.'

'Indeed not. Yes, my wife and I enjoyed it immensely.'

'And our young Oriel – a touching performance was it not?'

'I do think so, Miss Jewsbury.' Dickens felt nervous, he did not want further discourse about Oriel. Sam saw his anxiety.

'My wife much enjoyed your book, *The Half Sisters*, Miss Jewsbury. She would be vexed if I had not taken the opportunity to tell you so. She admires your views on the lives of, er – women – and, er – their need for better education.' Sam seemed to Dickens uncharacteristically flustered – what had he been going to say before he paused at the word 'women'? Did he think Miss Jewsbury might bridle at the word 'ladies'?

'I am very glad – please tell her so.'

'It has been a pleasure to see you, Miss Jewsbury, and I look forward to working with you. And now we must go. Mr Jones and I must return to Manchester for we have to meet someone from the London train.'

'Thank you for calling. It has been good to see you and I hope I can write something to your taste.' Dickens wondered if there was a hint of irony in that last remark – perhaps she thought he might have doubts about her work which promulgated women's freedom – and he did, remembering the outrage that had greeted her first novel, a tale of the unconsummated love between a married woman and a Catholic priest; even Jane Carlyle, Miss Jewsbury's close friend, had told him that she thought it indecent. That Oriel Greenwood had read them, he didn't doubt. Forbidden love.

'I do not doubt that my readers will enjoy something from the pen of the lady who wrote *Zoe*.' Dickens's compliment was not without its own ambiguity – he had thought Miss Jewsbury's novel rather too sensational, but he dared not refer to *The Half Sisters* again – the heroine was an actress, and he was too afraid that the reference to its heroine, Bianca, might open further discussion of Oriel.

They walked quickly away, as if they were afraid she might summon them back to ask about Oriel Greenwood. Sam was smiling.

'I knew as soon as I mentioned *The Half Sisters* that I had made an error – I nearly went on to say something about the actress, and then I thought she might return to Oriel Greenwood.'

Dickens laughed. 'And there was I thinking that you were overpowered in the presence of a bluestocking! Anyhow, I am glad you diverted her – I was sinking into quicksand just then myself. Have you read any of Miss Jewsbury's books?'

'No, but Elizabeth has – I'm too busy reading Charles Dickens.'

'Exactly as it should be, Superintedent Jones. And now to what Mrs Gamp might call a bit of pickled salmon, a cowcumber and a mossel of cheese.'

'A slice of cold beef?' asked Sam, who knew the answer already.

'Don't have nothink to say of the cold meat, for it tastes of the stable.'

10

AMAZED AND CONFOUNDED

Hot beef, rich gravy and mashed potato furnished their lunch at The Bull Hotel, not far from London Road Station. Pickled salmon was off and there were no cowcumbers to be got for love or money, much to Sam's gratification. Like Doctor Johnson, he thought the cucumber was a vegetable to be well sliced, dressed with pepper and vinegar, and then thrown out as good for nothing. He chuckled at the thought.

'Penny for 'em?' asked Dickens.

'I was thinking of Doctor Johnson and cucumbers.'

'A witty fellow, he. I was thinking what to do with this,' Dickens pointed his fork at the piece of tripe lying uneaten on his otherwise clean plate. 'Is it a piece of sponge with which to wipe our chins?'

'Tripe!' Sam knew very well that Dickens had eaten tripe before. He remembered Mr Filer's disquisition on the wastefulness of tripe in *The Chimes*.

'Well, really, Mr Jones! Nay, I cannot think it is to be eaten – not even finely broil'd – a thought expressed, if you please, by Mr Shakespeare himself.'

'Never!'

''Tis true, 'tis pity, and pity 'tis, 'tis true – tripe occurs just once in Shakespeare, as far as I know – *The Taming of the Shrew*.'

'Stewed, they say, is the best ever.'

The landlord, a man whose sanguinary complexion was the colour of ox-blood, and whose head, neck and shoulders were so constituted as to give him the solid, muscly appearance of the bull pictured on the inn sign outside, approached to clear the plates. Dickens amused himself by speculating as to the appearance of the landlord of The Lamb and Flag, a pub they had passed on the way to The Bull.

'Tha's not 'ad thy tripe, sirs. 'Tis good for the blood – the owd lady there swears by it.' The landlord gestured towards a remarkably bloodless-looking dame seated behind the bar. She was no puff for the invigorating effects of tripe, unless she was made of it – her pallid face had the colour and texture of tripe.

'Forgive us, sir, your beef has proved more than a sufficiency if we are to do justice to your apple pie.'

Sam looked appalled – he had eaten quite enough, what with the oatcakes earlier. If the apple pie came in the quantity that the beef had, he would burst.

'No more for me, if you please, landlord.'

'Ah, my friend has a weak constitution, alas – he looks strong, but is prey to a kind of wasting sickness. A ruined piece of nature, he is, Mr …?'

'Lamb, sir, Abe Lamb.' Then the landlord of The Lamb must be Mr Bull.

Well, Mr Lamb, I cannot be so unfeeling as to consume apple pie before him. As Doctor Johnson wisely observed, a man who aspires to be a hero must drink brandy – a brandy-and-water warm will set him up so bring us two of those, if you will.'

'Yon doctor mun be a good 'un. I'd like to shake 'is 'and.'

At the conclusion of this affecting narrative, Sam seemed unable to speak – no doubt on account of his weak constitution, but he appeared to have developed a tickling cough which the landlord assured him would be 'put to reets' by the brandy prescribed by 'yon doctor'. So saying, he repaired to the bar to prepare the medicine.

'A sheep in bull's clothing,' murmured Dickens. Sam was once more afflicted by his cough. Mr Lamb returned with the warming potion which Sam sipped whilst wiping his watering eyes.

'You are in a nice state of confugion, Mr Jones, you are, an' half a dudgeon of fresh young lively leeches on your temple wouldn't be too much to clear your mind,' observed Dickens sagely, though so much in the manner of Mrs Gamp that Sam was overcome again.

'Enough,' he spluttered, seeing the mischievous glint in Dickens's eye. 'Stop it, I beg you.'

Dickens took pity on him. They finished their brandies, paid the bill, bade farewell to Mr Lamb and the woman at the bar, and went out to the station. After the warmth and laughter at lunch, they felt the cold. The day had darkened even more now. They looked at each other. Time to meet Rogers and poor Mrs Bell.

There was not long to wait for the London train. It was somehow comforting, Dickens thought, to see the homely face of Constable Rogers, who was in plain clothes, as he escorted two ladies to meet Superintendent Jones and Mr Dickens. Rogers introduced Mrs Bell and her companion, Mrs Stark. Mrs Bell was small and obviously with child. She lifted her black veil and Dickens saw how fragile she looked. She was pretty in a delicate way. She reminded him of Dora Spenlow. Dickens glanced at Sam and saw the pity in his eyes. The other woman was taller, dark with a determined air.

'Mrs Stark, sir, has come to look after Mrs Bell,' Rogers explained.

Mrs Stark smiled and her stern features softened. 'I am Mrs Bell's cousin. I should like to be with her when she has to identify her husband. Will you be able to arrange an hotel for us? We had no time.'

'We can do that, Mrs Stark, of course,' said Sam, then he turned to the other woman. 'I am very sorry, Mrs Bell, that we have had to bring you, but we knew of no one else. It must be very distressing for you.'

Mrs Bell spoke. 'Thank you, Superintendent. What can you tell me about poor Clement?'

What could he tell her? He took her small hand. 'I cannot tell you very much except that Inspector Hardacre of the Manchester Police is doing all he can to find out who has done this.' He felt how inadequate his words were and he was glad that it would be Hardacre who would have to question her about her husband. Surely, she would not have to know about Mrs Ginger and Oriel Greenwood – it would be too much for her to bear. Perhaps the Inspector could find out more about him from Mrs Stark.

They took a cab to the mortuary at the Infirmary where Inspector Hardacre waited. Dickens saw his quick, appraising glance take in the woman and her condition. When he spoke, his voice was gentle.

'Perhaps Mrs Stark could identify your husband, Mrs Bell? It would distress you greatly, I think.'

'No, Inspector. I must see him. I am his wife; it is my duty, but I should like Ruth to come with me.'

They went down the stone steps to the mortuary. As they descended, Dickens was aware that the air was colder here; it was like going down into a vault – where Bell lay festering in his shroud. The Inspector led the way, his uniform black like a suit of mourning. He seemed to vanish eerily round a bend in the stairs. Mrs Bell's face was ghostly pale under the shadow of her black bonnet with its veil hanging on her shoulders, and Mrs Stark's face was stern again, grim in the bluish shadows.

The staircase twisted and they found themselves by a huge wooden door studded with iron. It might have been a gaol, thought Dickens. He looked at Mrs Bell again. Her eyes were huge in her pale face; she reached out for Mrs Stark to steady herself, and he heard her take a breath as the Inspector opened the door into a white-tiled room, where the attendant waited by something covered in a sheet on a huge marble slab. Water dripped somewhere. The air was still as a tomb and even colder than outside. The loathsome smell of death and carbolic soap. Chamber of horrors.

Inspector Hardacre took Mrs Bell's arm and led her to the marble slab. The attendant folded back the white sheet to uncover the face. Mrs Bell raised her head to look. A half-stifled cry came from her. 'It is not —' then she staggered back a step, and the Inspector caught her as she fainted. Sam hurried forward and took her in his arms.

'Take her out,' said Hardacre. 'There is a bench outside.' Sam carried her away. Dickens and Hardacre looked at Mrs Stark, who was staring at the corpse, her face transfixed in horror.

'What is it, Mrs Stark?' asked Hardacre. He knew that there was something wrong.

Mrs Stark turned to him. 'It is not Clement Bell – it is not. What have you done? It is not her husband. I must go to her.' She hurried out.

Hardacre looked at Dickens, who stood amazed and confounded, his face drained of all colour. He could not speak for it was true. The dead face, although very similar to

Clement Bell's, was not his face. Oh, God, he thought, what *have* I done?

Hardacre spoke at last, his words dropping like metal strokes on Dickens's ears. 'Well, Mr Dickens?'

'I have made a dreadful mistake – it is not Clement Bell. The man here looks like him, but he is not the man I knew. I am profoundly sorry, Inspector – what can I say? That poor woman – to have put her through this without need.'

'My mistake, too, Mr Dickens. I should have brought you to look at the body more closely. I took Tom Watson's word for it, but I should have made sure. I can see that you would have assumed it was Mr Bell – him being dressed like the dead man, on stage in the dead man's seat —'

'And the hair, Inspector – it is just like Bell's. And the hand, the hand I saw hanging down. That long, thin, white hand was exactly the same as Bell's.'

'Well, no sense in mithering about what's done. Two questions occur to me: who is this? And, where is Clement Bell?'

'I can answer the first, if not the second, Inspector.' Mrs Stark had come back into the room. Her face had relaxed somewhat and her voice was steady. 'That man is Edwin Bell, Clement's older brother who lived here, in Manchester.'

11

ANGEL MEADOW

Later in the evening, when Mrs Bell had been tended to by a doctor, and Mrs Stark and she were safely in their room in the Palatine Hotel, and Rogers had taken the train back to London, Hardacre, Dickens and Jones sat in Hardacre's office at King Street to review the situation. Sam had been told of the revelation about Clement Bell and was pleasantly surprised by the Inspector's forbearance in the matter of Dickens's mistake. He had agreed that it had been natural for Dickens to assume that the man on stage was Clement Bell.

'I dare not say the word "assume",' Dickens was saying, 'but I rather think that the man in the auditorium was Clement Bell – I said to Sam that it was just the sort of thing he would have done if he were not dead. And he is not.'

'That explains the mystery of the coat,' said Sam. 'He needed that. He could hardly travel about without it. He took his brother's coat, money and train ticket – he was not going back to Mrs Ginger's, but he left the other things, the bag and the suit, to allay her suspicion. She thought he was coming back. And therefore, she had no need to go to the theatre. She'd sent Amy Sweet home so she could be sure to be alone with him.'

'Of course she would think he was coming back – the play had another night to run, and when he didn't come she'd think, perhaps, he was with us – or with another woman.'

'Miss Greenwood, if she knew about her – not that it matters now.'

'Except,' Dickens said, 'I'm wondering when he intended to go, given that there was another night of the play. Why would he leave before it was over?'

'Perhaps he hadn't planned to,' Sam answered. 'It was his brother's death that prompted his disappearance. He knew he'd be a suspect.'

'Odd, though, that none of the things in the bag were marked – something distinctly rum about your Mr Bell,' said Hardacre.

'Separate clothes for a separate life,' observed Dickens.

'Right enough – there's plenty about your Mr Bell that makes me want to know all about him. I went to the firm of solicitors that Mrs Stark said Edwin Bell worked for and I have his address. Mrs Stark met Edwin Bell in London, but she didn't know his Manchester address. I do not relish having to tell another lady that her husband is dead and that we suspect his brother, but it must be done – and soon, and I must find out what I can about the relationship between these two brothers. Mrs Stark didn't know much and Mrs Bell's not fit to be questioned.'

'I wonder if Bell has returned to London, or, Charles, as you thought, to Liverpool,' queried Sam.

'Not unlikely,' Hardacre answered. 'Liverpool is a port – you know what that might mean. I've sent my sub-Inspector already. He's to find out if a man and a woman answering Bell and Miss Greenwood's description are on the passenger lists for any of the ships sailing in the next few days – I've sent a telegraph to the shipping office with the name – that might help. *The Robert Burton* sails to New York tomorrow. There's a transport ship to Australia in three days, and *The Henrietta* sails for Durban day after tomorrow – take your pick.'

'It will be America,' said Sam confidently.

'Why?' asked Hardacre.

'The gun – you said it was American.'

'So I did. I suppose it's possible that he has been in America – we can ask his wife when she's fit. And New York's quicker than Australia or the Cape – he'll want to be away and into a city as soon as he can. It wouldn't be difficult to vanish in New York.'

'Where he can take a different name; remember, he's an actor – he can be anyone he wants. Plenty of theatres in New York.' Dickens was convinced that New York was where a man like Clement Bell would make himself at home.

Sam frowned as he thought of something. 'I don't think he'll have taken Oriel Greenwood. He's not in love with her – she would be an encumbrance to a man on the run, even if she wanted to go. And, now I think of it, he's too clever to go straight to Liverpool. It's too obvious – he must know that you would question Mrs Ginger and find out about their connection with Liverpool, and make enquiries there. And where better to go than the place that we might think would be the last place he'd go?'

'London?' asked Hardacre.

'London, Inspector,' said Dickens, picking up Sam's theory. 'There's no place like a great city when you are once in it. He'll not break cover too soon. He can lie close and wait till things slacken, then try the open – make his escape to foreign air.'

'Exactly,' said Sam. 'Plenty of places to hide there for a man who knows the city. And he could take a ship to America from the Pool of London. He could go anywhere – France, for example. But, I think that he will lie low for a time and there we must seek him through his friends and relations. Someone will know something.'

Hardacre thought about it. 'Then I suggest that you get back there as soon as you can. You can, perhaps, take Mrs Bell and Mrs Stark – you can question them as easily in London as here, find out about his life. I'll have a telegraph back from my sub-Inspector later – if he has found them. If not, I'll keep looking here – Mrs Ginger might know something, and Edwin Bell's family.'

'What about Oriel?' asked Dickens suddenly. 'If he has killed his own brother, what might he have done to her? If, as you say Sam, he has not taken her, if …' He stopped. The thought was unbearable. The man was ruthless – he had abandoned Marion Ginger when he had no further use for her. What was Oriel's fate?

Sam came to his aid. 'She may not know anything, Charles. She may have run away simply because he had told her he was not coming back. She would be too distressed to go home.'

Inspector Hardacre agreed. 'I'll try everyone that knows her – she might be in hiding with someone – some friend – I'll have to keep digging. Meanwhile, I ought to go to Edwin Bell's house. Will you come back here in the morning?'

'We will,' said Sam. 'We can take the noon train to London and begin our investigations into Bell's London life.'

They put on their greatcoats and hats and went out into the dark. As they walked down the great steps leading to the Town Hall, Kettle came running round the corner from Cross Street, very much out of breath. They looked at his anxious face.

'A body's been found, sir, a woman. Met 'Obson from B division. 'E wor comin' to yor. Knew about the murder and the missin' lass – dead woman's a stranger in them parts.'

Dickens felt his legs weaken. Not Oriel, please not Oriel.

'Where?'

'St Michael's – the old buryin' ground.'

'Any more details?'

'A woman found her, went to look for a policeman, found 'Obson and Potter. Potter's with the body. 'Obson's gone back. Young woman, 'e says, not the usual type.'

'Right, we'll come. Get a cab, Kettle.' Hardacre turned to Dickens and Sam. 'You'd best come – if it is Miss Greenwood then I'll need you to identify her, Mr Dickens.'

'I would recognise her,' said Sam hurriedly as they walked to the cab. 'I saw her in the play.' He had seen Dickens's sick face, and wanted to spare him the sight of the girl for whom he had felt such tenderness. He could not judge him; he thought that Dickens would not have acted on his feelings, but he felt pity for him. He often thought that for all his success and fame, for all his wife and children, there was a restlessness in his friend, an unassuaged longing for something that he had never found.

'No, Mr Jones,' the Inspector's tone was firm. 'No mistakes, this time – for either of us.' He looked hard at Dickens, who saw that the Inspector would brook no opposition – he had been forbearing about the matter of Clement Bell and Dickens knew he must make amends for that mistake by identifying Oriel Greenwood, if, God forbid, the body was hers.

St Michaels's Church was in Angel Meadow, the place Engels had described as 'Hell on earth'. It was not the refuge of angels, and the word 'meadow' had long since ceased to be a fitting description. Long ago, there had been fields and woods, and clear streams flowing there. Now, only the clogged and filthy River Irk flowed sluggishly by and the meanest, most squalid alleys were lined with the back-to-back houses, hovels and cellars where there was no clean water, only a pump for as many as twenty families.

The streets were dark, but noisy with brawling, shouting, wild people. Children, half-naked except for pitiful rags, played in the slimy gutters. Everywhere they saw faces marked by want and desperation, or disfigured by rage, cunning, brutality, every kind of wickedness, for this was the haunt of murderers, thieves, prostitutes, pimps, cadgers, coiners, all who were without hope.

Even the red-brick St Michael's Church was called the ugliest church in Manchester. The cab stopped and they got out to hurry through the churchyard to the old burying ground, a place so terrible it was beyond description on this dark night. Hardacre and Kettle had bull's-eye lanterns, which cast a liverish gleam on to the crumbling brick archway that led into the graveyard.

Dickens saw the arch ahead of him – no ivy, just decaying brickwork. He looked up to see not the full moon of his dream, but a thin, shrunken eye of a moon which looked down sickly as if in horror at what it saw. God, he thought, this is worse than any dream, any nightmare, because it is real. And the stench. Death and contagion. Water oozed up from the swampy ground filling the air with noxious gases. Here there had been plague and pestilence. Forty thousand dead, including the children who gave the place its name – Angel Meadow, haunted by the spectres of the plague victims. You could smell it. Here was waste, wilderness; every place of desolation you could imagine was not so horrible as this. It was an abomination, an open wound on the body of the nation – worse, he thought, by far than Seven Dials or St Giles's, the places he had written of in London. This is hell, and I am in it.

He and Sam stopped just before the archway. Sam looked at him – he, too, recalled Dickens's dream. He had seen the picture Dickens had mentioned. This was no romanticised gothic scene. And the song? *The Ivy Green*? Only the cat-calls and yells of the drunks and brawlers who infested the ginnels that wound round the church and burial ground into which they must follow Inspector Hardacre, who was shining his lamp back at them as if to hurry them on.

Steps led down through the archway into the burial ground and they followed the sour lamplight to find themselves where the two constables and two women waited by the body. One was a poor-looking, middle-aged woman with a brown shawl covering her head. The other looked respectable, younger, better dressed in a black cloak and dark dress. She was wearing a black velvet bonnet, but they could see her pale face and dark, anxious eyes. Who was she? Dickens stepped forward to look at the dead face of Oriel Greenwood.

'It is she,' he murmured, sick to the heart.

She lay on her back amid the rubble of bricks, stones and slime, and in the yellow light her face was still, and white as marble. She wore a dark cloak which spread about the ground and he could see the dark dress underneath. There was white lace at the neck and the cuffs of her hands – hands which lay on her breast. She might have been sculpted in stone, an effigy you might see and wonder at in a quiet country church. But she was here, in this dreadful place. The pitiless moon looked down and Dickens saw the blood, which soaked the dress and stained the white lace at the sleeves.

Hardacre nodded. His face was set as iron. 'You know what to do,' he said to the two constables. 'She must be got away from here as soon as possible.'

'Bring her to my house.' The younger women spoke. Her voice was soft and low, educated. 'It is better – it will take too long to get your men. Besides, it is not safe here – not even for you.' She looked at Hardacre.

'Did you find her?' he asked.

'No, Inspector, but I know her, and I will tell you all when we've got her to a better place. It is not fitting for her to be here.' Hardacre heard the determination in her quiet voice, and if she could tell them about Miss Greenwood, then so be it.

'You are right, Mrs …?'

'Mrs Dale – Constance Dale.'

'How far is your house?'

'Not far – by St George's Chapel. I am the Minister's wife. It is down by Sharp Street, on Rochdale Road. You know it?'

'I do.'

Kettle lifted Oriel Greenwood and placed her gently into the waiting arms of Constable Potter, a thickset young man in whose hold she appeared weightless. Inspector Hardacre led the way with Mrs Dale and the other woman. Constable Potter went after them, carrying the body, followed by Dickens and Superintendent Jones. Kettle and the other constable came last. They went into Style Street, turned right then left into Angel Street, the street which William Gadsby, pastor at St George's for forty years, had said ought to be named Black Angel Street. They passed by the factory yards, the reservoir, the warehouses, the iron foundry and the saw mill, past the rows of back-to-back houses, the dark courts and alleys where families of ten lived in cellars, and the teeming lodging houses where thirty people might live.

No one paid much attention to them; occasionally a wide-eyed urchin looked up from the gutter; women standing on their doorsteps gazed curiously, but said nothing when they saw the Minister's wife. A group of men coming out of the foundry gates stood and let them go by, wondering for a moment the meaning of this strange procession, but the pub or the fish shop claimed them; near The Weaver's Arms, a girl in a tawdry red dress gave a frightened glance at the police and saw that they were carrying a girl. Beaten up, mebbe, she thought. Well, it 'apppened. She hurried on, but when Dickens looked back, he saw her standing under the gas lamp, staring after them, her face blotched with shadow, as if it were diseased.

No one spoke as the silent procession made its way into Rochdale Road to the chapel where Mrs Dale let them into her house through a backyard, into the scullery and then to her parlour. Oriel Greenwood was taken upstairs and the two constables sent to King Street to bring the mortuary van.

The parlour, lit by oil lamps, doubled as a study. On the desk near the window were papers, an inkstand, pens and a Bible. There were bookshelves filled with an assortment of books, some of which Dickens recognised as his own works.

Mrs Dale turned to him. Now that she had taken off her bonnet he could see that she was perhaps about thirty, with a pale oval face, calm grey eyes, and smooth, shining brown hair, parted in the middle and gathered into a knot at the back. Her dress was plain black with just a watch pinned below the shoulder.

'I know who you are, Mr Dickens. Margaret spoke warmly of you. Had you come in search of her?'

'We had. This is Inspector Hardacre from King Street Police Station and this is Superintendent Jones from London. Perhaps you would tell us what you know of Miss Greenwood?'

'Yes, I will, though how this dreadful thing has come about, I do not know.'

Inspector Hardacre spoke. 'Mrs Dale, it would help if you could start with the finding of Miss Greenwood.'

'Martha can tell you about that first. This is Martha Boot, who works with me sometimes.'

Martha had taken the brown shawl from off her head. They saw a kindly face on which hardship had scored its lines, and a pair of faded blue eyes which showed distress at the memory of what she had seen. 'I wor cummin' from t'chapel through the alley into Style Street where I live. Two lads come out o' the burial ground – screechin' they'd found a body. I went in to look. Oh, it wor terrible to see that poor girl lyin' so still in the bricks an' mud. I shan't forget it. I sent one to find a policeman and while I was waitin' I 'ad a look. I knew she wor the lady that was stayin' with Mrs Dale so I give the other boy a penny to go an' get 'er. The police cum an' told me to wait. 'Tis all.'

'Mrs Dale, how is it that Miss Greenwood was staying with you?' asked Hardacre.

'I knew Margaret and her family from Whaley Bridge where I was born and lived as a girl. Though Margaret is —' she stopped suddenly before composing herself. 'Margaret was younger than I, but we were friends before I married and came here to work with my husband – he is Mr Gadsby's successor. You knew him, Inspector?'

Hardacre nodded. Who did not know of William Gadsby, a man whose compassion for the poor, whose benevolence, radicalism and eloquent preaching were a legend in Manchester?

Mrs Dale was speaking. 'Margaret came here two nights ago. She asked if she might stay before she went to London – she was expecting a gentleman from the theatre to come for her. She said her mother knew all about it. But, Inspector, I was doubtful. She seemed too anxious, as if she were afraid and excited at the same time. I did not think she was well and I could not understand why she would be going to London with a gentleman. She said that you, Mr Dickens, and the other company members would be going too, but I thought there was something wrong: why should she come here of all places? I tried to persuade her to wait until I could write to her mother. She agreed, but when I returned last evening she was gone. She left a note to say that she was sorry she could not wait for me.'

'No gentleman came?' asked Hardacre.

'No, but I assumed she had arranged for him to come while I was out, that she had gone to London. Then the boy came with the message from Martha – he said it was urgent. I had no idea until I saw her there. Has this man done this? Who is he?'

'We think he is a man called Clement Bell,' said Hardacre.

Mrs Dale's eyes widened in recognition. 'She spoke of him – she cared for him. But I could not believe that Mrs Greenwood knew of all this and had sanctioned it. But if she loved him and he her, then why?'

'We don't know, Mrs Dale. We suspect him of another murder and we need to find him. Did Miss Greenwood tell you anything about him?'

'Very little, apart from the fact that he was an actor and that your company, Mr Dickens, would be performing in London. I think she wanted me to believe that it was all in your hands.'

Dickens had to tell her. 'The company was not going to London, Mrs Dale – the play was to end tonight, and I thought Miss Greenwood would go home to Whaley Bridge.'

Mrs Dale looked grave. 'I see. Then she was running away with him.'

'She thought so.'

There was a knock at the front door. The mortuary van had arrived. Mrs Dale looked at the Inspector. 'Is it possible for you to wait for my husband? He will be home in the next half an hour. I should like him to see her. She will have most need of blessing, Inspector.'

12

LYING AWAKE

Dickens and Jones left Mrs Dale's house; Inspector Hardacre had agreed to wait for Mr Dale.

'A compassionate man, the Inspector,' observed Dickens. 'The more I know him, the better I like him. Straightforward and earnest, resolute and tough, yet he was prepared to wait even though he has much to do.'

'He is a man whom one respects,' agreed Sam, nodding, before changing the subject. 'I think Bell will be gone. Miss Greenwood was killed yesterday – poor girl. He must have promised to take her to London when all the time he intended her death. We must get back to London and find out what we can.'

Dickens did not answer and for a time they walked on in silence, following Kettle who was to see them back to the Palatine Hotel. Sam observed Dickens, saw how that finely cut face, delicate yet decisive, was deeply troubled, his shoulders sagged. Exhaustion, thought Sam. He would feel the death of that girl, not because he loved her, more because it was the death of promise, of what she might have been. He thought of his only daughter, Edith, dead at twenty-one, and her child.

'Food, and warmth, and sleep,' he prescribed his friend. 'You are exhausted.'

Dickens smiled at him, his face brightening for a moment. 'Sleep that knits up the ravell'd sleeve of care —'

'Sore labour's bath. Balm of hurt minds,' Sam continued the quotation.

'Would that it were so. But Macbeth murdered sleep – I think that Bell has murdered mine. What dreams may come? There is no place so lonely as dreamland, land of unspeakable terrors where none can share the agony of the dreamer. I am afraid, Sam, after what we have seen here. And of my part in Oriel's death.'

'What do you mean? You can't think it is anything to do with you.'

'Only that he hated me.'

'But he didn't kill her because he hated you.' Sam was stern. 'No, Charles, no. He killed his brother – we're sure of it now. I suspect there must be money in it. Edwin Bell seems to have been a successful lawyer, Clement Bell, perhaps an unsuccessful journalist. Perhaps he asked for money and was denied. Oriel Greenwood may have known something. How many times have we discussed motive? The murderer hates his victim, fears him or her —'

'And there is no hatred deeper than that rooted in fear. She was guileless. She may not have known what she knew, but he could not risk it.'

'Exactly. He's ruthless. Yes, he disliked you, was envious, perhaps. He may even have seduced Oriel because he knew you were fond of her, but he did not kill her for that. He killed her because after the first murder, the second comes easy. What is there to lose? Hanged for a sheep as for a lamb.'

'Or the other way round. Very apt, Sam, but I know what you mean, and, as ever, you have done me good.'

They walked on, each preoccupied with his own thoughts. Kettle was silent, too, thinking of the girl they had found, and the murderer who, perhaps, was far away now, in London. Inspector Hardacre would keep searching in Manchester and they would keep an eye on the passenger lists of ships out of Liverpool. But he could be anywhere. Murder. What a terrible thing – to kill that poor young lady. Downright wicked.

Kettle left them at the Palatine Hotel. Dickens and Jones went in to order their supper, though neither felt much like eating when it came. No tripe – that was a mercy. Roast chicken and roast potatoes. They ate some of it and took a glass of wine apiece to the fire.

'We ought to see Hardacre tomorrow before we go,' said Sam. 'I should like to know about Edwin Bell. The Inspector will want to know if there is anyone else who might have had cause to murder him.'

'I am convinced that it is Clement Bell after tonight,' responded Dickens. 'I no more doubt it than that the Old Bailey is not Westminster Abbey.'

'I agree, but Hardacre's job is to investigate all possibilities. I wonder what Edwin Bell's family can tell us about Clement Bell and his relationship with his brother.'

'You may find out something useful tomorrow, agreed Dickens. 'I must go to see the boy, Jo. I thought I might try to find him a place with the Grants. He is a bright lad. I am sure he will do well if he can be found employment. I shall seek him out while you see the Inspector. What are we to do with Mrs Bell and Mrs Stark?'

'If Mrs Bell is well enough, I think we could find a first-class carriage to take them back to London. I should think Mrs Stark will have given Hardacre as much information as she can – I will have to interview Mrs Bell when we get back to London. We need to know about her husband's financial circumstances – was he in debt, for example? What was his life in London?'

'I can go to see Costello, find out what he knows,' said Dickens. 'Of course, he may know only that part of Bell's life that Bell chose to reveal. I still find it extraordinary that Costello should have written so warmly of him.'

'Hmm – a man of many parts. His wife would not know. She is a delicate girl, and as we saw, pregnant. He is a man of appetite, as we know. Perhaps he took his pleasures elsewhere in London – women, gambling, clubs. He probably lived beyond his means. Debtors closing in – bills not met. Desperate, he ...'

'... sought to get money from his brother, who refused,' finished Dickens.

'But why did Oriel Greenwood disappear?' asked Sam. 'You said yourself that she wouldn't have simply abandoned the play. She must have known about the murder and fled – to Mrs Dale, as we now know. No one would think to seek her there. But if she knew, then why did she consent to go to London with him? That's the puzzle.'

'I do not want to believe that she knew about the murder,' said Dickens. 'No, Sam, it is inconceivable. Perhaps she wasn't as innocent as I thought, but she couldn't have been in the theatre when Edwin Bell was murdered. Jo heard only one person leave, and Tom Watson would have seen her, surely? Bell knew she was at Mrs Dale's, but how?'

'Let us suppose that she didn't know about the murder,' pondered Sam. 'Suppose she was waiting for him somewhere. A hotel, perhaps – he went somewhere after the murder of Edwin Bell. Try this for size: he goes to her, tells her that someone has been shot, that the play is withdrawn, that he will take her to London – they can be together there. Tells her she must hide away – she suggests Mrs Dale's. He tells her that he will come for her. He has to get her away from the theatre, from the certainty that she will be questioned because —'

Dickens finished the sentence for him. 'Because he let something slip to Oriel about his brother. He would know that we would question her, and she, in her innocence, would tell us that he was to meet his brother. That would be enough, surely, to make her a danger to him.'

'It would,' agreed Sam.

They were silent then. Dickens thought about the girl whom Mrs Entwistle had thought was a bit spoilt. He thought of Robert Alston, who was not enough for Oriel who had not wanted to settle down. And the play: Clement Bell had played the noble Alfred Evelyn – how easy it would have been for Oriel to believe that Clement Bell was the same. He knew how hard it was to come back to reality after the magic of acting, how hard it was to leave those with whom one had lived so intensely. She would see herself as Clara, faithful, unwavering in her devotion – she would sacrifice everything for him. And she had.

Sam spoke again. 'Clement Bell had a gun in his pocket when he met his brother – did he think only to threaten Edwin, or did he, anticipating a refusal, intend to kill him?'

'Perhaps the first. What makes a man a murderer? When comes the moment that he steps off the precipice into the abyss? When exactly does he condemn himself?'

Sam wondered what emotions had pushed Bell to that first reckless act from which there was no going back, and said, 'We don't know into what toils he has entangled himself. His brother's refusal may have been the end of his last hope of escape from debt, let's say. He uses the gun as a threat to try to force the matter. They're both angry – Tom Watson heard high words – and Bell shoots his brother.'

'But then I heard his applause when I discovered the body,' pointed out Dickens. 'If he was angry and desperate he would have fled. There is something cold-blooded in his watching me. What was he doing there in the stalls?'

'You said that he might have hidden up the stairs – perhaps he heard you come in, came down a bit, saw it was you, and couldn't resist applauding to see what you would do.'

'He took a risk – what a nerve he has! I thought he was gone when I fired the gun, but he must have stayed there in the stalls. He must have been delighted to see me arrested. He saw it all.'

'And all he had to do was slip back onto the stage and get out the back way.'

'And Jo heard him. I tell you, Sam, that coolness frightens me. What else might he do?'

'You mean beyond killing two innocent people?'

'Let us hope it is only two.'

Upon that sombre note it was time to retire. They agreed to meet at the station for the two o'clock train to London. Dickens thought that would give him time to see Jo, and to find some refuge for him, even if he could only leave him in Tom Watson's care for the time being. Something positive must come of these dark days in Manchester – someone could, perhaps, be saved.

Lying awake, sleep evaded Dickens, slipping from him like one of those satiny counterpanes which would slide from the bed when the restless occupant turned over. He was glaringly, persistently and obstinately awake. I must not allow my mind to wander, he thought, or I shall be awake all night. But his mind refused to obey. Ideas like fleas leaped up, touched down, then off again. *David Copperfield* – that's it. Think of the next instalment. I am like Mr Dick, he thought, into whose head King Charles I would keep popping. Betsey Trotwood popped her head in, then he was in Dover – wherefore to Dover? King Lear popped in, pushing Miss Trotwood unceremoniously out – every inch a king. Our foster-nurse of nature is repose – even the mad old king slept. Macbeth popped in, and old King Lear simply vanished. Macbeth, Macready – dear old Macready whose performance of Macbeth had harrowed him with fear and wonder. Theatre. Oriel Greenwood. Bell. Death.

It was no good. He got out of bed and went to the window. The pane of glass felt cool to his heated brow. He thought of the old remedy which said that if you beat the pillow and shake the bedclothes twenty times you will have sweet and pleasant sleep. Unlikely. He stared out at the night, across the street to where the dark shapes of the mills loomed, and beyond them, clustering about the walls of the factories, the little houses and mean streets where even now the mill workers, the foundry men, the spinners, the weavers and their wives and children were getting up in the dark to start their long, relentless day. He could see the bulk of the engine house, and heard the stirring of machinery and steam, and fire. A terrible emptiness possessed him. It was time to go home.

13

MRS GASKELL

Dickens and Jones parted the next morning at the Town Hall. The Superintendent went in to see Inspector Hardacre, and Dickens walked along to Spring Gardens and the Queen's Theatre. Tom Watson was in his watchman's box with Jo. They were sharing a breakfast of cold sausage and bread.

Dickens took Jo into the dressing room that had been his own – how long ago it seemed that he had looked out from the stage at the bright faces, all laughing, earnest and intent. They faded away like figures in a dream to be replaced by that jeering applause in the dark where a murderer had sat and watched a scene of his own devising.

Jo was looking at him, waiting for him to speak.

'Where is home, Jo?' he asked the boy.

'Nowhere, sir. Don't have one now.'

'But you did, once?'

'Till mam died, yes. We lived over the bridge, in Salford, behind the blackin' works, alley off Egerton Street.'

The reference to the blacking works took him back, just for a moment, to Hungerford Stairs, to the dilapidated old room with its rats where he had laboured over his pots of blacking and thought he would never escape. He looked at his hands. He had thought they would never be clean. Dickens, who took a shower every day, looked at the dirty, lonely boy.

'And when your mother died?'

'I had a stepfather, Mr Dickens. Hard, he wor. I hated him. He brought his woman to live with us, but that didn't stop him.' The boy's eyes filled with tears at some memory. Beaten, Dickens supposed, abused and used when the mother had gone.

Jo wiped his eyes on his ragged sleeve. 'He pretended to be blind or crippled. I wor meant to beg for him, or steal, so I ran away. Best to live on my own.'

'Can you read or write?'

'Went to the Temple – Sunday School, sir, and mam taught me too. She went to school. Said I mun talk properly. She loved me an' I loved her. I miss her.'

'Would you like to get work – a situation as a messenger boy, perhaps?' Dickens thought perhaps Jo could be got out of Manchester – to Ramsbottom where the Grant Brothers had their mill. Jo looked anxiously at him. 'You might become a clerk, a young man in an office – if you practise your reading and writing. There is a school at the mill. An opportunity, Jo, for a better life.'

'I cannot, sir.'

'Why not, surely it would be better than living on the street?'

Jo wept then. Dickens did not understand. He had offered the boy a chance, yet it seemed to distress him.

'Jo, what is it? How can I help you?'

'I cannot be a clerk in a mill. I cannot be a messenger boy – I cannot – I'm a girl.' Jo lifted up a mass of unruly hair and pulled it back to gather her hair into a knot behind her head. Under the dirt Dickens saw the delicate profile, the small chin, and the long, dark lashes that made a fan on the cheek when the child closed her eyes. Jo was most definitely a girl.

She was weeping again, the wrenching, choking sobs of a child grieving for all she had lost. The loneliness of it pierced him. What to do now? He dared not touch her, dared not enfold the lost child in his arms. He must be practical. There must be something. Then he had a thought. Come to it gently.

'What is your real name?'

'Joanna – 't'was easy to call myself Jo; but what can I do, sir? I cannot go into service. I cannot live in a strange house. What if they were cruel?'

'An apprentice, Joanna, a job in a milliner's or dressmaker's?'

'I cannot, sir. I cannot sew or make dresses. No one taught me. Mam taught me readin'. She wanted me to go to school – I wanted to learn things. I could stay with Tom – he donnot know the truth. I could stay here – be here when you come back, sir.' She looked at him with a kind of hopefulness.

'I do not know when I might come back. And you need a life, Jo, a future, more than just with Tom, kind as he is. What if I took you to a lady I know who has a school? She would find a place for you there. You could learn things.'

He had thought of Mrs Gaskell. He had received a letter from her in January. She had asked for his help in finding a family to take a girl to South Africa, a girl who had been in prison, but whom Mrs Gaskell thought was worth saving. He had consulted Miss Burdett-Coutts with whom he had established his Home for Fallen Women in Shepherd's Bush. Some of the girls had sailed for Australia to start new lives. Miss Coutts had found a family going to the Cape, willing to look after Mrs Gaskell's protégée. Perhaps she would now help him to find shelter and a home for Jo.

Jo looked doubtful. It was clear that she had no faith. She was afraid of the idea of a new life – the old one was bad enough, but it was what she knew. She had survived.

123

'Let me try her, Jo. She is a good woman. She would not be cruel, and, as I say, you could go to school, I know it, and then there will be hope for a future. Let me try.'

The girl nodded. He would have to move fast, he thought, get a cab to Upper Rumford Street – he remembered the address, but he was blowed if he knew where it was. A cabman would. Meanwhile, Jo could stay here.

'I will bring my friend, Jo, and you can see if you like her. I think you will. She is kindness itself.'

'Donnot tell Tom about me, will you, sir. I'll tell him myself if I'm goin' with the lady.' He noted the word 'if' and saw the uncertainty in her eyes.

'I will come back before I go to London to tell you what I have arranged.'

Dickens went out into King Street to leave a note for Sam at the police station – to tell him that, at all costs, he must wait at the station. Dickens might be late, but he would come. Then he found a cabman to take him to Mrs Gaskell's house, a mile and a half from the city centre at the end of the very long Upper Rumford Street, one end of which touched the town and the other where number 121 was situated, the last house which overlooked some fields. There was still some countryside here, even a mile or so from the middle of the seething, noisy town.

Dickens rang the bell and gave his card to a maidservant. He waited, looking at the cows in the nearby field until Mrs Gaskell came out to meet him. She looked astonished at his being there, and not a little flustered.

'Mr Dickens, I had no thought to see you here. You must come in. What a very great surprise.'

He grinned at her. 'I am sorry, ma'am. Thou art gloppened, I see. An' not a bit o' flesh meat in t'ouse.'

She could not help laughing at his Lancashire accent, and at the use of the word 'gloppened' – she had used it in *Mary Barton*, and he had remembered.

'Come in, come in. Awn downreet glad to see yo'. Thou mun tek a sup o' tea.' She paid him back in kind. The awkwardness was over, and she took him into a drawing room where a fire was lit, and where two little girls played on the carpet, and a third sat at the piano. Three of Mrs Gaskell's daughters, Meta aged thirteen, Flossy aged eight, and the youngest, Julia, aged four, all of whom looked at him with wide eyes. They were pretty, fair-haired girls with sweet faces like their mother's. Mrs Gaskell introduced them to Mr Dickens, and then they went away to their nurse.

Mrs Gaskell sat down opposite Dickens. Now her eyes were troubled beyond the fluster of an unexpected guest.

'You have come about Margaret Greenwood? Miss Jewsbury sent me a message this morning. What has happened, Mr Dickens? A young man shot, too.'

'It is thought that a man called Clement Bell has murdered his brother, and that he killed Miss Greenwood.'

'But why should he murder Margaret? It seems impossible. They were in the play – oh, heavens, was she …?' she faltered.

Dickens did not wish to say too much. Oriel's life should not be the subject of talk – not that he thought Mrs Gaskell would gossip, but still, it should not come from him. He saw that in the silence she was uncomfortable that she had leaped to such a conclusion.

'I do not want to speculate. The case is in the hands of Inspector Hardacre. He would not be pleased if I were to say too much – he is a capable man and will, I hope, find out the truth. I am deeply sorry about Miss Greenwood – she was such a talented girl. It is monstrous.'

'Yes, that is the word.'

'But, I came about another matter, too. It is not connected, but it involves a young girl whom I hope you might help.'

Dickens told her about Jo. Mrs Gaskell was all sympathy and agreed to go and see Jo.

'There must be something I can do,' she said, 'perhaps find her lodgings with some respectable family until I can find a permanent place. There will be someone in Mr Gaskell's congregation at Cross Street. She could go to the industrial school at Swinton – it is a good place, well run. It has gardens, play areas, sports fields – fresh air and good food – I could find her a place there. How old is she?'

'I do not know – eleven or twelve.'

'And she is at the theatre?'

'Yes, I have left her in the charge of the watchman there. He does not know she is a girl. She is afraid, I think – she feels safer as a boy, and she is right. I will go back and ask him to keep her until you can see her.'

'Yes, that would be best – I will think of whom I can ask to look after her. I will do all I can, Mr Dickens. You gave me help in the matter of my girl from the New Bailey Prison. Miss Coutts writes that she will find some people to accompany her to the Cape. I think she will do well in another world, as your Jo will. It is a reflection on our society, is it not, that a girl must masquerade as a boy for her safety – and women must masquerade as men for theirs – or for their success. Do you know, Mr Dickens, that I began writing under a man's name – Cotton Mather Mills. Appropriate, was it not?

'Very – but you became Mrs Gaskell with *Mary Barton* just as Boz became Charles Dickens.'

'And the Miss Brontës left off being Currer, Ellis and Acton Bell – three brothers became three sisters, and two are now dead. It is very sad. I think of poor Miss Brontë away up there in the Yorkshire hills.' She sighed. 'Well, I will do as much as I can for that poor girl of yours. We cannot do much now for Margaret Greenwood – it is tragic. I wish she had not changed her name.'

'I thought Oriel a most pretty name,' said Dickens.

'It is, but she seemed to us not quite herself – I changed back to my own name and you to yours. We wanted to be ourselves, but Margaret I thought wanted to be someone else. I suppose that is why she wanted to be an actress.'

'What do you mean she was "not quite herself"?' Dickens asked.

'I do not know exactly. I suppose a little distant to her old friends. We thought she might have married a young man called Robert Alston – a fine young man. We all had hopes, but she wanted something else; perhaps she thought she had found it in the theatre – I wondered if she had met someone else, she had no time for Robert. He was hurt, we could tell. Oh, it is all so dreadful. Her mother will be deeply distressed – her only child. And your Jo with no mother to protect her. I will go to see her as soon as I can.'

'Thank you. Now I must go – I have a train to catch. In the meantime, I look forward to receiving your story of Lizzie Leigh – I should like it for the first edition of *Household Words* in March.'

'You shall have it.'

She accompanied him to the front door – if he walked a little along the street he would find a cab, she was sure. She watched him as he left – an extraordinary man. She had not altogether liked him when she had dined at Devonshire Terrace in 1849. Too much the centre of attention, she had thought. A bit too much of the flatterer – too much soft sawder, as they said in the north. But now she had seen his concern for that poor child and that he had found time to come to see her and enlist her help. She remembered his prompt reply to her January letter about Miss Palsey, the girl in prison. When he made a promise he kept it. Well, she must keep hers – finish *Lizzie Leigh*, and set about finding a home for Jo.

He had just time, Dickens thought, to go back to the theatre and tell Jo that someone would come, and to give a sovereign to Tom to look after her, and then, pray the Lord, the train.

He managed it. Jo had gone on an errand, just across to the Concert Tavern for Tom's beer, but Dickens could not wait. He gave Tom the sovereign with instructions to look after Jo until Mrs Gaskell should come.

Two o'clock found him and Superintendent Jones in a comfortable first-class carriage. Mrs Bell and Mrs Stark were there, too. Mrs Bell, looking pale and fragile, sat with her eyes closed. She did not speak and they asked her no questions. All that would keep until she was back in London.

'*Go where we may, rest where we will. Eternal London haunts us still.*' Dickens whispered More's words to Sam, and then they sat quietly, watching the country and the towns fly by, hearing the shriek of the engine as it passed through trembling stations, the wheels on the rails, sounding their music, taking them home.

PART II

LONDON

'Calm and unmoved amidst the scenes that darkness favours, the giant heart of London throbs in
its Giant's breast ... In that close corner where
the roofs shrink down and cower together as if to
hide their secrets from the handsome street hard
by, there are such dark crimes, such miseries and
horrors, as could be hardly told in whispers.'

Charles Dickens, *Master Humphrey's Clock*

14

AN INTERLUDE

Dickens sat at his desk, contemplating a little green cup ornamented with the leaves and blossoms of the cowslip in which there was a posy of yellow crocuses, like little suns brightening the gloom of this early spring morning in February. Winter still, really, he thought. Ice on the Thames, and then floods for the tides had been exceptionally high in February. Not the weather for searching. Clement Bell had not been found. Perhaps he had slipped out of the country – gone to America where even now he might be walking the streets of New York. Costello's affable friend or Dickens's enemy, the murderer of Edwin Bell and Oriel Greenwood? Dickens still could not fathom the difference. He had talked to Dudley Costello, who still insisted that the Clement Bell he knew was a harmless, good-natured, not very successful journalist. Costello had shaken his head – not a murderer, surely. Sam had reported much the same thing from his interviews with those who knew the man. Yet he had vanished, and two people connected to him had been murdered.

Dickens bent his head to the papers on his desk, the blue slips upon which he had written the latest instalment of *David Copperfield*. David was enmeshed in his courtship of Dora Spenlow, girlish, bright-eyed, lovely Dora. He thought of Mrs Bell, Clement Bell's wife, who had no understanding of her husband's disappearance. Mrs Stark, her companion, had told Sam that she was too ill to be questioned, and she herelf had been unable to tell the police anything much about Clement Bell's life in London. It was a blank, and Sam was doubtful that they would find the truth. In Manchester, Inspector Hardacre was pursuing his enquiries, but there had been no news.

There was a letter from Mrs Gaskell telling him about the progress of her story *Lizzie Leigh*, the tale of the seduction of an innocent country girl employed in Manchester. He would have it by the end of the month, she wrote. And, there was more:

> *I must tell you, too, about Jo. I am afraid there is no news of her. I have been back to the theatre twice now to see Tom Watson, but he has not seen her. She has vanished, it seems. I rather think she did so on that day you came to see me. Tom Watson remembered your coming, and that Jo had gone for his beer. She did not come back. I asked him to send me a note if he should see her, but I have not heard anything. I went to speak to the landlord of the Concert Tavern; she did not go for the beer. She must have gone away then – with only the tuppence for the ale. Tom Watson did not begrudge the tuppence. Wise old man, he knew she was just a bird of passage.*
>
> *I am so very sorry, Mr Dickens. You hoped for a happy conclusion to her story, and so did I. There are too many abandoned children here in Manchester, and in London, also. They are helpless to protect themselves. I look at my own daughters, so rosy and happy, and cannot help but think of the injustices of fortune that create such lives for my unfortunate girl in prison and your Jo …*

Indeed so, thought Dickens. Oh Jo, why did you not wait for Mrs Gaskell? He had promised that someone would come for her. But she had been doubtful, he had seen it in her eyes. Jo wanted to go to school, had been tempted, but something wild in her had claimed her. He had seen it at the Home for Fallen Women he had established. Not all the girls wanted to stay – some were too restless; they chafed at the lack of freedom, the regulations – not that they were harsh, but the streets called, the wild, noisy streets. He thought about one of those girls, Isabella Gordon, who had disguised herself as a man for safety's sake, and for the freedom it gave her. Jo as a boy, too, roaming the streets, afraid to enter a world she did not know. She would never be found, he thought.

There was a knock on the door and in came Katey, his second daughter who was always sent as ambassador for the others when there was a boon to be asked. He could see Mamie, her shy head just peeping round the door. She came in when she saw that he was smiling and happy to be disturbed.

Katey was eager. 'Papa, we have something for the little girl at the stationer's. You said it was her birthday soon, and as she has no mama to look after her, and no sister to make her something, we have made this.'

She handed him a little picture frame, inside which was an illustrated copy of Isaac Watts's poem *'Tis The Voice of the Sluggard*, a great favourite of the family's.

'You made this?'

'I did the pictures and Mamie copied the words. Aunt Georgy found us the frame. Will she like it?'

'You are dear good girls to think of it. I am certain that Eleanor Brim will love it, and I shall take it to the stationery shop this very day after lunch. Can I fetch anything for you from the shop? A treat of any kind?'

'Are there coloured inks?'

'Every colour of the rainbow – let me see, yellow, the colour of a Chinaman's ear, purple, the hue of witches' lips, and green, the green of a dragon's scales. Rhia Rhama Roos, the magician might drink these inks, though you must not, or you will be yellow, or purple, or green forever.' Rhia Rhama Roos was the Unparalleled Necromancer who appeared at Christmas parties, who could make dolls disappear, plum puddings spring out of top hats, and, most extraordinary of all, could conjure guinea pigs from a box of bran. And only Papa knew who he was.

They looked at him with wide, round eyes. Papa the magician, the spinner of tales. Was it true? It must be. He knew things which others did not. Mama did not know these things. Nor Aunt Georgy.

'Oh, and there is a strange ink that only spies use which, of course, is invisible, and comes in an invisible bottle. I shall put it in my pocket. Of course it won't stain if the bottle breaks.'

'Oh Papa, how will I know I have it if it is invisible?'

'You must trust me. And Mamie, what shall you have?'

'Some sealing wax, please.'

'You must be careful not to burn yourself if you use it.'

'Oh, I shall not use it,' said Mamie gravely. 'I just want to look at it on my desk.'

'I see.' He understood that she would not want to spoil the sticks by burning them. She was a neat, serious little girl. Katey will want to burn it, he thought. She was the fiery one. Lucifer Box, he called her, while Mamie was Mild Glos'ter

'Is there invisible sealing wax?' Katey asked, a glint of mischief in her eyes.

He turned to his desk and palmed a stick of wax. 'If you look on my desk you will see two sticks of wax with what seems like a space between. But in there is the invisible stick. Don't breathe too hard or it will melt into thin air.'

They looked, and held their breath. To be sure there was a space, just big enough for a stick of wax.

'And,' said Dickens, 'all you have to do is toss it into the air like this.' He picked up the imaginary stick, threw it up in the air, caught it and opened his palm. 'Abracadabra – it turns into a visible stick of red sealing wax!' And there it was. 'Very convenient, eh?'

The two girls clapped and laughed.

Mamie pointed out, 'It is lunchtime, Papa. Are you coming in now?'

'I am.'

They danced ahead of him out of the library to the dining room where Aunt Georgy was waiting. Mrs Dickens was upstairs with Henry, the baby, just over a year old, and the little boys, Francis, Alfred and Sydney, were in the nursery upstairs. A quiet lunch, thought Dickens, sitting down on one of the green leather-covered chairs. Through the bay window with its crimson damask curtains he could see the leaden sky. Still, he would go out, keep his promise to buy the inks and wax. And he would take Eleanor a gift – a first edition of *A Christmas Carol*, bound in red cloth with gilt-edged pages. She would like that.

At Bow Street, Superintendent Jones was reading a letter from Inspector Hardacre. Clement Bell had still not been found. There had been no trace of him at Liverpool. Of course, he might have gone under a false name – he was an actor, after all. Marion Ginger had told them nothing more. Clement Bell had not contacted her; of course not, thought Sam, he had abandoned her now that he had no further use for her, just as he had abandoned his wife. The letter made mention of Edwin Bell:

On the night of the murder, Edwin Bell was in the audience watching his brother play the role of Alfred Evelyn. His wife had not accompanied him to the theatre. She was staying in the country, and there was no reason for the servants at home in Chorlton to be concerned as Edwin often stayed in an hotel if he was to be at a late function, or to be in his office early. No one missed him – he was a partner in the law firm in John Dalton Street – he could come and go as he pleased.

Edwin had told his wife that Clement would be in Mr Dickens's play at the Queen's Theatre. She assumed that they would meet as Clement did not often come to Manchester. Edwin rarely saw his brother, but they were not estranged. He did not often talk of Clement, though she did say that Edwin felt his brother might have done better to take up the law rather than journalism at which he was not, apparently, very successful. Still, his wife had money from her father. The settlements at the marriage were such as kept the father in control rather than the husband, which suggests to me that Clement was not entirely to be trusted. Perhaps, as we thought, he had debts which he had to conceal from his wife and father-in-law.

I did find out something interesting from the friend who accompanied Edwin Bell to the theatre. Edwin seemed tense and somehow angry, the friend said. He muttered something which sounded like the word 'blackguard' when Clement Bell came on, but that was all. I wonder if Edwin had some idea that Clement wanted money from him. Anyhow, the friend left Edwin at the end of the play. Bell said he was going to see his brother, and that he was going to have it out with him. The friend got the impression that there was bad blood between them. Of course, this does not fit with what Edwin's wife told me about the brothers' relationship, but men don't tell their wives everything. However, it does fit the account Tom Watson gave us of the high words spoken …

It did, thought Sam. Perhaps Edwin had suspected that his brother was leading a double life. He may even have wondered about his relationship with Oriel Greenwood. He may have known something about Marion Ginger. But it was all supposition. Edwin could tell them nothing now, and Clement might be far away in America – or anywhere. Dickens had made enquiries about him, but had found out nothing useful. Bell seemed such an unremarkable man. People knew him in the offices of various periodicals and newspapers and at a few clubs, but no one could say more than that he was pleasant, good humoured, and seemed happy enough with his wife.

Perhaps that was the point. Clement Bell adopted this perfectly ordinary, decent character to conceal the man within. Murderers did that. Look at Greenacre – a grocer and sweet manufacturer hanged for the murder and mutilation of his sweetheart. And Wainewright, poet, artist and critic. Who would have thought that a man like that would murder his uncle, his mother-in-law and sister-in-law? Dickens said that he had seen him in Newgate where that once polished young man had untidy hair and a dirty moustache – well that was prison for you. Money was the cause in both cases – want of it was a powerful motive.

But all this speculating didn't do much good. Besides, there were other cases to be dealt with. There had been a spate of robberies in and about Bedford Square; a child had been found murdered in a squalid alley in Seven Dials – oddly the newspapers were not so interested in this as in the theft of plate from the Cavendish house.

But they had made progress – some of the plate had turned up at Fikey Chubb's. Fikey, well-known to Sam, called himself a respectable businessman. In truth he was a fence, and Stemp, one of Sam's most trusted constables, liked to keep his eye on Fikey which was how he came upon the silver plate. Fikey, of course, had no knowledge of how it came to be stashed behind his counter. Sam smiled as he thought of the interview with the sweating Fikey – a man whose stench could pollute the Thames. Fikey had pleaded a frame-up, of course. Some bleeder had planted it all. A friggin' disgrace, it woz when a man o' business woz 'arrassed like 'e woz. Yer couldn't trust anyone. Sam had asked if there was a particular anyone not to be trusted, a question to which Fikey had scowled and declared 'e dint know no bleedin' perticulers. And there Sam had left it, abandoning Fikey to a cell where he could think upon his acquaintances, particular or not as the case may be. Constable Stemp had taken Fikey to the cell, holding him by the scruff of his neck, like the rat he was. Fikey was frightened of Stemp. Sam had had to open all the windows in his office to rid himself of the smell of the man.

Alas, there had not been any progress in the case of the murdered child, and that was because no one claimed her. And as there were an estimated thirty thousand children roaming the streets, filthy, half-naked, half-starved, most thieving for their living, and not enough places in the Foundling hospital, the workhouses or the ragged schools, it was not surprising that one murdered child was of no interest to most. She had probably been orphaned or simply abandoned, left on the street to make her own way. They may never know.

A Mrs Belinda Timmins, a respectable woman who lived off Parker Street, had come to ask about the dead girl. Her own six-year-old daughter, Polly, had vanished from the backyard of their house. Mrs Timmins had gone out to call her in and had found the door to the yard open, and Polly gone. She couldn't have opened it herself, Mrs Timmins insisted. 'Someone 'as took 'er, I knows it.' Sam had taken her down to the mortuary where the dead child lay; clean now, he had thought, so innocent in the white gown, but, underneath it, he knew there were bruises which no amount of washing could remove – the stains left by the murderer who had vanished into the labyrinth of alleys in the city.

Mrs Timmins had forced herself to look. It was not her Polly; she didn't know the child, but 'oh, Gawd, wot a terrible thing'. Sam did not know whether to be glad for her or sorry. Granted it was not Polly, but then where was she? Mrs Timmins who had spared a moment to lament the death of an unknown child, returned to her own grief.

Such things happened: children were taken from their homes, from the street while they were on an errand or coming from school, spirited away, sometimes found dead, sometimes never found. He thought of the empty place at the table, the empty bed or cot and the horror of never knowing to what end your child had come. He had put Inspector Bax on the case – he hoped that Polly Timmins's disappearance did not mean that there was some gang at work.

He looked back at Inspector Hardacre's letter. He suddenly felt a kind of rage against Clement Bell – what business had he, a comfortably off young man with a wife and child to come, to turn murderer? It was greed, no doubt, or envy, resentment. It was not poverty or misery or despair – you could understand that, if not forgive it. He recalled a man who had killed his wife and two children, and who had stayed in a foetid cellar with the bodies for weeks. He was found when the neighbours called a policeman – the stink had been unbearable. The man had died in the hospital at Newgate – because he did not want to live. Poverty and hopelessness had killed them all, Sam had thought at the time, unable to condemn the man as a murderer. But greed, the want of something that belonged to another when you had enough, that was insupportable.

He bent his head to finish his paperwork. It was time to go to Mr Brim's stationery shop; it was Eleanor Brim's birthday – she would be eleven. Sam's wife, Elizabeth, had proposed a small party, small because Mr Brim was ill in bed. This time, Elizabeth said, he might not recover from the consumption that was killing him – and what then? Elizabeth had already promised Robert Brim that she would look after his children. There was no one else, and she would also take care of the shop which would be left to the children. Sam did not know if it would work, but he had thought of someone who might run the shop when Elizabeth was too busy. Elizabeth had thought it a splendid idea. In the meantime, he hoped that the serious little girl could enjoy her party. She would – Mr Dickens, their best customer, was coming, and Constable Rogers.

When Sam and Rogers arrived at the shop in Crown Street, they found Dickens already there, and Eleanor opening her present, the sight of which drew a smile of joy. Sam saw Elizabeth look at the child with such love that it made his heart turn over.

Dickens, whose observant eye missed nothing, said, 'Blimey, it's the perlice – 'ide the swag, my dears. Scarce, scarce.' No longer Mr Dickens but the villainous Fagin, he continued, 'You'll 'ave to get up early in the morning to win against the Superintendent for all e's a rum lookin' cove.'

Everyone laughed; Sam went to wish Eleanor a happy birthday. Tom Brim was playing with a spinning top on the floor, and Poll, the dog, was eying it suspiciously. Scrap, the messenger boy was there, too, in charge of the cake and lemonade. Eleanor studied her picture and smiled delightedly when Dickens recited the first verse from memory and with comic actions. Dickens, who sang for his children before bedtime, sang especially for Eleanor one of the old Irish melodies he had sung years ago in Chatham with his sister Fanny:

What the bee is to the floweret,
When he looks for honeydew,
Through the leaves that close embower it,
That, my love, I'll be to you.

There was quiet for a moment as the song died away, but Dickens, ever alert to the need for a change of mood, lifted Tom onto the counter and began the round game, 'I love my love with an A, because she is —'

Tom thought a moment, and then came up with the deliciously absurd, 'An apple,' which led to all sorts of mad flights of fancy. The loved one was, by turns, beastly, crazy, dastardly, eleeomosynary – the last supplied by Dickens who swore that it was a true word, and had he a diction-ary in his pocket which as a writer he ought to have had, he would have proved it. Eleanor declared that Mr Dickens would never cheat, but she warned him that he must not do it again – only ordinary words were allowed. The mischief-maker could not resist another when it was next his turn.

'I love my love with an S, because she is —' he paused for dramatic effect. Sam took out his pocketwatch. 'She is – spoffish.'

There was an outcry. It was not an ordinary word – it was extraordinary. In fact, Eleanor insisted it could not be true. But it was, Dickens asserted. He knew it to be true for he had made it up himself. It meant, he told them, a busy, bustling sort of person. They agreed that it was a useful sort of word.

'Spoffish, spoffish,' cried Tom Brim, delighted with the word, and so it had to be allowed. And Tom was allowed the privilege of the last word of all, and he loved his love with a Z because, of course, she was zooey. No one had the heart to suggest that it was not a proper word, especially after Mr Dickens's contributions.

After the cake had been eaten, and the lemonade drunk with toasts to Eleanor, and after Dickens had conjured Sam's watch from his pocket, it was time to go, and for Eleanor to take her presents to show Papa who was waiting upstairs. Dickens did not forget the inks and sealing wax for his girls.

Dickens and Jones stood on the pavement outside with Scrap, who had noted Sam's gesture to him.

'Lookin' fer someone, Mr Jones? Want me ter 'ave a listen out?'

Scrap, Mr Brim's errand boy, acted for Dickens and Jones, too. He had been useful to them in two earlier cases: his sharp eyes had found a man with a crooked face, and he had a good pair of ears; he knew the streets, and the urchins who might know of a stranger. 'Newspaper offices, Fleet Street way — do you know it round there?' asked Sam.

'Yers — goes up ter Cloth Fair, that way about. Mr Brim does business wiv a stationer's there, and one in Cock Lane. 'Oo's the cove?'

'Name of Bell — Clement Bell. Not a cove to mess with, Scrap, so just listen in case anyone mentions him.'

'Got yer, Mr Jones. I won't do nuffink, jest listen about. Let yer know if I 'ears anyfink. Spoffish, that's me.' He winked at Dickens and then left them to it.

'Bright lad,' said Dickens. 'What will you do when …?'

'When Mr Brim is no longer here? Elizabeth and I have promised him we will look after the children, and Elizabeth will run the shop — but that cannot be forever. I have had an idea about that. Mollie Spoon.'

'And?'

'Well, she and Rogers are to be married at the end of next week — you are invited, of course — and Mollie Spoon will no longer be in service so I thought they could live at the shop, and Mollie could manage it when Elizabeth cannot be there. Scrap will still have his job, and he can, as he always does, flit between lodging there and making his occasional visits home.'

'Capital. You have spoken to Rogers, of course?'

'I have. He likes the idea very much. So does Scrap. A bright lad, as you say. He knows that there is no hope for Robert Brim and did wonder what was going to happen to them all. I assured him that he would still be needed by us.'

'You do not think there is much hope of our finding Clement Bell?'

'I am afraid not, I think we have lost him.'

'I think so too,' acknowledged Dickens.

They parted at Bow Street. Dickens made his way to the office of *Household Words* at number 16 Wellington Street North. The first edition of the new periodical was to be published in March at tuppence a copy. He wanted to see his sub-editor, Harry Wills, the thinnest man alive, Dickens thought, joking that Wills had been training all his life to go up a gas pipe. Things were going well; he had started on his preface, stating the intentions of the journal, Mrs Gaskell had promised her tale *Lizzie Leigh*, and there were to be articles on matters of topical interest and poetry, too.

He sat in the bow window looking at the fog thickening in the narrow street where the gas lamps were haloed in hazy greenness and the buildings opposite had almost disappeared. The office was empty now. Haunted place, he thought. The artist, Hogarth, had lived on this site where he had seen a woman in her coffin. It was time he went home. He went out into the dark street. He would not have been surprised to see Marley's face in the doorknocker of the next office; somewhere, he imagined, looking at the fog shifting down the alleys and courts, nature was brewing on a grand scale.

Dickens walked up to Oxford Street where the traffic was moving slowly; it would come to a standstill later. His way took him to Portland Place, and into Devonshire Place where once, on a foggy night, he had been pursued by a murderer. It was quiet here in the gathering dark, and he thought of his terror that night when he had heard soft footfalls behind him. The fog seemed to be denser here, suffocating as a musty old cloak thrown over the head. For a moment he was completely lost; he could neither tell where the pavement began nor how to cross the road. He stood still, straining to hear.

And then it came, a curiously uneven footfall followed by a sound like a knock, then a slight echo. He turned to where he thought the sound came from. No one. Turned again. No one. Yet the sound came on. He felt a tightening in his throat and his hand went involuntarily to his neck. He saw in a sudden movement of the fog that he was next to a passageway between two houses and darted in. The strange uneven tread came closer – he peeked out. A man came halting by – a man with a stick, and Dickens saw briefly the gleam of a white clerical collar. He felt weak with relief and hurried on, the follower now, not the pursued. The man had vanished but, somewhere ahead of him, he heard a curious sound like laughter. An impression of a cloak swirling, a figure in a top hat. Then it was gone.

Where was Clement Bell? He pictured him crouching in the dark, waiting. Waiting for what? The chance to run? Or was he waiting to strike again?

15

A DOOR CLOSES

The brown air smelt of smoke and sulphur; the sky had vanished. The fog had continued to thicken, so deep that it was impossible to see a yard in front. The garden in King Square, off Goswell Street, was wreathed in fog. Superintendent Jones and Constable Rogers had thought it quicker to walk when the message came from a beat constable. They had crept along, their bull's-eye lanterns creating little cones of light which illuminated the way for a few feet so that they had avoided passers-by whose faces loomed up suddenly in the gloom. It was slow going for the two men. The message had been an urgent one, but they could not stride out as they wanted. They had gone by Lincoln's Inn up to Holborn Hill, through the eerily deserted Smithfield Market, along St John's Street, cutting through Percival Street which took them to the quiet square of terraced houses where at number 24 lived Mrs Dora Bell.

There was faint yellowish light coming from an open door ahead of them. They saw the constable at the bottom of the steps lift his lamp, and as they drew near they could see Mrs Stark's white, anxious face looking out from the doorway.

They went up the steps. Mrs Stark opened the door wider; the fog swirled into the dimly lit hall, and they saw the body at the foot of the stairs. It looks unreal, thought Sam, like a scene from a play – the fog twisting itself round the body of the woman in her dark dress, the terrified maidservant and the frightened woman waiting for their cue.

Mrs Stark spoke, breaking the awful silence. 'I sent for you, Mr Jones – I did not know who else … I thought you ought to know … you knew her and —' she sat down suddenly on a hall chair. The maidservant was staring at the body of Mrs Bell, tears running down her horrified face.

Sam asked, 'Is there anyone else here? Any other servants?'

'No,' said Mrs Stark, 'it was cook's day off – as I was going out, I knew Dora wouldn't need her. Emma could give her something cold if she wanted it – or some soup …' her voice trailed away and she wiped her eyes.

'Then my constable will take your maid to the kitchen to make some tea.' He nodded to Rogers, who steered the girl away from the stairs, down the corridor to where he supposed the kitchen would be.

'Mrs Stark, will you come into the drawing room with me? You can tell me what happened in there.'

They went into a room where the remains of a fire smouldered; Sam added some coal. When it was going again, he turned to face Mrs Stark, who had sat on a sofa.

'Tell me,' he said, 'if you can. You went out?'

Mrs Stark looked exhausted, but he had to know. She took a deep breath and looked at him. 'Yes, I went out for the afternoon to visit my mother. She is old now, and misses me. I was to stay here with Dora until she was better, or until Mr Bell —' she broke off. What to say about Clement Bell?

'He's not been here?' asked Sam.

'No. Dora has been too ill to talk about it. She has not been herself …' she wiped her eyes again.

Sam's voice was gentle. 'In what way?'

'She speaks of Clement as if he were still in Manchester – she asks when he is coming home. It is as if she has forgotten we were there, and that we saw —'

Sam waited. The shock, perhaps, had affected Dora Bell's mind – she had erased what she did not wish to remember. He thought of how fragile she had seemed.

'Doctor Wells seemed to think that she would recover when Clement returned – I could not bear to tell him about that business in Manchester. Where can he be?'

'We don't know, I'm afraid. Inspector Hardacre in Manchester has no news – but tell me about tonight.'

'Dora, Mrs Bell, seemed a bit better. She was quite calm – we moved her to the sofa in her room. She said she would be all right. Emma – the maid – would look after her, she said. Emma is a nice, capable girl. I trusted her. I meant to come back by five o'clock but the fog – it took so long. The cab could hardly move, and there was an accident – a wagon and a cab collided in the fog. My cabman didn't want to go on. I thought I would walk, but it was so dark, Mr Jones. I hardly knew where I was going – it seemed like hours before I got back here and met Emma, who had got locked out, and we found poor Dora ...' She closed her eyes.

Rogers came in with the tea, the maidservant with him. She would have to be questioned.

'We will leave you for a few moments, Mrs Stark. I must make some arrangements.' Sam and Rogers went out to look again at the body lying at the foot of the stairs.

'We need to look carefully at this, Rogers, before she is taken away. It could be an accident, suicide, or, of course, someone might have pushed her, and we must find out what might have happened. Now, we must be swift.'

Sam looked at the position of the body. Mrs Bell lay on her back, and there was blood at the back of her head – the fall had caused her to crack her skull on the wooden floor. That had probably killed her. Had she fallen backwards, or had she twisted as she fell forward, tripping over something on the staircase? Sam mounted the stairs, looking carefully at the carpet and the stair rods for anything loose. He went to the landing at the top and examined the carpet there. There was a rug, rumpled – she might have tripped on that, and been unable to save herself. She might have been faint; on the other hand, the rumpled rug might suggest that there had been a struggle of some kind. He would have to find out if someone had been there that day. He thought of Clement Bell. Had he come to see his wife? Had there been some kind of argument? It was time to ask.

'Rogers, you'll have to send the constable outside for the mortuary van, but it will take hours in this fog. We must take her upstairs. We can't leave her here like this. Find out from the maid which is Mrs Bell's room.'

As Rogers went to ask, Sam looked again at the dead woman. She was wearing a loose, dark red dress; one arm was flung out, the other was underneath the body, where he could see the swelling of her pregnancy. The child dead too, he supposed. He could hardly believe that someone would have pushed her deliberately, knowing her condition. Surely no man could do that – only a fiend. He wondered whether there might be marks on the arms which might suggest that someone had held her. He would look when they took her upstairs.

When Rogers came back, he arranged the shawl so that the blood would not stain Sam's coat, then he lifted her into the Superintendent's arms. But when Rogers lifted her, they saw that the dress was soaked in blood. They both looked down to where she had lain and saw the blood which told them that the child would never be born. They carried her up to her room where there was a fire and the gas lamps were lit.

Laying her on the bed, Sam rolled up the loose sleeves of the dress to reveal the slender arms. The arm that had been flung out looked red round the elbow. She might have caught that as she fell, or the force of the fall had marked it. The other arm was broken – the fall had probably done that. Sam had seen plenty of dead bodies and he knew from experience that those livid red marks could show immediately after some violence done. The post-mortem might reveal other injuries, but there would be cadaveric lividity, mottled, sometimes purple marks covering the abdomen and back of the deceased. He didn't think it would be at all possible to tell if she had been pushed. Only the actual marks of fingers could tell that. In this case, Mrs Bell had been so frail that the lightest push could have sent her tumbling down the stairs, or she could easily have fallen. He rolled down the sleeves.

Rogers put the shawl on the pillow, and they arranged her carefully so that she looked to be sleeping. They looked round the room. Was there anything to suggest that Mrs Bell had received a visitor? The book she had been reading was on the floor by the chaise-longue.

'Sir – look at this.' Rogers was kneeling on the rug by the fire. His keen eye had spotted something. 'It's mud, sir. Someone stood here. It's still a bit wet.'

Possible, thought Sam. Someone who had been outside had stood here, perhaps looking down at a frightened woman. A gossamer clue, true, but worth asking about. Had the maid been outside during the afternoon?

They went downstairs again. Rogers went out to give the constable his instructions. However long it took, they must come with the mortuary van. Sam went in to question the maid. He wanted to know how she had been locked out.

He asked her had there been any visitors during Mrs Stark's absence. No one had been to the front door, but the butcher's boy had come to the kitchen door at four o'clock. Had Mrs Bell come down at all? No, Emma had taken her a cup of tea at about four thirty. Mrs Bell had asked about Mrs Stark, and Emma had told her about the fog. Mrs Bell had drunk the tea and eaten a sandwich. Emma had gone up to take away the tea things, leaving Mrs Bell reading on the chaise-longue in her bedroom. Emma had washed up the pots and had stayed in the kitchen by the fire to wait for Mrs Stark. She had read the paper.

'An' then I heard a knock at the front door. I thought it was Mrs Stark, that she might have forgotten her key. I went an' opened the door, but there was no one there. Just the fog, sir. I went down the steps to have a look up an' down the street. I couldn't see anythin' – it was so thick.'

'Did you hear anything? Footsteps?'

'I did hear something – someone was laughin' – I thought it was someone across the street, an' there was someone. I just had a glimpse then he was gone – swallowed up, if yer know what I mean – in the fog. I thought it might be boys – yer know larkin' about, knockin' on doors, laughin'. It happens sometimes. I went down the street a bit, but there was no one.'

'And then?'

'I went back up the steps, an' the door was closed – it had shut. I should have thought – I've done it before. Mr Bell laughed about it, but I should have thought. Mrs Bell mighta bin callin', she mighta wanted me ...' the girl burst into tears.

'Did you knock on the door, Emma?' asked Sam.

'No, I didn't want her comin' down them stairs.'

'Do not blame yourself. It was an accident.' Mrs Stark's voice was kind.

'How long were you outside the house?' queried Sam.

'Hard ter say, sir – five minutes or so.'

Time enough, thought Sam, for someone to steal into the house and shut the door. Someone, perhaps, who knew that Emma would think it had closed accidentally because it had happened before. 'And then?'

Emma recovered herself. 'I went down the area steps to see if the kitchen door was open, but I knew it wasn't. I always lock it at night. I waited for Mrs Stark. I walked up and down the street a bit to keep warm. I went as far as the end – just to see if Mrs Stark might be coming. There's a cab stand in Goswell Street. I talked to the cabman there, but he said no cabs had come 'cos of the fog.'

Whoever had come in would have had time to do whatever he had done and go out again, Sam thought, but he only said, 'Thank you, Emma. One more thing. When the butcher's boy came did you go out of the kitchen into the area?'

'Yes, he sometimes leaves the gate open – despite me tellin' 'im – so I went out ter make sure he closed it.'

'Then you made the tea and took it up to Mrs Bell?'

'Yes, sir.'

'That is all, Emma, thank you.' Sam saw her frightened eyes. He smiled and said, 'I just need to know the timing of everything. You needn't worry. And now I must speak to Mrs Stark.'

As the door closed, Mrs Stark turned to Sam. 'You think he has been here – that he knocked at the door and sneaked in when Emma went down the street. He would not, could not have killed her. I do not believe it.'

'It is possible that someone came in. Tell me about Bell and why you cannot believe he would harm his wife.'

'I thought him weak, he was not a success as a writer. He thought the connection with Mr Dickens would lead to greater things. That is why he insisted on going to

Manchester even though Dora was not well. But she could never deny him, and so she asked me to come.'

'Why weak?' Sam was interested.

'He went through money like water. He had inherited money and lived like a fine gentleman – clubs, cards, but he earned little. It was a pretence at working to appease old Mr Richards – Dora's father. He did not approve of Clement, and the settlements at the marriage provided an income for them, but the capital was in trust. Dora would inherit, and there was money for when the child came. But he was always out – men have secret lives, Mr Jones, of which their wives know nothing. Double lives.'

She paused, and Sam saw her face darken at some memory. He waited.

'My husband had a mistress. I did not know until after his death. She had a child. I had none, and now Dora's child will never be born. How sad it all is. But I cannot believe, even for all his weakness, that he killed her. He was fond of her, careless, yes, but he did not hurt her, and she loved him.' Mrs Stark looked into the fire. He saw her tears for the unborn child.

In the silence that followed, Sam reflected on the lives of Mrs Stark and Dora – forced into patient acceptance of what could not be changed. Their husbands had the freedom to come and go as they pleased, to lead their varied and interesting lives, to spend so often what was not theirs except by law. He thought of Edith, his dead daughter, whose husband was married again now, living in Manchester, and who had two children – bitter thought.

'I did not speak of any of this to Dora,' said Mrs Stark, breaking the silence. 'What good would it have done? It would not have changed anything. Her father could do nothing – he lives in Devon and is a sick man. This will kill him. No, Mr Jones, Clement was selfish in a careless way, but people liked him. Easygoing, good tempered – and why not? He had nothing much to disturb his pleasant life. I cannot believe he is a murderer.'

Easygoing, good tempered. Just what Costello had said of Bell when he had recommended him to Dickens.

'Well, we must find him and prove that he is not,' said Sam, 'and then Inspector Hardacre can look elsewhere in Manchester for whoever killed Edwin Bell, and Oriel Greenwood.'

'I hope that you will find him. Now, I shall go upstairs and wait with Dora until she can be taken away. You will tell me when the inquest is to be?'

Sam assured her that he would and, after wishing each other goodnight, she went upstairs to keep her lonely vigil with the dead woman. He sat on, thinking. Clement Bell, weak, selfish, but apparently too easygoing to be a murderer, but Mrs Stark had wondered about a secret life. She thought that he might have kept a mistress, as her own husband had done. She had said nothing about any trips to Manchester or Liverpool, but as she had not lived with them she would not have known.

Accidental death, maybe. The mud on the carpet might have been left by Emma after she had been outside. The whole story could be simple – Mrs Bell, realising that Emma was not answering her summons, might well have tried to come downstairs, tripped on that rumpled rug and fallen to her death. But the front door had closed. Someone had been in the street. Bell must have come in. Mrs Stark had said that Dora believed he would come home. Perhaps he had been desperate, angry – she might have run from him and fallen, or he might have pushed her.

Constable Rogers came in. 'Are we ter wait, sir?'

'I think we must. We should not leave them alone here.'

'You think it's murder, sir?'

'It might be. I think on that mud, Rogers, and the convenient locking out of the maid, and the deaths of Clement Bell's wife, his brother, and Oriel Greenwood, and I say to myself that I do not believe it is just coincidence.'

16

SWEET SALLY DIBBS

'We've lost him,' Sam had told Dickens. Now, in his office, in the darkness of early morning, Superintendent Jones wondered. Yes, they hadn't found him, but he was some-where. Why had he gone back to his old home? For money? For papers? For clothes? And what had happened between him and his wife that she should end up at the bottom of those stairs?

He must have some refuge. Had someone taken him in? There were hundreds of lodging houses and cheap hotels – places where a man might hide and never be found. He could disguise himself – dye his hair, wear spectacles, dress himself in a poor man's clothes, walk out of London, sleep in a ditch and make his way to some port from where he might sail anywhere.

Would it help if he sent Inspector Grove to search the house? Neither Mrs Stark nor Dora Bell could tell him what might be missing. Emma might know if clothes were missing, but one man's clothes were very like another's – unless you were Dickens, he thought, smiling a little at the thought of the old white hat Dickens sometimes wore, and the plaid trousers and bright waistcoats. If he could look out of his window now, he would see an army of black coats and top hats, plush ones or battered ones, new ones or second-hand ones, low-crowned hats, felt caps or cloth caps – in that army you could not pick out one man and say, 'It is he – the murderer.'

He thought of Inspector Hardacre. Perhaps he would find out something. He wouldn't give up, that was certain. Perhaps Mrs Ginger knew more than she was telling. Well, he could hope, and in the meanwhile it wasn't as if he had nothing else to do. He ought to go over to Wellington Street to tell Dickens about Dora Bell, and he should go to the shop, tell Scrap they didn't need him to search for Clement Bell anymore. No, he didn't want Scrap walking into danger.

He stood up and was putting on his coat when the door opened to reveal Dickens – Dickens with a face alight with information.

'Tidings, my lord, tidings swift as the posts could run. Behold the Sparkler with —' he saw Sam's face. 'Something's happened. What?'

Sam told him about Mrs Bell. 'I can't be sure it's murder – she might have fallen. It could have been an accident, but that closed door tells me otherwise.'

'Poor thing – and her child, too. But why should Bell kill his wife? She couldn't have known anything about his doings in Manchester.'

'No idea. And I've just been thinking that we have no idea where to look for him.'

'Well, I have something to tell you which might be of use. I had a visitor at the office this morning.'

'Someone who knows where Bell is, I hope,' said Sam.

'Not exactly. A man called James Flay,' Dickens noticed Sam's raised eyebrows and grinned back, 'Flay, I say, a wet curl paper of a lad, with hair of the hearth-broom variety, and something of a poet, who came to offer me a parcel of verses for the new publication, and in our meanderings about the perils of the literary life he mentioned Clement Bell. Knew he was missing – the word has got round. Flay had known Bell before his marriage to Dora and he knew that Clement Bell had a mistress, a pretty little widow in a pretty little house in Hampstead. Mr Flay thought that he had given her up when he married, but I rather thought we might seek her out.'

'And did Mr Flay know exactly where the pretty little house is?' asked Sam.

'Ah, not exactly, but he did mention a little white house with a shiny black door.'

'A dozen or more like it, I daresay,' sighed Sam.

'Samivel, Samivel, don't put yourself in a perspiration – I'm a comin' on ter the kernel o' the matter as the old gentleman said ter—'

'Don't, Mr Weller – leave the old gentleman out of it, I beg you,' but Sam was smiling.

'Mr Flay, being of a poetical turn, remembered the very street – Downshire Hill – because he once took a stroll down to Lawn Cottage where Keats once lived. It was called Wentworth Place then. He and Bell and the pretty widow were going to take tea with an old actress, Eliza Chester, who owned Lawn Cottage then. Famous in her day – mistress of one Calcraft —'

'Not the hangman!' Horrified, Sam was distracted from the important matter.

'No, thank goodness or I should have to give up the stage in grief. Politician.'

'I might have preferred the hangman, but never mind all that. Where's this house?'

'Well, along a' the aforementioned Downshire Hill is a little lane with a terrace of houses in which, Mr Flay seems to recall, is the little white house with the shiny black door.'

'Which might have been painted green since then,' Sam pointed out.

'Ah, but Sammy, my boy, we only have to knock at a few doors and ask for a Viennese widow.'

'Viennese?'

'Oh, didn't I say? Yes, a Viennese lady.' Dickens's expression of innocent regret didn't fool Sam.

'Name of?'

'Ha! Madame Lottie Moser.'

'Money?'

'Plenty.'

'Then I'll believe it — a rich little widow. Very much in Bell's line, I'm sure. We shall go there directly.' Sam was on his feet and at the door. 'What are you awaiting fer?'

At the cab stand at the end of Wellington Street they found the obliging Hob, a favourite of Dickens's.

'Hobnob, my old friend, would ye take Mr Jones and me to Hampstead?'

'Gladly, Mr Dickens, Mr Jones, sir. I'll take ye an' I'll wait if yer wants.'

'We do, Hob, if old Bob here will oblige us.' Dickens indicated the cab horse. Hob and Bob — how they came by their harmonious names Dickens never knew, but Bob, like his master, had a cheerful mien and a healthy stoutness which betokened good food and care.

'Git up, Bob — Mr Dickens wants ter go ter 'Ampstead, an' if yer takes 'im steady 'e'll put yer in a book, I daresay. An 'ero yer'll be, old Bob.'

'That he will, Hob. Let's get aboard.'

They were silent as the cab took them at the promised steady pace up Oxford Street and along Tottenham Court Road. Dickens thought about Lawn Cottage and

Charles Wentworth Dilke who had owned it when it was called Wentworth Place. Charles Dilke had worked for the Navy Pay Office and had known Dickens's father. Dickens remembered meeting him. He'd been a boy then, working at Warren's Blacking near The Strand after the business had moved from Hungerford Stairs. His father and Dilke had walked by and Mr Dilke had given him half a crown.

'What's up?' asked Sam.

'Just thinking – echoes from the caverns of memory. I used to come up to Hampstead in my youth to tramp across the heath and I knows a very good 'ous where you can get a red-hot chop and a glass of good wine – Jack Straw's Castle.'

'I know it, but not today, alas.'

'I suppose not.'

The cab took them by Regent's Park and up Haverstock Hill to Hampstead where Hob and Bob dropped them on the corner of Downshire Hill and High Street. He would wait, Hob said, at the end of John Street near Lawn Cottage.

In the little lane, which they found about halfway along Downshire Hill, they discovered the house. It was the middle house of three and it still had a black door, newly painted. Dickens grinned at Sam.

'Ring the bell then,' the Superintendant said. 'You can ask for Madam – the ladies always like you.' Sam waited at the bottom of the steps with his hat tipped over his eyes.

The bell brought forth a pretty little maid – engaged, thought Dickens, to match the pretty little widow.

'Is Madame Moser at home?' he asked politely.

'No, sir, she's in Paris with —' the maid blushed.

Dickens seized the advantage of the blush. 'Her maiden aunt?'

The girl smiled a dimpled smile. 'Not exactly, sir.'

'Ah, the maiden aunt's maiden aunt.'

'Oh, sir, it's not my place to say. Madame is very respectable, and lovely to work for. As sweet a lady as —'

'Any lady with a family of maiden aunts, I daresay.' The dimples appeared again. 'Now, my dear …?'

'Sally, sir, Sally Dibbs.'

'Ah, sweet Sally, I wonder if you might help me and my companion here. We are in search of an old friend of Madame Moser's – a Mr Bell. Do you know the name?'

'No, sir.'

'You'd remember if a gentleman of that name came here recently?'

'I would, sir, and 'e didn't come here. Perhaps 'e's a very old friend who's gone off now.'

'And that might be because Madame Moser has some new friends, or a particular new friend with whom she has gone to Paris, perhaps?'

Sally giggled. 'Get away, sir – an' if she has, what business is it of yours? Or his?' She looked down at Sam. 'Who's your friend?'

'Nobody important – just an old uncle who comes about with me. No need to bother about him.' Sam tipped his hat to the girl.

'Anyone else come in the last few days?' Dickens pressed.

'Only her maiden aunt, sir.' The dimples again.

'Very droll, Mistress Sally. You'd tell me if any gentleman has called in the last few days, wouldn't you?'

'No one's been, honest, sir. No one, only the grocer's boy and the post and they ain't gentlemen, that I can tell you.'

'And Paris, Sally? I won't breathe a word to Mr Bell, if I find him.'

'With Mr Clarke – Adolphus. She calls 'im Dolly an' 'e's a very nice gentleman and they're engaged to be married.'

'Well I wish them very well, Sally, and you, too.'

Dickens bade her farewell and slipped her a half-crown piece before turning from the door and walking down the steps to where Sam was waiting.

'Paris, eh, old 'un?' he said.

Sam saw a familiar gleam in Dickens's eye. 'No, Charles, not this time. We are not chasing to Paris in pursuit of "Mr Clarke". And no trying to tempt me with talk of fine wine and beefsteak.' That was how Dickens had persuaded Sam to go to Paris in search of another murderer.

'Ah, well, just a thought. I suppose we must accept that Clarke is not Bell and that Bell has not been here.'

'I think we must,' said Sam. 'It was worth a try, if only to see you inveigle that innocent Miss into revealing her mistress's private business. I'd treat you to chops at Jack Straw's but I must get back. Are you going back to Wellington Street?'

'Yes, why?' asked Dickens.

'I wondered if you would go to Brim's shop. I want you to tell Scrap to stop asking about Bell. After what happened to Mrs Bell, I don't want him to get into danger.'

'Yes, I'll tell him. The cab can drop me by St Giles's Church.'

17

THE CRYPT

Scrap ran like the wind through Smithfield Market, dodging the porters, the drovers, the butchers, the idlers and thieves; leaping over piles of mud and straw; slipping on rotten cabbage leaves; plunging headlong past the pens of squealing pigs and bellowing cattle, sparing no thought for the bleating sheep calling for the green fields from where they had been driven. He ignored the stench of blood and manure; hurled himself by waggons and trucks, dashed past the slaughterhouses, the triperies, the bone-boiling houses; twisted into alleys no wider than tunnels; flew by forgotten graveyards and tumble-down houses; darted across Faringdon Road, into Shoe Lane; stopped to take a breath, and was off again. A knot of alleys took him by Lincoln's Inn, through Portugal Street, and, at last, to Bow Street.

Perlice'd likely go by Skinner Street an' 'Olborn – wider but slower, Scrap had thought. He wanted to be first with the news. He'd seen the police at the church of St Bartholomew the Great, just by Cloth Fair where he'd taken a delivery of stationery. He'd heard the talk – dead man in the church. Mightn't be the one Mr Jones woz lookin' fer, but it woz a dead man, an' 'e would be the one to tell Mr Jones. Matter of pride it woz. Mr Jones 'ad asked 'im to look an' listen. Well, 'e 'ad.

Dickens had returned to Bow Street after enquiring at the shop for Scrap. 'Out on an errand up by Cloth Fair,' he told Sam. 'I spoke to Elizabeth and asked her to tell Scrap to report in. Professional matter, I said to tell him. I thought it might tempt him to come quickly.'

Sam smiled. Scrap took his responsibilities to the police very seriously. 'Mr Brim?'

Dickens looked solemn. 'In bed. Elizabeth sent for the nurse. He's not well at all so I didn't linger. He seemed to be a bit better on the day of the party.'

'For Eleanor's sake, I think. It's only those children keep him going.'

'Horrible disease. Poor Keats died of it even though he went to Rome.'

'Indeed.'

'Perhaps someone else will turn up to tell us that Bell is living in another snug cottage with another little widow.'

'And I'm the emperor of —'

Dickens was never to know which emperor for Scrap burst in with Rogers at his heels.

'Dead man – St Bartholomew's Church. Perlice there, but I came as fast as I could. Knew yer'd wanter know.' Scrap's eyes gleamed – he was first, could tell by Mr Jones's astonished face. 'Don't know nothin' else. Could be the cove yer lookin' fer.'

Or someone else entirely, thought Sam, but he did not say so. He saw how Scrap was pleased to have brought the news. 'Well done, Scrap. Right, we'll be on our way. Charles?'

'I'll come.'

Constable Stemp, a man not much inclined to imaginative flights, was astonished to see Superintendent Jones materialise in the churchyard as if some magic had summoned him from Bow Street. Constable Feak, who had been sent to fetch him, had gone only ten minutes ago. Then Stemp saw the boy, Scrap, and understood.

Dickens, Jones and Rogers, followed by Scrap who was determined to fulfil his commission to the end, came through the narrow passage into the burial ground, a place of rank grasses and weed, interspersed with decaying and tottering gravestones. It was dark, here, the graveyard hemmed in by the crumbling houses of Cloth Fair, ancient lath and plaster tenements, dilapidated and dirty, their lower timbers bulging and the upper storeys festooned with patched and ragged clothing hung out to dry, so many that Dickens wondered if the denizens of these tenements were cowering inside, naked, waiting until the sun shone so that they might dress themselves again. Cloth Fair, once the home of Elizabethan merchant princes, had fallen into near ruin, though the old house that was once the Earl of Warwick's still stood; admittedly, it was a tallow-chandler's shop now. The poet Milton had lived nearby, and Hogarth had been baptised in the church. A black cat perched on one of the gravestones. It gazed at them malevolently, adding to the eeriness of the scene.

There was nothing left of the twelfth-century church but the choir, the first bay of the nave and parts of the transepts. A blacksmith worked at his forge inside; a fringe factory occupied the former Lady Chapel, and it was in the cellars of this manufactory that the corpse had been found by a workman who was waiting with Constable Stemp.

'We don't 'ardly use the cellars nowadays, but I thought I 'eard somethin',' the man – one Matthew Duddy – said. He was a tall, spare man of middle age.

'What did you hear?' asked Sam sharply.

'I dunno exactly, sir —' Duddy looked puzzled. 'Sounded like a child cryin' – I dunno – mighta bin a cat. That great black thing's allus about. Anyways, I thought mebbe a child was down there. There was a baby once.'

'And?'

'The baby was abandoned. It was took to th'orphanage, poor thing. Anyways, I remembered that so I went down. Couldn't 'ear anything, but I went right in and turned over some sacks and old lumber, and then I found —' he broke off, his face paling at the memory.

'Take us down to where you found him,' said Sam.

They went into the church and Duddy led them to the rickety steps that went down to the cellars – surely, thought Dickens, once the crypt of the ancient church. Rogers had his bull's-eye lamp and Duddy had a lantern. They picked their way through the lumber of decades: bales of mouldering cloth, bits of old furniture, what looked to Dickens suspiciously like a coffin, huge slabs of crumbling stonework. There was vaulting above them, great stone arches, and it was very cold. Near the far wall at the end of the cellar they could see that some of the lumber had been moved and Sam noticed another set of steps leading upwards – to a door, perhaps. Where might that lead to?

The body lay by the wall, half hidden by some mounds of cloth. Rogers shone his lamp. Dickens stepped forward. The dead man had been shot. He could see the encrusted blood on the shirt front and more on the thick coat he wore. He looked at the dead face. Sam heard his quick intake of breath.

'Do you know who it is?'

'It is not Clement Bell, but he looks very like him.'

'Then who?' Sam looked down at the dead man and saw the resemblance to Edwin Bell, whose face he had seen as still as this on the mortuary slab in Manchester. 'Not another brother, surely?'

Rogers knelt down to look more closely. Under the travelling coat, the man wore a dark suit. Rogers felt in the pockets of the suit. Nothing. He felt in the pocket of the coat – that part of the coat which spread out on the stone floor. Nothing. He bent over and pulled at that part of the coat which was under the body, and from the deep pocket he pulled out a book. There was nothing else to identify the man. Rogers handed the volume to Sam who passed it to Dickens. In the light of the lamp, they peered at the writing on the cover. It was a copy of Bulwer-Lytton's play *Money* and on the inside of the cover was written: C.L. Bell, February, 1850. Dickens flicked through the pages. They could see how some lines had been underscored in pencil – the lines belonging to Alfred Evelyn, the hero of the play.

In the lamplight Sam saw the astonishment on Dickens's face.

'This is the copy of the play that I sent to Dudley Costello – he would have passed it on to Clement Bell.'

'So this could be Clement Bell?' Sam said.

They stared at the dead man's face.

'It must be – his initials in the script. Who else would have a copy of the play with Clement Bell's lines marked?' said Dickens.

'So if it is, who is the man who acted the part in Manchester?'

'An imposter, a man who took on another man's identity,' said Dickens.

'Mrs Stark didn't mention another brother, nor did Inspector Hardacre after he had seen Edwin Bell's wife. It is very curious indeed. Would you look again at the face? See if you can discern the difference between this man and the one you knew – it might help if we're to find him, to have him clear in your mind.'

Dickens stepped forward again to look at the dead face in the wavering lamplight. The dead eyes stared upwards; he looked surprised, and well he might at the sight of the man who was almost his double, and who had pointed a gun at him. He tried to conjure the face of the actor whom he had known as Clement Bell and compare the two. He was aware of the silence down here: the face before him seemed to move in the shadows and he saw, suddenly, the face of the other man which seemed older, harder, marked by experience. Rogers steadied the lamp and Clement Bell, if it were he, came back. It was a weaker face, softer, rounder, the mouth fuller – the face of a man who had been amiable, easygoing, likeable, Costello's friend.

'I shall know him when we find him.' Dickens's voice sounded grim. He remembered what had been done to Oriel Greenwood, and to Edwin Bell, and, perhaps, to Dora Bell and her unborn child A harder man had done these things, a ruthless man, a man who could kill and walk away.

'I shall have to ask Mrs Stark if she knows of any other relative, a cousin, perhaps,' said Sam. 'In the meantime, I must send Stemp to organise the mortuary van. We will need a proper identification. I don't want a repeat of what happened in Manchester. I want to know for sure if this is Clement Bell. Do you think Costello will do it? I don't want to ask Mrs Stark after what she has endured.'

'I am sure he will. I can send him a note.'

'Sir,' called Rogers, who had moved beyond the body to look about. 'There's a door up 'ere.'

'Where does that lead to, Mr Duddy?' Sam asked the workman.

'Into the 'ouse next door – nobody uses it now.'

'Does anyone live in the house?'

'Lodgin' 'ouse, sir. All kinds of folk, mostly poor – the place is fallin' down.'

'Shall I go up, sir?' asked Rogers.

'Yes, but be careful.'

'I'll go up into the church,' said Dickens. 'Scrap?' Scrap was there, of course. Dickens saw his eager face. 'Will you take a message to Mr Dudley Costello at the offices of *The Examiner*. Beaufort Buildings on The Strand – do you know it?'

'Yers, I knows it.'

'Sam, I'll write the note upstairs, just asking him to meet me at Bow Street – what time shall I say?'

'Five o'clock should give us time to get back to the mortuary, and to have a look round here. Will you ask Stemp to go back to Bow Street for the mortuary van?'

Dickens and Scrap went back up the steps into the church where Dickens gave Stemp Sam's instruction and wrote the note to Costello. Scrap went off.

Dickens prowled round the church – he could hear the clang of the blacksmith's hammer on the anvil and the sound of children's voices in the yard of the school next door. He had a look at the tomb of the founder, Rehere, whose painted effigy lay with the hands joined in prayer. He studied the monument to Percival Smalpace and his wife, Agnes, their brown marbled heads gazing out into the half-darkness. They looked suitably solemn, their mouths closed rather disapprovingly, Dickens fancied. The date of Percival's death was 1568 and the inscription had a warning for the viewer:

Behold yourselves by us
Such once we were as you
And you in time shall be
Even dust as we are now

Memento Mori. Dickens shivered slightly in the cold air. He wandered on, peering at the tablets on the floor. Nicholas Orme, dead at twenty-eight in 1628. Here, it said, he lay at peace with his two brothers, laid in this dust before him.

Three brothers. Three Bell brothers perhaps, he thought, remembering suddenly Mrs Gaskell's talk of Currer, Ellis and Acton Bell, the pen names of the Brontë sisters. Two brothers dead before Currer Bell. Here, too, a pair of brothers dead before a third. Death closes all, Tennyson had written. No it does not. Not death by murder. Murder. Dread word. It opened up graves, disturbed the sleeping dead – and the quick. Edwin Bell, Oriel Greenwood, Dora Bell, and now, it seemed, Clement Bell. And the murderer? Did he lie sleepless?

He had to think! Were there three brothers? Did the third have a name beginning with A? Currer, Ellis, Acton – Clement, Edwin and who? In any case, it might be a cousin, as Sam had suggested. Or it might be a man who resembled the two brothers. A man might have a double – that was well known. A darker side of the self. Clement Bell's amiable face had its darker counterpart in the man who had played Alfred Evelyn. If there were another brother, then he might have reason to dispose of his kin – money, perhaps, inheritance. Powerful motives for murder: greed, envy, resentment.

He stood in the dark choir. All sound seemed to have ceased. They were there, the dead: in the shiver of a gleam of lamplight where a shadow stirred; in the momentary lifting of a piece of carpet; in the dust that shifted in the draught, and showed for a moment a half footprint which vanished as though someone had stopped there on tiptoe and then moved on; in the air which moved because someone had passed through an open door. Do something useful, he thought gloomily, other than reminding us that we are mortal. You saw him. Tell us where he is.

The face came back to him again as he sat in the choir, as vividly as if the murderer stood before him. He saw again the leaner face, the thinner lips and he remembered the sardonic gleam in the eyes when he, Dickens, had passed him as he went on stage to hear the cheers that greeted Mr Charles Dickens. No one had cheered when Alfred Evelyn had stepped on stage. In more senses than one, no one knew him.

A noise on the steps signalled the arrival of Sam.

'Find anything interesting?' Dickens asked.

'Rogers worked his way up those steps into the abutting house – it is a lodging house, so one Nicholas Orme told us. He is a poor old man who lives in one room – lived there for years, he said.'

Nicholas Orme, thought Dickens, descendant of the brothers in their tomb.

'We surmise that the dead man was dragged down the steps into the crypt, dumped there. The murderer must have thought that the body might lie undiscovered at the back of the crypt. It wouldn't have been easy to manoeuvre a body down there – that's how he overlooked the book, I assume. The coat was caught under the body and he didn't realise that there was something in the pocket, though he must have taken everything else. Rogers is looking for clues – of course, the population of these rooms is so transient that it's not going to be easy to find out if the murderer stayed here. Mr Orme couldn't tell us anything. But Rogers and Feak, and Stemp, when he comes back, can pursue that line of enquiry. I've told Mr Duddy that he must not repeat anything that he heard. If asked, he is to say that the police have no clue as to the identity of the dead man.'

'You would rather the murderer did not know that we have found the body of Clement Bell.'

'Precisely. Had it not been for Mr Duddy's hearing the sound of a child or a cat, we might not have found him. If he thinks we don't know it is Clement Bell, he might come out of hiding. We can't conceal it for long, but it gives us some time.'

'If it is Clement Bell, when was he killed? Surely if he's been there a week there would be a smell. The body would be putrefying by now.'

'Not necessarily,' said Sam. 'It's dry and cold down there. In any case, I've known cases in which a body hasn't putrefied for more than a week. There was a case a few years ago – a young man died suddenly and it was twenty-eight days before signs of putrefaction were observed. The opposite can be true, too. Putrefaction can begin quickly – on the first day after death. Depends on the temperature and on the condition of the deceased – flabby people decompose sooner.'

'So he could have been dead for more than a week?' Dickens asked.

'He could indeed.'

'And now?'

'We go back to Bow Street to wait for Mr Costello to tell us if this is Clement Bell.'

18

STAPLE INN

Costello had gone, a little white in the face, to be sure, but that was to be expected of one who had looked upon a murdered man whom he had known and liked. For it was Clement Bell. Costello was sure. It was the man he had recommended to Dickens, the man to whom he had sent the copy of the play – the real Clement Bell, the easygoing, good-natured journalist who had been keen to work with Mr Dickens, who had said that he could learn the part ready for the rehearsals in Manchester, the man for whom Costello had been glad to do a favour, and who had neither betrayed nor murdered his fragile, innocent wife. Dickens was pleased that it should be so.

Dickens and Jones sat in the Superintendent's office at Bow Street, wondering what it all meant. They were waiting for Rogers to report any findings. Sam had telegraphed the news to Inspector Hardacre in Manchester who would need to know that they were no longer looking for Clement Bell, but for another man whose name and identity they did not yet know, and who might be using another name altogether. Not much help, thought Sam.

Dickens thought about the dead man, Clement Bell – at least the puzzle was answered. It was clear now why the man who had played the part of Alfred Evelyn was so unlike Dudley Costello's description of Clement Bell's character.

'Another brother, I am certain,' he said aloud. 'I noticed the dead man's hand – exactly like the hand of the man who played Alfred Evelyn, and exactly like the hand of Edwin Bell, hanging down over that wretched gun I fired. Granted the faces are different —'

'But no one mentioned another brother,' interjected Sam. 'Neither Mrs Stark nor Mrs Edwin Bell, that's what puzzles me – yet, all three are so alike that I am inclined to think you're right.'

'There must be a lawyer – remember what Mrs Stark said about marriage settlements, and that Clement Bell inherited money. Clement Bell must have a lawyer who can tell us something about Bell's family.'

Sam agreed. 'I'll send to Mrs Stark for the name and address. Semple can go now.' He went out to find the constable. When he came back, Dickens continued, 'Suppose this brother is a kind of black sheep. Say he was sent abroad?'

'America – the gun.'

'Exactly – and the carpetbag, perhaps that was American. It was very worn – the bag of a man who had travelled far, maybe. Suppose he came back to demand money – what he thought he had a right to. Clement and Edwin Bell refused him, and he murdered them.'

'But it's not practical – their money would not necessarily go to him, and how would he claim it anyway? He can hardly just turn up after all this, saying how sorry he is about his brothers' deaths and can he have his inheritance? It makes no sense.'

'True, but the mind of the killer is a horrible wonder apart. There's a twisted kind of logic in all murderers – they are possessed of such strange absorbing selfishness that they see the world only through their own eyes. Look at the Stanfield Hall murders – Rush intended to kill the whole

Jermy family so that Isaac Jermy would not foreclose on the mortgages. Rush knew he would be ruined and came up with the notion that he could wipe out the whole family to save himself – it didn't make sense. Whoever inherited would still demand that Rush paid his debts.'

'The murderer looks only to the gain he wants to make. You could be right about money. Mrs Stark said that Clement inherited money – we may suppose that Edwin did. Therefore, it would be feasible that a third brother would come for his share – if the third brother exists. But what about Dora Bell? Why kill her?'

'Perhaps it was an accident. He went to the house to ask about Clement, pretending he was still alive to cover his tracks. He frightened Mrs Bell – she tried to get away, and fell. He had no reason to kill her if, as we surmise, there was some inheritance from the Bell family to which he believed he was entitled.'

'A lot of surmise, Charles. We need some facts – we need to know about the Bell family.'

Rogers came in then to tell them what he had found in the lodging house.

'Some old dame who lets the rooms, collects the rent, does for them what can afford it, said there was a lodger who stayed a week – she don't remember exactly. But he vanished without a word. Not that she thought anythin' of it – 'appens all the time. She don't care as long as she gets the money. About a week ago or so. Name of Percival Smalpace.'

'It is he,' stated Dickens.

Sam and Rogers stared at him. 'How can you know?' asked Sam.

'Saw the name on a tomb in the church. He took it. A joke. It is a rather fine tomb with an inscription warning the living that they will be dust when their time comes. Just the sort of thing that would appeal to the man who applauded in the theatre when he saw me find the body of Edwin Bell.'

'Could the old woman describe him?' Sam asked.

'Tall, bushy beard, dark eyes.'

'Beard?'

'Disguise, I suppose,' said Dickens.

'An 'e won't 'ave one now. It don't 'elp much. I 'ad a look in the room, but nothing to see. Too clever to leave any trace.'

'And if he had left anything it won't be there now. You did ask?'

'I thought o' that, sir, but she said there was nothin'. Well, she would.'

'And, of course, she did not hear anything so convenient as a shot from a gun?'

Rogers grinned, hearing the irony in Sam's voice. 'Not a thing, sir, an' it's that noisy in 'ouses like that – folk screechin', fightin', all sorts goin' on – people in an out at all hours. I asked some of the other lodgers, but no one could tell me anythin' – not interested. But there's something else which might be interestin'.'

'Please tell me you found a tangible clue – the murderer's name chalked on a wall. That would do me nicely.'

'Sorry, sir, I wish I 'ad, but Stemp 'ad another look round the crypt and there was signs that someone 'ad bin sleepin' there – he found a couple o' beer bottles, some bread an' some sackin' what looked like it 'ad bin used as a bed.'

'A tramp?'

'No, sir, a woman – well she could 'ave bin a tramp, I suppose, but there was a bit of chewed ribbon, an' a baby's shoe. That's what made us think it was a woman.'

'The child crying – the one that Matthew Duddy heard,' Dickens interposed.

'A homeless woman with a child who took refuge down there. I wonder if she saw the body. She might have left in a hurry – she left a ribbon and the child's shoe, and her bread. I wonder if she'd been living there.'

'Not before the murder, sir, or she wouldn't 'ave stayed if she'd seen that.'

'True, but get Stemp to make enquiries. Someone might remember a woman and a child – she might have seen the man who was calling himself Percival Smalpace. It's worth a try.'

A knock on the door brought in Semple with the name and address of Bell's solicitor: Staple Inn, just beyond Lincoln's Inn off Chancery Lane.

'Tape and Binding,' Sam repeated. 'I know them – or rather Mr Tape. He is Robert Brim's solicitor. He came to the shop when Robert wanted to make me executor of his will, and to make legal my guardianship of the children.'

A brisk ten-minute walk took them up Drury Lane, along High Holborn to the old gabled black and white front of Staple Inn, through the archway into the quiet old court, a place Dickens knew from his time as a clerk to Ellis and Blackmore in Gray's Inn. It was his first job, got for him by his mother's introduction to Mr Blackmore by her aunt, Mrs Charlton. He had begun at Gray's Inn when he was fifteen and many a time he had run errands to Staple Inn, weaving his way through the narrow courts and alleys so often cast in the shade that he had felt that he existed in the dark most of the time, which indeed he had when traversing what he had called the perplexed and troublous valley of the law. He remembered the Inn's two irregular quadrangles, the quiet stillness contrasting with the clashing street, giving the visitor the sensation of having put cotton in his ears and velvet soles on his boots.

It had not changed in those twenty years; the same smoky sparrows seemed to be twittering in the same smoky trees which still grew from the grass plot in the courtyard. Well, he was sure he could hear the sound of birds. Too dark to see. Not changed since yon doctor's day, thought Dickens, remembering Abe Lamb, the landlord of The Bull in Manchester. Doctor Johnson had lived at Staple Inn in 1759 where he wrote *Rasselas*. They walked past number 10 which he recalled had a curious inscription above the door:

P

J   T

1747

Pretty Jolly, Too, he had once joked. No one seemed to know what it meant. Another mystery of the law.

Number 11 was the home of Bell's solicitors. Inside an ill-lit hall, they discovered a thin woman with a razor blade of a nose leaning by the newel post of an ancient staircase. She was wringing her hands.

The nose sniffed. 'Blood,' she said in a tone that would have guaranteed her the role of Lady Macbeth if the wringing hands had not.

'Out damned spot,' Dickens said and immediately wished he had not for she glared at him coldly.

'Yer might say so. I've said so. But it don't do no good. It will keep comin'.'

'The blood?' Dickens had to ask.

She sniffed again, 'Said so, dint I? Blood. I sees it. I rubs at it. I scrubs at it. But there it is.'

Dickens and Jones could not forbear looking. It was true that there was a mark on the floor, but whether it was blood they could not tell. The woman took a bucket which was at the foot of the stairs and knelt down with her scrubbing brush at the ready.

'Tape and Binding?' asked Sam.

'Tape only, yer honour. No Binding.'

'None at all?' This was Dickens.

'Dead. Dead as a doornail.' He would be, thought Dickens. They generally are. Look at Marley. She glanced meaningfully at the stain on the floor from which action they deduced that perhaps the unfortunate Binding had expired on that very spot.

'Mr Tape, then?'

'Upstairs. The boy'll be there.'

They made to walk across to the stairs. She spoke again, holding up a skinny hand as if to warn them of some prophecy to come.

'Don't —'

'Kick the bucket?' Dickens interrupted mischievously.

She fixed him with another cold look – she might, he thought, be measuring me for my coffin.

'Step on the blood, or yer might. It's 'appened. Shouldn't make light o' these things, sir. Yer niver knows the day.' And with that gnomic warning, she set to her scrubbing.

'Thank you, Mrs…?' Sam enquired.

She looked up. 'Stabb – Eva Stabb, laundress.'

Sam forced himself not to look at Dickens – he had heard the intake of breath through the nose to stifle laughter.

'Much obliged, ma'am,' he said.

Mrs Stabb dipped her head graciously to the taller man.

They went upstairs, Dickens ruminating on the appositeness of her name. When they gained the safety of the landing he whispered to Sam, 'Blood will have blood – stabbed Binding, I bet.'

There was a sound as of spectral chains clanking.

'It was the bucket – she kicked it.' Sam grinned.

'Inspissated gloom.'

'What?'

'Yon doctor – he lived at Staple Inn.'

'What doctor? Oh, Abe Lamb. I remember. And it means?' Sam was curious, forgetting for a moment why they were there.

'Darkness thickening. Johnson was discussing *Macbeth* which was why it came to me. Lady Macbeth down there, bloodstains, and, you must admit, it is dark up here. And look at that door – the entrance to a tomb, I should think.'

And indeed it looked rather forbidding, a black slab of a door, though there was a slice of cheerful light coming from it as it was just ajar. Sam knocked and an amiable voice invited them to come in.

'Mind the —' the voice enjoined them. It was going to say 'step' but too late, Sam had already stumbled into the room with Dickens hard on his heels. They righted themselves as the voice apologised. 'Sorry, so sorry – always mean to tell people to mind the step first and invite them in afterwards, but it seems more natural the other way round. Get it right someday I daresay. Oh, I say, Mr Dickens, Mr Dickens, Mr Dickens!' His voice rose a note each time he uttered the name.

'Mr Tiplady!'

Ambrose Tiplady had been a clerk at the offices of Ducat, a solicitor at Gray's Inn where they had gone in search of the man with the crooked face, a suspect in an earlier case. Now, as if conjured by magic, he was here, looking exactly the same: fresh-faced, innocent, apologetic, and astounded to see Mr Dickens and the Superintendent.

'Mr Ducat and I parted, yes, parted. I am afraid he did not quite get on with me nor I with him – something amiss between us, yes, amiss, that's it, though I am not quite sure what it was. He suggested I move on – just after that business with the clerk – you remember Mr Blackledge?'

They remembered all right. Smooth as barristers' silk, Mr Ducat had not cared much for their company at all when they questioned him about Blackledge, his clerk, a suspect in the murder of a girl called Patience Brooke. Dickens was not surprised that Ambrose Tiplady had been asked to find another place. Mr Ducat would not want to be reminded of any irregularity in the affairs of his chambers.

'And the bent old man? What happened to him?' Dickens asked.

'Old Badsgallop?'

'Badsgallop!'

Ambrose Tiplady laughed. 'I know, Mr Dickens, ridiculous ain't it, but he's still there. Knows all the secrets I daresay.'

'How came you here?' Dickens wondered if this set of chambers were any more congenial than the other for this good-natured youth.

'My uncle knows Mr Tape and he recommended me so here I am.'

'Do you get along with Mr Tape?'

'Oh yes, awfully kind man.'

'And Mrs Stabb?'

Ambrose Tiplady grinned at them. 'Ghastly old spectre, ain't she? Obsessed with bloodstains. I never see anything, but I always step over the spot just to please her. Mr Tape says she's harmless enough – awfully kind man, awfully kind. Do you want to see him? He's inside.'

'Yes, if you will tell him that we are here.'

Just then the inner door opened to show beaming Mr Tape, a small, broad, cheerful man whose dark hair was just touched with grey, and whose eyes twinkling like beads looked at them benignly over his half-moon spectacles. Awfully kind indeed, thought Dickens, glad for Ambrose Tiplady.

'Mr Dickens, good Lord. You know my boy, here – always talks about when he met you. Never thought I'd meet you, too. An honour, sir, an honour, and Mr Jones – this is not about Robert Brim is it?'

'No, I am here on police business I'm afraid,' Sam answered.

'Now that sounds serious, Mr Jones.'

'It is. We are here about a client of yours, Mr Clement Bell.'

'I see. Well come through, come through.'

They went in to an unusually bright office, all spick and span with a glowing coal fire. In that familiar atmosphere of pounce and parchment, red tape, ink-jars, brief and draft paper, law reports, writs, declarations, and bills of cost, Mr Matthew Tape welcomed them as to an evening party.

'Sit down, sirs, sit and be comfortable. I like things bright, Mr Dickens. The law can be dark, sir, dark and impenetrable, but it was what I was born to. Should have liked to be a sailor, but Mr Binding, my guardian, was a grave man – still is, of course. Dead now, dead as a – but you know that, Mr Dickens – like Marley, eh? Well, Binding bound me here, bound me here in the ropes of the law. "Matthew Tape," he said, "you cannot change your destiny. Your name calls you to it as mine did." No choice, sirs, but I can make it as bright as I can. Brighten it, brighten it, that's what I say, and Lord knows this place needs it. What with Mrs Stabb and her bloodstains – and the ghost upstairs.'

Dickens glanced at Sam who concealed a grin behind his hand. 'Ghost, Mr Tape?'

'We sing it away, me and Mr Tiplady. When we hear the footsteps we break out into a shanty or two and a good, loud bow-wow chorus. That shuts him up. Rum tale, though …' he looked at them, his eyes winking, waiting, hoping to tell.

Dickens, the collector of tales, obliged. 'A rum tale's best for winter.'

Matthew Tape smiled. 'True, sir, very true. Before my time, and Binding's, come to that, on a dark and stormy night when the casements were rattling and the wind whooshed down the chimney, wailing like some lost soul, and the candlelight flickered and died, old Cecil Mould who had the chambers above, received a letter. A letter telling him of the death of a woman he once loved – loved and lost, so they say, to a rival, a man who swore his love to the lady and betrayed her. He, Cecil Mould, had not forgiven her, though she was cruelly used, and now it was too late. Hanged himself – ropes of the law, sirs, ropes of the law. And he walks. Always on the anniversary of that letter. No rest, see. Love, sirs, turned to hate. Poor soul. But still, can't have him disturbing our peace. So, brighten it, I say. Not everyone can – Mrs Stabb can't, but you can, Mr Dickens, laughter and tears, eh? Not sure about you, Superintendent, and, by your looks, I suspect something very dark brings ye to Staple Inn.'

'It does, Mr Tape. Your client, Mr Bell, is dead – murdered, I am afraid, and I need to know about his affairs.' Sam was brisk now. Time to get to the point.

Mr Tape sat up straight in his chair, the humorous eyes darker now.

'That is bad news, Mr Jones. A young man. A young wife too, and a child on the way.'

'She is dead, too. An accident, possibly – a fall down the stairs.'

'This is sad, indeed. But what is it you wish to know?'

'What do you know of Bell's family?'

'There was a brother in Manchester, a lawyer, but my business was really with Mrs Bell's father, Mr Richards, who was concerned to keep hold of his daughter's fortune.

Mr Bell, he thought, was rather – irresponsible – a spender not a saver, but a nice lad for all that and his daughter loved him. Their income came from capital. There was plenty for the young pair to live on.'

'No man knows how much he can spend until he tries,' Dickens observed.

'Very true, Mr Dickens, very true. Money is a necessary evil, I always think. Why, when I —'

'According to Mrs Stark,' Sam interrupted before the storyteller could get going again, 'Clement Bell was a man who spent money like water.'

Mr Tape's eyes twinkled at Sam, 'I think he did. Mr Richards is a wise old bird. Clement Bell couldn't touch the capital. There was a trust to safeguard the capital settled on Mrs Bell by her father. If she died the money was to go to her heirs – of course, there are none now.' Mr Tape stared at the papers, his bright face sombre. 'What a pity, what a pity.'

'You know nothing of another brother?' asked Sam.

Mr Tape's eyes were puzzled. 'No, though there was a great uncle. And there was a lawyer in Dorchester. I'll ask Mr Tiplady for the box.'

He went to the door to ask Ambrose Tiplady to bring out the box containing the information about the Bells, and came back with a black deed box, the kind with which Dickens was familiar. Men's lives could be buried in those boxes; secrets bound fast in red tape, sealed with red wax, a bloody full stop on the parchment. Mr Tape spread the papers on the desk and looked through them.

'Yes, the marriage certificate, the settlements. Ah, here are the addresses of the uncle and of the lawyer. The uncle lives at Middleton House, Winterborne Steeple and the solicitor's office is in High Street, Dorchester, name of Cake. He'll know all about the family.'

'Thank you, Mr Tape. We're sorry to have brought such bad news. And now we must go.'

They bade farewell to the kindly lawyer and Ambrose Tiplady and went downstairs to the empty hall. Mrs Stabb had vanished, but Dickens peered at the floor where she had scrubbed. It was still damp, but he could not see the stain. Perhaps it did disappear only to rise to the surface again, a ghostly reminder of some long ago death like the footsteps in the top floor chamber.

Dickens took Sam's hand and gazed at his open palm. 'Well, Mr Jones, what now? I sees a journey, a long journey to a far country.'

Sam grinned. 'Not Paris, I hope. Dorchester far enough for you? What Inspector Hardacre would call a little jaunt to the countryside. Can you come?'

'I ought not to, but I will. I shall go back to Wellington Street, leave divers and many decrees for my faithful Harry Wills with regard to *Household Words*, and I shall meet you at Waterloo Bridge Station for the earliest possible train tomorrow morning. Bradshaw will tell us – I'll stop by your office on my way to Wellington Street.'

'You don't, perchance, see the name of a murderer written on my palm. If not, I'll have it back.'

'Alas, no, but I see something dark which might be a bushy beard.'

'Ah, yes, the master of disguise – you noted Rogers' description of the bushy beard, and he can take any name he pleases. Percival Smalpace, forsooth. Good job you saw that tomb.'

'Trust the observant eye of the Inimitable, Samivel, and trust the same man for a box of mutton sandwiches, some captain's biscuits and a bottle of porter. Sich a basket will see us right.'

'You might leave the biscuits, Mr Weller, dry as dust and fatal to the teeth.'

'Sammy, my boy, you'll find my biscuits a most jovial and moist sort of viand as my friend Tom Pinch found when he dined in state with Mr Pecksniff.'

Sam sniffed very much in the manner of Eva Stabb.

19

NAMES ON A GRAVE

After their four-hour train journey to Dorchester, Dickens and Jones took a fly to the village of Winterbourne Steepleton, just a few miles from Dorchester. They were standing in the quiet old churchyard of St Michael deep in a wooded valley, gazing at the grave of Edgar and Catherine Bell. Both had died in 1823, over twenty-five years ago. The parents of Edwin and Clement Bell, and, possibly, a third brother, as yet unknown.

They had been to the old grey house, set a little way from the village: Middleton House, the home of Edward Bell, great-uncle to the brothers, Edwin and Clement. A cheerful woman had opened the door, but when they had asked to see Mr Bell, she had shaken her head. The master was not well enough for visitors. 'Bless thee, he is nigh a hundred year old – he cannot be spoke to, zirs, for he can remember nought – like a child, he is. Blind these last twenty years.'

Sam had asked if she could tell them anything about the Bell family, Mr Bell's great nephews, for example. But she could not, she said. It was all before her time. Her own aunt, Miss Sparks would know. She had been housekeeper to Mr Bell for years, but she was very deaf now. It might be difficult to explain to her what they wanted. They might try at the church where the Bells were buried. The vicar might help, though he hadn't been there that long. Sorry, she was.

They had made to walk away when Sam turned suddenly just as she was closing the door.

'Mrs …?'

'Dear, zir, Etheland Dear.' She noticed the surprise on Dickens's face. 'I know, zir, my mother liked it – name of a grand lady her mother worked for.'

'It is very pretty,' said Dickens. 'I like it.'

'Has anyone else been here, any other stranger, asking about Mr Bell?' Sam asked.

She thought about the question. 'A year ago or more, zir, a man came – said he was from America, a distant relative of the Bell family, but I told him what I told you, Mr Bell couldn't be spoke to.'

'Did he give a name?'

'Mr Clarke.' Sam stole a glance at Dickens. Etheland Dear was speaking again. 'An', I remember, zir, he was a clergyman. He wore a collar. He had a beard, too, quite a bushy one – not quite right, I thought, for a young man.'

'Did he come in the house?'

'Well, he'd come such a long way I thought it wouldn't be any harm. I let him look round the rooms. He liked the library, stayed there while I went up to the master. He asked if he could zee 'm, but I said not. One strange thing, though. When he went, I heard him laughing as he went down the lane.' Her pleasant, open face looked puzzled at the memory.

They had walked thoughtfully down the lane to the church, Dickens remembering a man with a clerical collar and a stick who had passed him in the fog in London, and the eerie sound of laughter that had come from somewhere in the dark.

So, here they were in the churchyard with its mossy tombstones and velvety mounds under which were buried the dead of eight centuries. It was very still here, just a faint breeze rippling through the crowded trees where rooks made their nests, and where the early spring buds were just showing. There were patches of the yellow lesser celandine, shining like tiny coins, and the white snowdrops, their bells delicate as glass. A thrush sang somewhere, the liquid notes clear as water drops. They heard the clip-clop of a horse's hooves and the bleat of sheep in the fields beyond. How peaceful it was. Time had stood still; the dead were quiet here in their graves. It was hard not to think of poor Oriel Greenwood lying in that terrible burial ground in Manchester. She should have been here, thought Dickens, beneath the silent turf. Perhaps Edwin and Clement Bell could be brought here to lie with their parents – probably not. Edwin would be buried in Chorlton and Clement in Kensal Green, more than likely. I should like to be buried here, he thought, or at least in some quiet place in Kent where my bones will not be disturbed.

They looked at the little church with its squat tower and, as they did so, a young man came out and approached them, asking if he could help.

'We wish to find out about the Bell family,' said Sam. 'I am Superintendent Jones from London. I need information in connection with a crime.'

'You will have to look at the records. I am fairly new here. I know nothing of the family.'

The rector led them into his church, a cool, simple place with pine pews, an ancient font and stone-flagged floor. It was a peaceful place, where Dickens felt again the sense of timelessness away from the thump of the machines, the pistons and the engines of the great cities – London, Manchester, so far from here.

In one of the old dusty registers, some of which went back to the sixteenth century, they found him at last:

Edwin Arthur Bell, born 1817
Clement Leonard Bell, born 1818

And the final child, the third son:

Austin Frederick Bell, born 1822

So there *were* three Bell brothers. Three young men, two of whom were now dead, and very possibly by the hand of the third, the youngest. Dickens thought of a baby over whose cradle two small boys peered curiously. He remembered his own sons, Charley, aged nine and Walter, only three, gazing at baby Francis. They hadn't been much impressed, but they got on well enough now. So what had occurred to make this brother the enemy of the other two? What indeed?

They left the church to sleep on in its wooded hollow where the thrush still sang, and the narrow River Winterborne wound gently like a silver ribbon through the fields and villages, making its undisturbed way to the sea.

Sam spoke. 'Clarke is the fiancé of the Viennese widow.'

'She who was mistress of dead Clement Bell. It cannot be, Sam, it's too ...'

'Coincidental?'

'Improbable, impossible. In any case Clarke is not an uncommon name.'

'Two Clarkes connected to the same case? I don't know, Charles, but let's get on to Dorchester and the solicitor who, I hope, can tell us about the three brothers and what happened to those children after the deaths of their parents. How young they were. Austin Bell, a baby. Who took them, and to where?'

'I wonder if they were separated?' Dickens said. 'Perhaps Austin Bell was taken away – out of England ...' his eyes lit up. 'America, Sam, America.'

The fly was waiting to take them back to Dorchester. It was a bustling town with its railway station, circulating libraries, a theatre, a modern gaol, newly built Town Hall, market twice a week, its busy shops and offices lining the steeply rising high street. Their driver pointed their way down the street where they would find the office of Cake, the Bell family solicitor. They looked at the plates on the doors as they passed. By a passage with the name of Greyhound Yard, Dickens saw a small curly-haired boy wearing a brown knickerbocker suit and carrying a satchel of books, a noticing sort of boy with bright eyes.

'Know where the solicitor Cake has his office?' Dickens asked.

'Over the road,' the boy replied. Then another boy's voice was heard, calling for Tom, and off the curly-haired boy went, looking back once, wondering about the stranger with the pair of blue eyes that had looked so keenly at him.

Cake's office was over the road and in they went, up the staircase to enquire. Odd name, thought Dickens, who had rather hoped Mr Cake might have a partner called Loaf, or Bun at the very least. Bunkin he'd used himself in *Pickwick*, and Bung. Bud would be a good name – a nice little girl called Rose. He had felt a momentary start of laughter when he saw the first three letters of the first name: S-I-M – Simnel, it must be. But no, it was only Simeon. Pity. Dickens loved names – he could never begin a new book unless he had the names. He tried them out, rolling them round his tongue, writing them down to see what they looked like. David Copperfield had emerged from the improbable Magsby and Topflower, then Copperboy and Copperstone.

Sam was already knocking at the door. There was a boy, of course, a red-faced well-built boy who might have been more at home on the farm, but who went into the inner office and then motioned them to meet the longed-for Mr Cake whose eyes, Dickens insisted later, were exactly like currants.

'Complexion like pastry,' Dickens recalled on the train afterwards. 'Cake by name, cake by nature, I daresay.'

Which was not at all apt since Simeon Cake wore an expression of anxiety which seemed to be habitual. He was tall and thin with the rounded shoulders of a man who spent his time at a desk. Sam explained who he was, introduced his colleague, Mr Dickens, broke the news of the older Bell brothers' deaths, their suspicion that the youngest brother was somehow involved, and impressed upon Mr Cake the urgent need for information.

During this recital, Mr Cake's eyes widened as much as their smallness would allow. He was an ordinary man with ordinary feelings of dismay, shock, disbelief and horror, those emotions flickering across his unremarkable face as he took in the details.

'A bad business, Superintendent Jones. I can scarce believe it. Why, I have not seen those boys for well over twenty years. Thought they might come back some time. Expected them when old Mr Bell dies – won't be long now.'

'Did you expect Austin Bell?' Sam asked.

The currant eyes looked at him shrewdly. 'No, I did not. I'd best tell you the story. You'll want to know what happened to them after Mr and Mrs Bell passed on.'

'We do.'

'Edwin Bell was taken to Manchester by Mr Bell's sister, Caroline, who adopted him. She had two boys of her own. Couldn't – or wouldn't – take all three. Clement Bell stayed with his uncle – seems he was the favourite. Went to school in London and stayed there – a journalist, I think.' Sam nodded. Mr Cake continued. 'Austin Bell, the baby, was taken by Mrs Bell's sister who was emigrating to America with her husband, Mr Clarke.'

Clarke, the name given to the bearded clergyman who had visited Middleton House, and who had laughed to himself as he went away. The same Clarke who was engaged to the widow Moser?

'Anything heard of him afterwards?' Sam asked.

'That's the thing. At first, yes – Mrs Clarke wrote frequently from New York. She'd want to keep the connection – the boy would inherit a third of old Mr Bell's money, and he's a wealthy man. I'll come to that in a bit. Then, about fifteen years ago, Mr Clarke wrote to old Mr Bell to say that his wife had died in New York – he was going to the west and he would let him know when he was settled, send news of the boy and so on. But he didn't. Never heard another word. Old Mr Bell wrote of course to New York, to the address he had, but no news came, and that was it.'

'And the inheritance?'

'The children inherited an equal share of their parents' money, held by the adoptive parents. Edwin Bell came into his when he was twenty-one, and Clement the same. Austin Bell's share was given to Mr and Mrs Clarke. They were to hold it in trust for the boy. Naturally, they could spend on his education, upkeep and so forth, but it was expected that there would be a portion for him to have when he turned twenty-one. Old Mr Bell changed his will when he eventually came to believe that Austin Bell and Mr Clarke were dead, so his money will go to —' he recalled Edwin's and Clement Bell's deaths – 'to Edwin's children. Are you certain about Austin Bell, Superintendent? It hardly seems possible.'

'Someone went to Middleton House about a year ago, a man who gave his name as Clarke and said he was a distant relation of old Mr Bell. Suggestive, is it not?'

'It is. Clarke, eh? Surely not just a coincidence.'

'I doubt it, Mr Cake, and someone impersonated Clement Bell, someone who looks very like the two dead brothers, and Edwin Bell was shot with a gun which came from America. Unless it is a distant cousin, then I think we must assume that the killer is Austin Bell.'

It was time to go. They wanted to catch the four o'clock train back to London. Mr Cake looked grave as he bade them farewell and asked them to let him know if they found Austin Bell.

'And,' added Sam, 'you must of course let us know immediately if you hear from him. He might appear in time, the long-lost brother from America astonished to discover that he has a claim to half the fortune of old Mr Bell.'

'He will bide his time, I think. Mr Bell cannot live much longer. Then he will make his move. He is resourceful enough to find out when Mr Bell dies,' Dickens said.

'What am I to do if he comes here?' Mr Cake looked more anxious than ever at the thought. 'What do I tell him?'

'You treat him with every courtesy and you explain that the law takes time. You ask him what proof he has; you will take opinion. You are very pleased to see him after so long. You suggest he puts up at an hotel in Dorchester and you telegraph to me at Bow Street immediately.'

Mr Cake bade them a nervous farewell and out they went into the busy High Street to make their way to the station.

'America, eh, Sam? By God, I was right.'

Sam laughed. 'Inimitable, Mr Dickens.'

'And it all fits,' said Dickens. 'The beard matches the description given by the lodging housekeeper, the name Clarke, and I thought of something else. The night when Mrs Bell fell down the stairs, I saw a man in a clerical collar. He came behind me in the fog.'

'But that could have been anybody,' objected Sam.

'I heard laughter, too, someone laughing in the fog. What?' He saw Sam's expression change at some memory.

'Mrs Bell's maid, Emma, heard someone laughing when she got locked out. Someone laughing in the fog.'

They looked at each other.

'He knows me,' said Dickens. 'He must know that I know about Oriel Greenwood – where was he after the murder of Edwin Bell? Was he watching us?'

20

MR DICKENS TELLS A STORY

They watched the fields and the trees vanish, the villages and hamlets disappear; the church spires came and went; they saw cows in a field and then they were gone; smoke from chimneys curled away as Dorset was left behind as if a map were being rolled up.

Old Mr Bell slept his innocent sleep; Etheland Dear wondered about the strangers as she blacked the kitchen range; Cake's beefy boy copied his documents, and Simeon Cake went home to think about three boys separated as children, and the third, come back from the dead. How, he thought, did a child become a murderer? He felt a shiver touch the back of his neck.

'Pretty place,' said Sam. 'Could you live in the quiet countryside, in a house like Middleton House?'

'I doubt it; you know when I was in Switzerland and writing *Dombey and Son*, I could not get on fast enough, and I knew what I was missing – London. The weather was beautiful, so clear that I could see the whole of Mont Blanc six miles distant, but what I wanted was streets, and crowds, faces to feed my invention. Could you have lived there?'

'I doubt it; too quiet, I suppose. I somehow felt we had spoilt it – taking murder to that quiet house and churchyard.'

'I know what you mean – like a dirty mark on a picture. Murder and its ripples, eh? The stone in the water.'

Sam looked weary. 'We know now that there is a third brother, we know that he has been to Dorset, but where does it get us, really? We don't know where he is. Do you know, none of it seems real – Manchester is like a terrible dream, that night in the fog, a figure stealing into a house, a woman dead at the foot of the stairs, the crypt – all so nebulous.'

'What about Clarke? What do we do about him?'

Sam looked worried. 'We can't go haring off to Paris. I'll send a man to see your sweet Sally Dibbs – we need to know all about Adolphus Clarke and fast. I want him to be an innocent stockbroker, or a lawyer, or anything – just to clear him from our investigation.' Sam closed his eyes. He looked weary and grey in the feeble light of the oil pot lamp, and his face seemed to have shrunk a little.

They stopped at Bristol where they got out to stretch their legs and Dickens stopped a food vendor whose tray had some squashed looking buns and cakes for sale. He only did it so that he could say to Sam, 'Madeira, Cake?' It wasn't, but it didn't matter for Sam smiled and his face became his own again. They bought a bun each and a bottle of something gaseous.

They got back into the carriage; only one other passenger boarded at Bristol. He tucked himself into a corner, arranged his greatcoat about him, and closed his eyes.

'Now, Samivel, I hope I knows what my duties is. I have seen a great deal of trouble of my own self, and can feel for them as has their feelings tried in this mortal vale. You must be cheered up, that's wot, an' I knows jest the thing, the next best thing to a little sip of liquor which God knows I niver puts more than my lips to.'

Samivel could not forbear laughing at the sight of Dickens's face which had fallen into that of Mrs Gamp, last heard of in The Bull Inn at Manchester. 'And that thing is, Mrs Gamp?'

Dickens glanced at the other passenger, but he was asleep as his snores testified.

'A story, Mr Jones, which will take us from Bristol up to London, wot I call a Piljian's Projiss.'

'My ears are at your service, Mrs Gamp.'

Dickens resumed his familiar tones. 'Imagine a boy brought up in America, in New York, a boy who is named Frederick Clarke, whose mother calls him Freddie which she likes better than Austin – well she is not his true mother, but she is the nearest thing. She tells him tales of a family in England, a family with a rich uncle who lives in a fine house where they will go some day when they have saved enough, and this rich uncle will leave him a fortune. And there are two brothers who will share that fortune with him. And the boy is entranced; he dreams of this golden future and forgets for a time the poverty of the back streets of the glittering city where they live, and he forgets the coldness of his father – not his real father. He knows that his real father is dead, but one day there will be an uncle and two brothers, and he can wait, as children can. Patient, they are, and they are comforted by tales told when the candlelight is flickering and the fire lends a warm glow to a dingy room. Perhaps they kept alive his hope of something beyond that place and time.

'But the mother dies, and the father who is left dislikes the boy for he is not his own son. And there had been money – but it was gone, even though it had been meant for the boy. Mrs Clarke had worried, but what were they to do? Her husband enjoyed spending the money. It was theirs by right. They'd taken the child, hadn't they? And what did it matter since the boy would be getting more from the rich folks in England?

'Mr Clarke takes the boy with him to the west where he thinks he might make his fortune, and the boy knows somehow – do not ask me how – that the train is taking him further and further away from all his dreams. In a small town the train stops right in the middle of the street. Imagine if you will the main street: the pigs burrowing, and the boys flying kites and playing marbles, and men smoking, and women talking, and children crawling, and unaccustomed horses plunging and rearing, close to the very rails. Imagine two or three loafers loitering out with their hands in their pockets, or kicking their heels in rocking chairs, chewing tobacco, just idly staring at the train – there is no fortune to be made here.'

Dickens paused. Sam said, 'I see it in my mind's eye, Horatio.'

'The story of the rich uncle and the welcoming brothers becomes a bitter litany of rejection: couldn't wait to be rid of you, Clarke tells him. You weren't wanted there. Paid to take you away. Mr Clarke sinks into apathy and drink. There is no fortune in the west, just a job in a dry goods store, and errands for the boy to run, a life of drudgery and violence from the drunken man who is not his father, and whom he grows to hate. And upon whose dying he looks with contempt.

'In an old trunk he finds a few papers, nothing much of interest, except a letter which outlines the adoption of Austin Frederick Bell, son of Edgar Bell of Middleton House, Winterbourne Steepleton, Dorset, England. He will go there, he tells himself, and he will claim what's his by right.

'But, not yet, not yet. The boy must work first, work back to the east, and he does. There is a theatre in the little town —' Dickens saw a touch of scepticism in Sam's eye and grinned – 'you must allow me the licence of invention.'

Sam laughed. 'How could I not?'

'Travelling players, then, if you will. He gets a place with them. He can read and write, and he is intelligent and quick. He makes himself useful and he is given small roles, he understudies – and he move on. He finds he can be anyone he wants: Frederick Clarke, Austin Bell, Frederick Bell, Austin Clarke, Edgar Bell, Edgar Clarke – any combination. He gets to Philadelphia – a handsome city, but distractingly regular, I thought; I seemed to stiffen under its quakery influence; my very hands folded themselves upon my breast of their own calm accord ...' he stopped. Sam was laughing at the prospect of Dickens in Quaker garb with his hands folded in an attitude of prayer. He had cheered up.

'I beg your pardon; I was beguiled by memory for a moment. Philadelphia – it has theatres. Frederick Clarke does well, he is talented, acts Shakespeare, Sheridan, Goldsmith. New York next. A stint at the Olympic, per-haps, under Mr Mitchell, a comic actor of great originality, or Niblo's in the hot summer. Money in his pocket, and a desire in his heart. He has struggled, worked hard, and it is time the rich folks in England paid up. Those rich folks who had never given him a moment's thought, who had never written, as Mr Clarke had told him so often.

'He knows the address of that house by heart. There he will go to find out if the rich uncle still lives; he will go as Mr Clarke, a clergyman from America – he will be let in – perhaps if the rich uncle is alive he will say who he really is. Of course, the rich uncle is too ill to see him, but the housekeeper leaves him in the library. He is quick enough to look in the desk, to find the information he wants about those brothers to whom he meant nothing, and who would find they had a debt to pay. Well?' Dickens asked Sam. 'Will it serve?'

'It will serve admirably. I believed every word until I remembered you were making it up!'

'I know, but it could be true – or something like it – some iron entered that man's soul to turn him into a murderer.'

'Indeed it did. You have given me a study of the murderer. A man who is possessed by one idea – to get what he is owed, and when the brothers refuse him or baulk him, he sweeps them out of the way, for he has no brotherly feeling for them. Why should he? He was forgotten, nobody gave a damn about him.'

'And when he confronted them they did not know who he was, had never thought about him. No welcome – just disbelief, suspicion, resentment perhaps. The will cannot be changed. The old man cannot write another, and Austin Bell is entitled to nothing under the will as it stands. He despises them – their easy lives. He will have the money, he will.'

'And he will have to wait – bide his time. He must reappear at some time – otherwise what is the point?'

'But when Sam, when?' Dickens asked.

The train pulled in to Waterloo Bridge Station; they stood up to put on their coats. The other passenger approached them, smiling. They had forgotten all about him.

'I beg your pardon, but I could not help overhearing your story, sir. Fascinating tale – you ought to send it to Mr Dickens. I bet he would make something of it. Most entertaining. I am obliged to you. Good evening to you both.'

The stranger went on his way, leaving Dickens and Sam much amused. 'Perhaps I will send it to Mr Dickens,' said Sam. 'He might improve it – perhaps Mrs Gamp could make an appearance and collar our suspect with her umbrella.'

'By the throat, preferably.'

They walked from the station across Waterloo Bridge and into Wellington Street. Dickens looked down towards his office – he was tempted, but he ought to go home, it had been a long day. They went up to Bow Street, but Sam did not go in. Rogers would send to him if there were any news. Their way took them across Oxford Street up into Portland Place where it joined Devonshire Street, from where Sam could cut through Carburton Street and go down to his house in Norfolk Street.

They stood for a moment. 'Where is he now, I wonder?' Dickens asked.

'London? Manchester? All this needs to be told to Inspector Hardacre. I've just thought – in his letter, Hardacre mentioned that a friend of Edwin Bell's was with him in the theatre that night. He told Hardacre that Bell muttered the word "blackguard" when Clement Bell came on. Edwin Bell knew it wasn't Clement. He knew who it was – and he went backstage to confront him. Perhaps Austin Bell told him that he had killed Clement and then it was too late for Edwin Bell. He had to die too. I must write to Hardacre and tell him that we know who the murderer is, and that he used the name Frederick Clarke. Our dogged Inspector will still be looking.'

21

INSPECTOR HARDACRE

'Frederick Clarke? You know the name?'

Inspector Hardacre's voice was mild enough, but Mrs Marion Ginger was not deceived; she saw the icy gleam in his eyes. He knew. He had taken her by surprise, coming to Kennedy Street so unexpectedly. And Mrs Chew had been hovering in the hall, waiting for her money. Mrs Ginger had been so concerned to get rid of her that she had not time to prepare herself. She had closed the door on Mrs Chew's avid eyes, and when she turned to speak to the Inspector in the hall, he had asked the question. No polite greeting, no request to ask his questions. He had done it on purpose.

The Inspector had been as dogged as Superintendent Jones had surmised. The death of Oriel Greenwood had stayed vivid in his mind, and though he thought that the murderer had probably gone to London, he was still determined to find out as much as he could. And Marion Ginger stayed in his mind. He was not finished with her yet. The news from Superintendent Jones that the murderer had not been Clement Bell had quickened his interest in her. Had she known?

He had mulled it over, going over it in his mind, reading his notes, and then he had remembered a little detail, something that had not seemed all that important. Oriel

Greenwood, according to Superintendent Jones, had changed towards her young man, Robert Alston, about six months previously when she had been engaged to act at the Theatre Royal. It had not been necessary to interview Robert Alston, not when all the evidence pointed to Bell as the killer. But now Inspector Hardacre thought about that detail, thought perhaps she had fallen in love with someone else, a man who called himself Clement Bell, but who was someone else entirely. Time to find out.

He had gone to see Miss Anderton. She had not acted with Oriel Greenwood then because she had been engaged to play Ophelia in Mr Macready's farewell performance of *Hamlet*, which had taken place in October. However, she had been able to tell him that Oriel had played Celia in *As You Like It*, and that if he went to the Theatre Royal, he could find out who were the other members of the cast. That was how he came across the name of Frederick Clarke, a young actor who had, apparently, come from Liverpool. He had questioned the watchman, who remembered the actor. 'Oh, aye, generous with 'is tips.'

'Tips for what?'

The old man winked. 'Sumtimes I'd turn a blind eye, tha knows – if 'e wanted to stay a bit late, 'ave a bite o' supper in the dressin' room with 'is lass. No 'arm, I thought.'

'And the lass? Remember her?'

'Aye, Miss Greenwood. Nice young lass – very fond o' Mr Clarke.'

So, Oriel Greenwood had been fond of Frederick Clarke, and Frederick Clarke used another name later – Clement Bell, and Oriel Greenwood had accepted that. She had changed her own name. She had been Margaret Greenwood – a nice, sensible name. Silly girl, he thought, what was she doing letting herself be taken in like that by Frederick Clarke? Then he thought of poor Oriel Greenwood lying dead in that burial ground. Silly, she might have been, but she'd not deserved that.

Wait a minute. If Clement Bell had been known as Frederick Clarke then, then Marion Ginger must have known that, and she had not thought to mention it. Why not? She had been angry with Clement Bell, as she called him; she had thought he had abandoned her so why should she not tell? She must have known about the murder of Oriel Greenwood – she must have known that her lover had done it. Well, unless he asked her, he would not know. On the day that Dickens and Jones took the train to Dorchester, Hardacre went to see Mrs Ginger.

And she gave herself away. He saw how she flinched when he said the name.

'Shall we go into the parlour?' he suggested.

She was reluctant, but she had no choice, and they went in to the empty room. The velvet sofa and round table with its green chenille cloth had been sold. Inspector Hardacre saw the trunks and bags on the floor. She was leaving. Mrs Ginger faced him. She had recovered some of her self-possession, but he would have the truth.

'Why didn't you tell me that he wasn't Clement Bell? You knew very well what he was – you heard about the murder of Oriel Greenwood. You must have read in the papers about the body of that poor girl found in that dreadful place. You knew that he was a wanted man, and you had vital information.' He heard his own voice in the empty room. Hard.

'I was afraid. If you were to start looking for Frederick Clarke, he would know I had told you. Of course, I know now what he is …' the black eyes flashed for a moment. 'Do you not think that every knock on the door terrifies me?

I dare not keep a servant to live here – what if he were to be let in? I have hidden here like a hunted thing. He knows that I know too much about him.'

'Then I need to know all, and then you can go to wherever you feel safe from him.'

'When I met him in Liverpool, he told me he had come from America, and that he was looking for his relatives. He was going to Dorset where he believed the family lived, a family from which he expected an inheritance. He said he would come to Manchester to see me after his visit to Dorset. When he came, he was delighted that he had discovered that he had two brothers and one lived in Manchester. He intended to find out all about him before he approached him. The family name was Bell, which he said he would take if it suited him. Meantime, he would make his living as an actor. He used the name Frederick Clarke at first, when he acted at the Theatre Royal, but later, when he was engaged at the Queen's Theatre, he used the name Clement Bell. He had been to London to seek out the other brother. He laughed about it when he came back – said it was his brother's name, and he would use it for a joke. He said they owed him, and when they paid, we would go to America and live on his fortune.'

She wept then, but he must know everything.

'You said before that he went to London. Did you write to him there?'

'Yes.'

'As Frederick Clarke?'

'Yes.'

'And where did you write to?'

'A post office.'

'Where?'

'St Martin Le Grand – the letters were to be collected.'

Inspector Hardacre wrote down the address of the post office – an address which he would pass on to Superintendent Jones.

'When did you last write to him?'

'I suppose before he came back for the play – two or three weeks ago.'

'What did you write to him about?'

'I sent him some money. I did not know when he was coming back – not until he said he had been engaged by Mr Dickens.'

'He lived off you?'

'He said that when he came into his fortune…' she laughed, a bitter little laugh. 'What a fool I've been.'

'Why did he go to London?'

'Family business, he said. I assumed it was to do with the money he hoped to get.'

'And he came back as Clement Bell?'

'Yes.'

An idea was beginning to take shape in the Inspector's mind. Frederick Clarke had not only killed Edwin Bell and Oriel Greenwood, but he had murdered Clement Bell. It had to be. The name Frederick Clarke might be an alias, too. He must pass all this on to Superintendent Jones. He turned his attention back to Marion Ginger.

'And where are you going?'

'Where he cannot find me – far away from here.'

'I need to know.' He felt sorry for her – she had been used, as had Oriel Greenwood. She had been seduced, no doubt, by talk of inheritance and a life in America. She was greedy, he thought, and probably unscrupulous. She had not cared that he was using other names. She was prepared to live with him, marry him, perhaps, though she had a husband. Anything was better than her life in Cheshire, chained to a madman in an asylum.

'I am going to Penrith. I have a cousin there. She is a widow who wants company.'

Her voice was bleak. The black eyes dulled now. Nothing to dazzle in Penrith, he thought. Still, Frederick Clarke would not find her. He believed her, but he would check up on her.

She wrote down the address for him, and he left. As he closed the parlour door, he looked back to where she stood in the empty room. She looked forlorn as she stared into her empty future.

22

A DEATH

Sam watched as Dickens walked away along Devonshire Street, then he turned to make his own way home where Elizabeth would be waiting in the firelight, and Posy would make him a cup of tea, and he could rest for a while in the warmth of his own home.

He put his key in the lock, but the door opened suddenly as if someone had been standing behind it, waiting for him. Somebody had for there was the little servant, Posy. She had been seated in the hall. He saw that she had been reading a periodical. It would be *The Finchley Manual of Industry*; Posy was determined to improve her household skills, and theirs, he thought. Posy had ideas about the way a Superintendent of the Police and his wife ought to conduct their lives – sometimes, alas, they fell short of her exacting standards. But now she was looking at him anxiously.

'What is it?' He was alarmed suddenly.

'Mrs Jones, sir, we 'ad a message from the nurse, Mrs Feak. Mr Brim 'as taken a bad turn. Mrs Jones 'as gone.'

Sam made to turn and go out again.

'No, sir, yer not to.' She looked up at him and he almost laughed at the challenging look in her eyes. He might be master here, but this girl had instructions to give.

'No, sir. Yer to come in first, and take some hot soup. Mrs Jones said. She said not to let yer go without some food.

Mrs Jones's orders, sir. Yer've bin out all day. Soup's ready. An' a fire in parlour, sir.'

He gave in. Clearly Mrs Jones's orders were not to be gainsaid, even by the Superintendent. 'Very well, I obey. I'll come to the kitchen, though, and eat it there.'

Posy looked doubtful, but she smiled benignly.

The kitchen fire was warm, and there was heat from the black-leaded range, and the soup smelt good. It was pea soup, hot and peppery, just as he liked it, and there was fresh crusty bread, and a cup of tea. He felt better immediately.

'I'll wait up,' said Posy as she closed the front door after him later on.

He chuckled to himself when he thought of the confidence she had gained, and the inches – only a couple, perhaps, but when he remembered the scrap of a girl whom Dickens had found in the street, selling her tattered artificial flowers, he was pleased. You couldn't save them all, but Dickens, bless the man, had done what he could. He had found employment for a crippled boy, had placed a shoe-black boy in a ragged school, and had established the Home for Fallen Women at Shepherd's Bush. That thought led him to Isabella Gordon and Anna Maria Sesina. They had been dismissed from the Home for bad conduct, but Dickens had met them again. They were working in a theatre somewhere in Soho – not, admittedly, much more than a penny gaff, but Austin Bell was an actor, and that might be a lead there for Charles to follow. He would think about that tomorrow. Now he ought to hurry.

He walked down Norfolk Street and back across Oxford Street, thinking about Mr Brim. He went into Dean Street, then through Seven Dials, crowded as always, and noisy. There were the piemen and baked potato men with their little tin stoves sending sparks up the street when the doors were opened; there were stalls selling all manner of goods: oysters and eels, bonnets and buckets, second-hand clothes, ancient boots and broken umbrellas, and there were drunks reeling against walls, and a knot of men watching two others beat each other to pulp. A girl with a bruised face and a scarlet gown falling off her scrawny shoulders stepped towards him, but he hurried on. He knew where she had probably got that bruise, and she would have more tonight if she did not find a customer. The brawling, brazen life of the city.

He thought of the quiet churchyard in Dorset. Was it only this afternoon that they had stood there? Yet he supposed Dorchester had its poor, no doubt – but not in such impossible legions. He dodged round a man carrying a tray of pies, and side-stepped a drunken woman dragging two barefoot children with her; she was singing a raucous, tuneless collection of words. You couldn't call it a song. Her children looked starved. He reached in his pocket, and gave her a shilling. 'Spend it on them,' he said, but she only looked at him with uncomprehending eyes.

He hurried on to the comparative quiet of Crown Street and the stationery shop. He knocked. The door was opened by Scrap who looked as though he ought to be in bed. But he wouldn't go, thought Sam, not if he were needed. The boy looked up at him with troubled eyes.

''E's bad, Mr Jones. Mrs Feak sent me for Mrs Jones. She thort – I dunno – 'e might die this time ...' Scrap's eyes filled. Not that he was without experience of death. Sam knew that he'd been about the streets and alleys enough in his short life to know what death looked like – how it could take a man, a woman, or a child: an accident, hunger, disease. The cholera epidemic last year had killed thousands. Some dropped in the street, dead where they lay. But this was different. Scrap had become part of this little family, and he would grieve, especially for Eleanor Brim whom he loved.

'Where are the children?'

'Tom's in bed wiv Poll ter keep 'im comp'ny. Miss Eleanor's wiv Mrs Jones in 'er own room. She don't wanter sleep – she knows wot's 'appenin', but Mrs Jones ses she must go ter bed soon in Tom's room in case 'e wakes up.'

Elizabeth came out. She had heard his voice. Scrap went back upstairs. 'I'll look arter Miss Nell whiles yer talk ter Mr Jones.'

'Thank you, Scrap. Try to persuade her to go to bed. She'll listen to you.' Scrap smiled, a smile that transformed his urchin face. Dickens was right when he had said that virtue shows in rags, and goes barefoot as well as shod. Not that Scrap was in rags now or without shoes, but he had been.

Elizabeth smiled at Sam. 'You have had your soup?'

'Force-fed by four foot six, and I'm to be sat up for.'

'Very good – I am glad you did as you were told.'

'No choice – but I had to come. What news?'

'He is dying, Sam. The doctor has been and has given him an opiate so that he sleeps without much pain now. Mrs Feak is so good, and she will sit up all night. But it has been dreadful …' Her eyes filled with tears, and he held her in the warm encirclement of his arms as he had held her when Edith died. They stood without speaking in the quiet shop where only a few days ago they had laughed over the word game on Eleanor's birthday.

'I love my love with an E,' murmured Sam after a while, 'because she is my Elizabeth, and she is my eternal love.'

'Oh, Sam, how fortunate we are in each other despite our losses. I cannot hope he will live if he is to suffer so, yet, poor Eleanor, poor Tom.'

'What must we do?'

'Wait through this night, and when he is gone I will take Eleanor and Tom home. I half thought I should do it earlier, but that little girl understands what is happening. She will not leave him.'

'I will stay with you, and tomorrow we will take them home.'

They went up together to the dying man's room. Robert Brim slept, his white face quiet now, and his breathing faint. It would not be long. Elizabeth sat down. Mrs Feak sat near the bed, watching her patient. The door opened and Eleanor Brim came in, a little white figure in her nightgown. The child went over to Elizabeth who took Eleanor in her arms, though her eyes were fixed on the man in the bed.

'You will need to say goodbye, Eleanor. You know that he is sleeping, and he is not suffering anymore.' Elizabeth whispered.

'He will not wake up?' asked the child.

'I do not think so, my child, but he will know that you are here.'

Eleanor slipped from Elizabeth's knee and went to the bed, where she touched her father's hand.

Robert Brim's eyes fluttered and they saw his hand move in hers. Eleanor stood for a while, then she came towards Sam, against whose solid form she leant her head. He put his hands gently on her thin shoulders, willing the tears not to come from his own eyes. She looked up at him, searching his face. Whatever she found, it was enough. Then she went away to her brother.

'She chooses you,' said Elizabeth. Sam wiped his eyes and Elizabeth went to the bed where she took Robert Brim's hand, and he heard her murmuring soft words to him. 'We will love them, Robert. Do not fear for them.'

Sam moved a chair to the bed for her so that she could sit by Robert. All the while, Mrs Feak sat still at the other side of the bed. There was nothing more for the nurse to do but to wait and watch.

The fire died down, the coals shifting, making their shushing sound. They sat through a long night until grey dawn slid in through the chink in the curtains. They heard the change in his breathing, the rattle in the throat, a long sigh. As if at a signal all three stood. Then he was gone.

Mrs Feak said quietly, 'I'll do what's needed, Mrs Jones. You should get them children away to your house now.'

They left her and saw Scrap asleep on the landing outside the door of the bedroom. There was no sound from within. Asleep, they hoped, and went down to the parlour behind the shop

'I will go in and tell them when it is light, and then we will take them home.'

23

A NARROW ESCAPE

By midday, Sam was back in his office. He had taken Elizabeth and the children home, leaving them in the care of Scrap who had assured him that he would look after them all. He had been back to the shop to see Mrs Feak and had arranged for the undertaker to call. The sleepless night had left him weary, but he had no choice. He had written a note to Dickens to tell him about Robert Brim, and he knew that Dickens would come as soon as he could. And he had sent Inspector Grove to Hampstead to question Sally Dibbs, the maid, and to follow up any information on Adolphus Clarke.

Inspector Hardacre's letter was in his hands. The post office address might be useful, he thought. Austin Bell – it was easier to call him that now – might not have collected his letters while he was planning his murder of Clement. There had been no money on the body; Austin Bell had helped himself, but soon he might be in need of ready cash, and there was a little packet waiting for him at St Martin Le Grand, at the post office there. He would send a man in plain clothes to keep watch.

The postmaster would have to be told that he must inform the constable when Frederick Clarke collected his letters. He would have to go himself, take Constable Semple with him, and explain what he wanted of the post office. What they needed was a sharp-eyed, quick-thinking clerk who would communicate fast enough for Semple to apprehend Austin Bell. Risky, but worth a go.

Hardacre had found out about Frederick Clarke, and he had worked out that he had killed Clement Bell. Hardacre had told him about Marion Ginger, her fear of Bell, and her intention to go to Penrith. He picked up his pen to write to the Inspector – he must tell him what they had found out about the Bell family in Dorset.

Rogers came in. He had already told him about Robert Brim. The shop would be closed for the time being, and then Rogers and Mollie would move in.

'This letter is from Inspector Hardacre,' Sam said, 'who tells me that our man went under the name of Frederick Clarke, and that his lady love, Mrs Ginger, sent him money a week or two ago.'

'To be collected?' Rogers was quick.

'At St Martin Le Grand.'

'You think 'e might want money?'

'It's possible. We'll have to see the postmaster. We need to know if there are any letters for Frederick Clarke. I'll put Semple in there. You never know.'

Dickens came in then. 'I went up to your house from Wellington Street to see if I could do anything. Nothing needed for the moment so I came here. I am at your disposal, if you need me.'

Sam told him about the post office, and the plan to watch for Austin Bell.

'I had a thought,' said Dickens, 'about the theatre.'

'So did I. I wondered about Isabella Gordon. Whether she might be worth asking. And, another thing – Hardacre tells me that Austin Bell met Oriel Greenwood when they were acting in *As You Like It* at the Theatre Royal in Manchester – he was using the name Frederick Clarke then.'

'And he was Clement Bell when they were with me at the Queen's Theatre. I wonder how he explained the change of name.'

'He'd have some story, I suppose – stage name, or something. Does it matter?'

'I suppose not, but it does shed more light on the murder of Oriel Greenwood. She knew that Clement Bell was not his real name – it made her a threat to him. We thought that he was afraid she might let something slip. Perhaps I should investigate productions of *As You Like It*, and I'll seek out Isabella Gordon – though I think he might look higher than the kind of theatre I went to with Isabella.'

'Not necessarily. He could disappear into a minor theatre, earn some money, bide his time. No one would ask questions, and he could move on when he felt like it.'

'True. I'll have to see if Isabella and Sesina are still where I left them last November – they could have moved on, of course. On my way home I'll have a look at the posters in Drury Lane and on The Strand to see if *As You Like* it is on anywhere.'

They parted on The Strand; Dickens intended to walk along to The Adelphi, and the Superintendent and Rogers made their way towards St Martin Le Grand and the post office.

Dickens walked briskly to the corner of Adam Street where he contemplated the imposing façade of The Adelphi with its wide archway and columns reaching up to a pedimented balcony. An adaptation of his Christmas story *The Haunted Man* had been on here in 1848. And he had come here as a young man to watch the comedian, Charles Matthews. That was in the days when he had thought acting might be his calling – only a swollen face had prevented him from attending an audition with Charles Kemble and the stage manager, Mr Bartley, at Covent Garden. He had not known then that he would be known for his stories rather than as an actor – destiny, he supposed. He had told Bartley that he would apply again for an audition, but he did not. Fate intended him for something other than the stage, but, he thought, how near I was to another sort of life.

There was no performance of *As You like It* at The Adelphi, but then, he reflected gloomily, Austin Bell could be in anything. *Othello*? No, he wouldn't be in a major role, but I can see him as Iago – not the rough, straightforward, seemingly honest Iago that Macready had played. Something slyer, meaner – Bell was nowhere near the actor Macready was.

He walked up to The Strand Theatre, and then to the Lyceum, the front of which was in Wellington Street, the dear old Lyceum where the adaptation of *Martin Chuzzlewit* had had a run of one hundred performances. Nothing. Then up to Covent Garden – he might have seen his own name on the bill if he had gone back. He was undecided – should he go back to Wellington Street? Or should he try one more – the Theatre Royal in Haymarket was not so far. This must be the last. He could walk to every theatre in London and not find him. He could, of course, seek out Isabella Gordon, and there was Alice Drown who had once been at the Home for Fallen Women and who had left to work in the theatre. She might still be on stage at the Victoria Theatre over the river. Later, perhaps.

His way took him across St Martin's Lane, through Leicester Square. The bill advertised Samuel Phelps in *As You Like It* – tonight! Good. He thought about going in to ask about Austin Bell, or Frederick Clarke, but stopped himself in time. That wouldn't do – what a fool he would look if the doorkeeper said that Bell was there and that he would take a message! And it would be no good if the watchman told Bell that someone had been asking for him – the play would be without one of its actors tonight, especially if the watchman had recognised him and told Bell that Mr Dickens had been asking for him. He did not want to come face to face with him – not now, not at all. He walked away swiftly.

He took a circuitous route, turning quickly into James Street where he knocked into a man wheeling a barrow with a wooden crate on top which tottered dangerously to the indignation of the hens inside. 'Blimey, wotchit mister!' the man cried out, but Dickens flew on, not daring to look back. He rushed down into Dorset Street, and into crowded Trafalgar Square, up into Adelaide Street, a series of left and right twists through into Covent Garden. He did not stop until he was at Bow Street Police Station.

Sam was back from the post office where he had seen the postmaster and had put Semple in place. He looked up when Dickens came in looking uncharacteristically flustered.

'What is it?'

'Sorry, Sam. Let me sit down and get my breath. I've just come from the Theatre Royal in Haymarket.'

'You haven't seen him?' Sam sounded alarmed.

'No, no, but I nearly made a foolish mistake; I almost went in to ask about Bell, then – you may well look relieved – I thought better of it. I had a horrible thought that the doorman might tell him that Mr Dickens had enquired. I ran off as fast as I could – imagine, the Inimitable seen running like a madman, holding onto his hat, panting as if the Furies were after him. I had a nasty moment with a crate of chickens.'

'But you don't know if he was there,' Sam pointed out reasonably.

Dickens looked at him wide-eyed. 'Your observation, Mr Jones, renders my conduct, as my father would say, manifest to any person of ordinary intelligence, if the term may be considered allowable, idiotic.'

Sam laughed. 'I do not say the word is apt – rash, perhaps. But, nevertheless, he might be there, and your caution, if not your later impetuous dashing away, renders your conduct advisable in the circumstances.'

'Much obliged, Mr Jones. I feel distinctly less of a stupendous jackass.'

'Well, he might be there. And I can tell you where he isn't.'

'Where isn't he?'

'He isn't in Paris. Inspector Grove found out about Mr Adolphus Clarke. Our Dolly is as innocent as a babe —'

'In Paris with a widow!'

'Innocent for our purposes. Mr Adolphus Clarke is a respectable stockbroker with a steady income and a reputation for honesty in his dealings.'

'Not a murderer then – just as well for the pretty widow, if not for us. Now, I did think that I might go to see the performance of *As You Like It*, see if our Mr Bell is in it. I could take Mark Lemon. He was with us in Manchester – two pairs of eyes to scan the stage.'

'Yes, but make sure you leave quickly – we don't want him seeing you if he's there, nor Mr Lemon.'

'True. We'll slip out at the interval – I'll know by then. What news from the post office?'

'There is an uncollected letter postmarked Manchester which we might assume is from Mrs Ginger. I didn't have it opened – I don't want him running off. I want him walking out like a respectable citizen, straight into the waiting arms of Semple.'

'If it's no-go tonight, I thought I might try Isabella Gordon or Alice Drown, and I thought discreet enquiries might be made to Macready. I know Phelps, Charles Selby and the Keeleys. I could ask about any new, promising actors from the provinces.'

'You could,' agreed Sam, 'though, of course, he might be using yet another name. Still, we have set our traps, as it were. Let us hope he walks into one of them.'

24

EYES ON HIM

Dickens went to his office in Wellington Street to write a note to Mark Lemon at the offices of *Punch* magazine in Bouverie Street, inviting him to join him at the performance of *As You Like it*. To tempt him further, he suggested that they dine early at The Athenaeum where they would meet at six o'clock, and in the way of tantalisation, he hinted at a mystery to be solved:

> *I really think this ought to be done, and indeed must be done. Write and say it shall be done. You shall pluck out the heart of my mystery.*
> *Ever affectionately*

That'll catch him, he thought. Dinner and a mystery. And so it did. Lemon's reply came by return. Now for *Household Words*. Mrs Gaskell's story *Lizzie Leigh* was on his desk, but he put it to one side. He did not want to think about Manchester just now – he knew that if he started, he might well be distracted. He turned to something that would keep his mind off murder. His eye fell upon the article he had written for the first edition: *Valentine's Day at the Post Office*. He pictured The Window Department where huge slits gaped for letters, whole sashes yawned for newspapers, and the wooden panes open for clerks to frame their huge faces, like giant visages in the slides of The Magic Lantern, and he thought of the 337,500,000 letters that passed through the post office in a year, and he thought of that one letter waiting for Austin Bell. He imagined the sloping handwriting in black. Mrs Ginger's hand. He hadn't liked her, but he felt pity for her now. She would know what kind of man she had loved. To work, he told himself and he turned to the title of the next: *The Amusements of the People* in which he intended to describe a night at the Victoria Theatre in the company of one Joe Whelks – *how all occasions do inform against me!* Everywhere he looked there were reminders of the case.

At seven o'clock, he and Lemon were sitting in the stalls at the Theatre Royal, Haymarket, waiting for the curtain to rise on the scene: an orchard near Oliver's house. He had told Mark that he was looking for the man they had known as Clement Bell. He had already looked at the programme, but of course there was no Frederick Clarke listed, no Clarke at all, and no Bell. He looked at the names of the actors: Phelps, Keeley, Mrs Warner, Miss Reynolds, Davenport – the American. That was a thought, he might know of an American actor newly come to London – Wallack, Cooper – whom Macready had called 'an incarnation of stupidity' as Iago – perhaps the part of William might suit him better. Some names he did not know: Mr Stephens, Mr Maxwell, Mr Lake – no clues there. He did not know what part Bell had played in the Manchester production. More likely in London that he would play a minor role – an anonymous lord, an attendant, a shepherd, perhaps.

The play was starting. He watched the first scenes, peering at the lords at the court of Duke Frederick, but it was no use – impossible to tell if any of them bore a likeness to Austin Bell. At the end of Act I, Celia and Rosalind were on stage after the exit of the Duke, and it was in that quiet scene that Dickens felt as though eyes were upon him. Not so unusual, but some sense told him that these eyes were hostile. He felt a touch of ice at his spine.

What made him look up he did not know, but there in the box was a man, his opera glasses trained upon Dickens. It is he. He can see me, thought Dickens. He can see my face, and I know the expression on his – that cold, appraising, contemptuous look he gave me when he had Oriel Greenwood in his arms. He hated me, and he hates me now. They might as well have been alone in the theatre as they had been in the darkened auditorium in Manchester when the man he had thought was Clement Bell had looked at him on the stage, and had applauded. Ill-met by ghostlight. The figure dropped the glasses from his eyes, bowed to Dickens, and was gone. It was Bell. Who else?

His instinct was to leap from his seat and rush to the door. But how could he? What a disturbance it would make, and what a palaver in the newspapers. *Mr Dickens taken ill at the theatre! Dickens flees from performance of 'As You Like It'!* He would have to sit it out. The time until the interval seemed interminable. Even Shakespeare could not distract him from his teeming thoughts. Had Bell seen him earlier at the theatre? Had he come tonight to convey a message? *I am watching you. I am not afraid of you. You cannot catch me.*

At the interval Dickens went to see the manager, Mr Webster, to ask who had been in that particular box. The answer was that the box had not been engaged. It was empty as far as he knew. Dickens explained that he thought he had seen an acquaintance there. Mr Webster doubted that one of Mr Dickens's acquaintances would purloin a box without paying for it, but a stranger might sneak in. Sometimes a box might be left open by mistake. Dickens apologised for troubling him and went to meet Lemon.

'No sign of him. Of course, it could have been anyone. I shall go home, I think. What about you?'

'Do you want me to stay,' Mark asked, 'see if he's in any of the forest scenes? I can let you know if he is. I'll take a different seat so that he'll think we've both gone. I could keep my eye discreetly on the box, and if Bell comes back —' Mark looked at Dickens's strained face. 'Should you be doing all this? Bell's dangerous. What if ...?' his voice trailed off.

'If he's after me? I have thought of it. I will go in a cab to see Superintendent Jones and tell him about tonight. And as for whether I should be involved, I cannot help it. I feel responsible. I engaged him – and Oriel Greenwood. I should have ...'

'What? Tried to intervene? I know you were fond of her, but she was not as fragile as you thought, you know. She was determined to have him.'

'You thought that I was deceived?' Dickens was offended.

'Dickens, old friend, of course you were. Don't be offended now. That poor girl did not deserve to die, but it was not your doing.'

Dickens looked at his friend's kindly face. Dear old Lemon. 'A weight is on my breast. The only difference between me and the murderer is that his weight is guilt and mine regret.'

'The funeral – Mr Brim. Do you want me to come?' Mark had been one of Mr Brim's customers, directed there by Dickens.

'God bless you, Mark. I would like it. It is at noon at Highgate – day after tomorrow. We meet at the shop.'

'Now get your cab,' Mark told Dickens, 'and tell Sam Jones everything. Then go home. I will go back in and keep my eyes peeled.'

'Lemon – aid, I will. Goodnight.'

Lemon smiled at the familiar pun. 'Goodnight, sweet prince.'

Dickens went out and darted into a waiting cab. But, there was someone there before him.

25

LOSS

At Norfolk Street, Elizabeth Jones was putting Tom Brim to bed. In the parlour Sam was sitting with Eleanor Brim, who was looking at the flames of the fire. He watched her and hoped that he would be able to answer whatever questions she was turning over in her mind. He saw how she frowned a little, and how grave her face was in the firelight. He waited.

She wept then, and turning to him, saw that his arms were waiting. The sobbing wrenched his heart, but he simply held her gently. His own heart seemed to splinter as he heard her say 'Mama'. That was it, too. She wanted her mama who had died so long ago.

When the tears stopped he wiped her eyes with his handkerchief.

'Is Papa with Mama now? Papa said she was waiting. Is it so?' She looked up at him.

'He is,' Sam answered.

'She has waited a long time,' she said. 'I miss them, but poor Papa was so ill – is it better for him now?'

'I think it is; the pain is over.'

'Are you our father now?' she asked, her solemn grey eyes fixed on his face.

'Your father will always be your father, Eleanor. I am here to look after you and Tom, and Scrap and Poll, of course. I will stand in for your father.'

'Did he ask you?'

'Yes, he did. He wanted to be sure that you and Tom would have a mother and father because he knew that he would not get better. You knew that, too.'

She nodded.

'Where is Papa now?'

'He is with Mrs Feak. She will look after him until —' he paused. If he was going to be her father then he must face the responsibility of an intelligent child who could not be fobbed off.

'I had a little girl once. When she grew up she was ill like your poor papa and she died. We had to say goodbye and leave her with the nurse who laid her in her coffin, and we buried her in the ground, but we knew that she was not really there. Her soul, the purest and best part of her, had gone to be in the care of our Lord Jesus.'

Eleanor asked nothing more. He did not know if it had been enough, but let her believe. He saw her eyes close. At last, she slept.

Elizabeth came in and Sam carried Eleanor upstairs to the bed next to Tom's. The little boy was fast asleep. Elizabeth would sit with them until she was sure that Eleanor would not wake.

Sam went back into the parlour. And then there came the little tap on the window which he had been expecting. He went to open the front door and there was Dickens. A cab was just rolling away – Rogers going home.

'Thank you, Sam. I was mightily glad to see Rogers when I got in the cab. What made you?'

'A pricking of my thumbs,' Sam said with a smile. 'I thought if Bell were at the theatre he might see you – I told Rogers to get to The Adelphi in time for the interval and to wait if you didn't come then, and to make sure he had a cab – just precaution.'

Elizabeth came down the stairs, having heard the murmur of voices. Dickens saw how Sam looked up at her, and how she answered his glance and nodded. Some unspoken message passed between them. He felt such a piercing ache of loneliness. That one happiness he had missed, the one friend and companion he had never had.

Elizabeth went back upstairs and Sam took Dickens into the parlour where he supplied him with brandy and water. 'What happened?' he asked.

Dickens told him about the man in the box, his conviction that it was Bell. 'He bowed, and though I could not see him clearly, I knew by that single gesture that it was he. You can imagine my feeling when I got into the cab and saw someone in there already.' He shivered at the memory and drank his brandy. 'Is he after me? I tell you, Sam, he frightens me.'

'He is taking too many chances, but we shall not take any more. No more sleuthing alone. You and I will visit the theatrical folk you mentioned, and we'll take Rogers with us to seek out Alice Drown and Isabella Gordon. I'll put Stemp at your house, too – no one will get past him, and he will have instructions to arrest anyone answering the description of Bell.' Sam's voice was uncharacteristically hard – a tone Dickens had heard only when the Superintendent had faced down some very hardened criminals.

'Has Stemp found out anything about the woman in the crypt?' Dickens asked.

'No. I'll put Feak on to that. Stemp's the man for watching your house.'

'But if we frighten Bell off, he might disappear.'

'That's a chance I'm willing to take – I will not put you in danger. Good Heavens, Charles, my career would be in shreds if it was discovered that I was using Mr Dickens as a stalking horse and put him in danger of his life. I'd be lynched by your legions of admirers!'

Dickens had to laugh. 'You are right, of course – and I admit I do not want to come face to face with that man on my own.'

'Then I shall escort you home. He may be watching, but he won't come near if there are two of us, and he'll see that you are under my protection. If he has been watching, he will know me.'

'Is all well here?' Dickens asked.

'I think so – Eleanor wept tonight. A good thing, I think. That dry-eyed grief was too much for a little girl to bear. Time will put it right. Elizabeth is to take them to her cousin in the country where there is a farm and trees and meadows. It will help.'

'It will indeed. Do them good to be out of London.'

'You are able to come to the funeral?'

'Of course. Mark Lemon will come, too. We will meet you at the shop. Now I must go. I'll be at home tomorrow morning until about eleven o'clock, then I shall go to Wellington Street, after which we might make our enquiries of my theatrical friends.'

'We will.'

'I knows where we might take what Sam Weller calls a nice little dinner, a pair of fowls and a weal cutlet, French beans, taturs, tart and tidiness. What say you?'

'I say aye to that,' smiled Sam.

Sam walked with Dickens to Devonshire Terrace. Dickens went in through the iron gate and stood for a moment looking up at the night sky. Not a star and no moon. How dark it was. Footsteps on the road outside. Slowing. Stopping. Then the footsteps went on. Dickens opened his door and went in.

26

A NIGHT AT THE CIRCUS

'A demnd, damp, moist, unpleasant body,' observed Dickens in the manner of Mr Mantilini as he and the Superintendent returned from the theatre in Drury Lane to Bow Street in the rain that the clouded darkness had foretold the night before. It had poured since daybreak. Not that you could say that day had ever broken, Dickens thought, as they trudged through streets steeped thick in mud, and endured the cold darts of rain, borne by a raw wind, flying in under their umbrellas to sting their faces. They had walked all over the place to talk to Dickens's friends at the various theatres, but had found out nothing at all about Austin Bell. No one had heard of him under any of the names their invention had provided.

They stood to cross the road when a gust of wind snatched Dickens's umbrella and hurled it backwards over the heads of those behind him. He thought of leaving it to its fate, but it dropped like a fallen crow by a billboard and, feeling a kind of pity for it, he stepped through the crowd to retrieve it. Looking up, his eye caught the wording of a rather sodden poster hanging from the wooden board. It was the word 'American' that he noticed first and his quick eye registered the banner headline: 'The American Equestrian Company'.

'Sam,' he called. The Superintendent went over to him and they read the whole:

A Matchless Stud of 40 American Horses
Barnell Runnells – Scenic Rider
MJ Bickley – The Great Star Rider of America

'Well?' said Dickens.

'Well, indeed.'

'Forty horses, Sam, and forty riders. Perhaps a night at the circus?'

'Madness!'

'He must be somewhere, and what a place to disappear. Our man of many parts, why should he not find a job in the American Circus? Remember my tale on the train – perhaps he joined as a boy after the death of Clarke. He is a man who had fought his way in a wild world.'

Dickens's eyes shone with eagerness. When he got an idea, nothing could shake him. His imagination, thought Sam, could easily conjure Austin Bell on horseback, disguised as The Indian Hunter, or perhaps The Flying Indian, two more delights offered by the soggy poster. I'd rather see him cleaning out the stables, Sam reflected, with those long white hands stained in muck. White hands did not quite fit with Dickens's conjuring of the tough American whirling his lasso about the circus ring, but he kindly forbore to say so.

Dickens noticed Sam's frown. 'Dang it, sir, you ain't convinced that a trip to the circus'll fix us.'

Sam laughed at Dickens's American drawl. 'I ain't, but we'll try it. It's as good an idea as any at the moment. He must be earning money somewhere as he has not been to the post office.'

'He won't – he may very well suspect that you know of his letter. So, shall we try tonight?'

'We shall.'

An interesting party found itself at Astley's near Westminster Bridge that evening. Dickens went round to the Box entrance, and the others went to the stalls. Sam had made careful plans. Constable Feak, in plain clothes, had been detailed to hang about the stables behind the theatre – he had already been there a couple of hours. His instructions were to listen for a possible name, not to ask, in case Bell vanished again. If they did not catch him tonight, then at least they might know if he worked there. Constables Dacre and Semple, in uniform, were stationed outside the entrance to the stable yard. Burly Stemp and Constable Rogers were to place themselves at the two entrances to the circus ring when they saw the horses and riders going in.

Sam, accompanied by his old friend Bridie O'Malley, dressed up to the nines in red velvet and black feathers, took seats in the stalls near the riders' exit on one side, and at the exit on the other side were Mrs Feak and Scrap, with another plain clothes constable beside them. Sam could see Scrap clearly enough to give or receive the signal. Scrap, having seen Clement Bell's body, might recognise their quarry, and the idea was that he should dart through the tunnel under cover of the horses and alert the policemen. Sam would leave by the other tunnel as fast as he could.

In his box, Dickens had a large white handkerchief to flourish if he saw Bell among the horses and riders and he had his opera glasses trained on the stalls. He could see Sam next to Bridie's red dress and large hat, and opposite he saw Scrap with Mrs Feak. A nice little family party, he thought, not unlike the Garland family's outing to Astley's that he had described in *The Old Curiosity Shop*. Scrap had not been to the circus before. Next time, Dickens would bring him when they were off duty and the boy could enjoy it all without the responsibility of keeping his sharp eyes open for the wanted man.

Dickens had been here many times; he always felt a thrill at the magic of it all. Astley's was a sumptuous palace, gilded and mirrored, decorated in yellow and white, green and gold with rich crimson hangings for the boxes. The circles were supported by eight Doric pillars and forty-six Corinthian columns – a very temple of pleasure. A great crystal and gold chandelier hung from a dome and the proscenium formed a magnificent triumphal arch over the great stage. And the smell of sawdust and horses – a smell he always thought that was never in any other place in the world.

The place was packed – two thousand people, perhaps, and most of them the ordinary working folk for whom this was a treat, a sight literally for sore eyes: the eyes of servant girls and laundresses that looked mostly on great foaming coppers full of other people's laundry; the tired eyes of grey-faced clerks bent all day over dusty ledgers, and the suddenly round eyes of children used to playing in narrow lanes or shabby courts. Here was an escape out of the literal world – and for a sixpence only. Dickens believed in the amusements of the people – his article on the same subject would be soon in *Household Words*.

The curtain was rising; the long brilliant row of lights came slowly up, and the music began. On the stage there was enacted *Othello* – on horseback, the Moor costumed as an African, his face blackened by tropic suns, his scimitar in his hand, and the horse caparisoned in a leopard skin. A fight to the death. Othello's enemy inflicts the fatal blow. Othello falls on to the horse's back, clutches the leopard skin, and is taken away to thunderous applause. Another horse and rider, a juggler who throws up two oranges and catches them on two forks. The Flying Indian somersaults on the horse's back and lands, shaking his headdress and brandishing his tomahawk, with his moccassined feet firmly in place, and he does it again – twice.

Dickens looked through his glasses. He could see Scrap and he could imagine his wonder at it all, but he wouldn't forget his responsibility – not Scrap, despite the Flying Indian. The glasses ranged over to the opposite side. Bridie O'Malley was enjoying herself, though Sam looked as if he were ready to spring up at once. As if he sensed Dickens looking at him, Sam glanced up at the box. Dickens lowered the glasses. Nothing yet.

Then, in they came, the great parade of forty horses, and their riders. Dickens saw Sam straighten up and Scrap lean forward as he scanned the riders. Some were Indian braves led by their chief, a commanding figure in his feathered headdress – the Flying Indian of before. The opposition were the cavalry soldiers at whom Dickens peered intently. They wheeled round and round the circle, then the cavalry stopped, ready for the charge, and there at the back of the troop, he felt certain, was Bell. He knew him immediately by the familiar long hands resting on the reins. Dickens flourished his handkerchief. Scrap and Sam looked up simultaneously. The horses wheeled again and the back row made its way to the exit tunnel next to where Scrap was sitting. Dickens saw the first man unfurl his flag. Bell was next – these cavalry men would return through the opposite entrance to trap the Indians. He hoped Bell would be trapped by the policemen waiting outside

Dickens did not wait to see Scrap dart from his seat. He left the box immediately. Sam saw and left his seat, climbed over into the ring and ran into the tunnel amid the horses. No one noticed. All eyes were on the Indian chief who led his braves once more round the ring, pursuing the cavalry. The air rang with their high yells.

As Bell trotted out behind the leader, he saw the uniformed policeman at the entrance to the tunnel, and he spurred on his horse, seizing the gun from his holster. The gun fired – a blank, but the report was loud enough. The policeman – Constable Semple – lunged at him, but Bell was already past him and in the stable yard. A boy started up from nowhere, but Bell charged on. Feak saw Scrap about to be mown down by the rider. He flung himself at the boy and was caught with a glancing blow in the chest from the wild hooves. The rider plunged on through the gateway, where another policeman made to grab the stirrup. He kicked him away and fired again. Another uniformed man waved his rattle. The horse reared and snorted, its eyes rolled white, but Bell kept his seat, turning the horse to the right. A man coming towards him shrank in fear. Bloody Mr Dickens! Bell looked at him and pointed the gun. Dickens flung himself away. Bell fired again over Dickens's head. Dickens smelt the tang of sulphur. Bell pulled at the reins and cantered away. The devil had been and gone.

27

A FOOTFALL ON THE STAIRS

Back in the stable yard filled with thirty-nine horses and their riders gaping at the scene, a horrified Sam saw Feak lying on the ground, Semple kneeling beside him. He heard the high shriek of the rattle and saw Dickens scrambling to his feet.

'Get after him!' he shouted to the policeman with the rattle, knowing it was no use. Catch a man on a galloping horse – a man who could ride like that – not possible.

Scrap was stretched out on the cobbled yard, but as Dickens went to him the boy sat up. His face was scraped where he had hit the cobbles. He would likely feel the bruises in the morning, but he was otherwise unharmed thanks to Constable Feak. Behind Dickens, Mrs Feak and Bridie O'Malley appeared. Mrs Feak saw her son.

'He's alive,' shouted Sam, seeing Mrs Feak's ashen face. Feak's eyes opened and he sat up.

'Jest winded, sir, I think. What about the boy?'

Dickens was helping Scrap to rise. Sam said, 'He's all right, thanks to you, Feak. You saved his life. Get a cab, Semple, and take Mrs Feak and her son home. Bridie, I beg your pardon – you'll go with them.'

'I will, Sam. To be sure, I never expected so much excitement. A night at the circus, you said.' She laughed, her black feathers shaking. 'A quiet dinner next time, perhaps.'

Semple went off to fetch a cab. Mrs Feak knelt by her son. 'Well, my boy, it's a mercy your head want in the way, and that you 'ad your thick coat to protect you. Can yer stand?'

'I think so.' Sam helped the constable up.

'You're a hero, Mr Feak. You deserve a medal.' That was Mr Dickens, smilin' at 'im as well. Ma looked pleased, too. She could fuss 'im when they got 'ome – not now, not wiv 'em all lookin'.

'Sorry we dint stop 'im, sir,' said Feak.

'We didn't expect to be chasing a horse, Feak. You did well, and we'll get him, don't worry.'

Semple returned. A cab was waiting. Scrap was persuaded that he must go, too. Semple would take him to Norfolk Street when Mrs Feak had looked at his scratches.

'Mind, Scrap, not a word about this to Mrs Jones,' said Sam.

'No, Mr Jones, yer can rely on me. I jest fell, that's all.'

Semple shepherded his flock to the cab just as Constable Dacre came through the gate leading the horse – without its rider, of course. It tossed its head and side-stepped, almost treading on Dacre, who pushed it away.

'My horse, I believe.' A deep voice caused Sam and Dickens to turn round. The speaker was the foremost rider, the Indian Chief, resplendent in his eagle-feathered headdress. Pitchlynn, thought Dickens, remembering the Chief of the Choctaw tribe whom he had met when travelling on a steamboat to St Louis. A surprising man who had been particularly attached to the poetry of Walter Scott. Not that Pitchlynn had been wearing his native dress, a fact that Dickens had regretted, though he recalled vividly how the chief had raised his arm like a man brandishing a weapon. Not that the present chief had a weapon, nor was he an Indian.

'Richard Sands, sirs, owner of these horses and employer of the man you were chasin'. Might I ask why?'

'A wanted man, sir,' said Sam. 'A murder suspect. What name do you know him by?'

Richard Sands looked hard at Sam. 'You sure of that, sir?'

'I am. I am Superintendent Jones of Bow Street. Who is he?'

It was an extraordinary, improbable scene: a London policeman and an Indian Chief facing each other. The stand-off was broken by the sudden snort of Bell's horse, and its hooves moving on the cobbles. Sam continued to look up at the Chief, who had the advantage of being on horseback, but Sam did not speak.

Richard Sands finally nodded. 'Freddie Clarke. Knew him before, years back – in New York. Did some ridin' for us then. Come from Philadelphia, trained at Welch's Circus there. Learned to ride with Napoleon Welch – a man who could ride four horses at once. Clarke was a handy rider, useful. Left us for the theatre. Lost sight of him till a few days ago.'

Philadelphia, thought Dickens, I was right. He glanced at Sam, but Sam was looking fixedly at Richard Sands.

'What did he tell you?' asked Sam.

'Said he'd come to England to look for his folks, but they was all gone. Family died out, so he needed a job. Said he'd come back to America with us. Wanted to go home. I needed a rider – one man injured, so I took him on.'

'Did he lodge here?'

'Bunked up with the troops.'

'Was he here last night?' Sam was thinking about the man Dickens had seen in the theatre.

'Had some business. Came back in time for the parade.'

It fitted. Bell could have come from the Haymarket. From what Dickens had told Sam, Bell had left the box well before the interval; in fact, before the end of the first act.

'I will need to look at where he slept. I need to see if he has left anything he might wish to come back for.' Sam looked at Richard Sands.

'Ain't much, I guess. You're askin' if I'll tell you if he comes back?'

'I am hoping you will, Mr Sands. I know he is a compatriot of yours, but murder is murder on both sides of the Atlantic.'

'It is.' Sands nodded. 'In the rooms over yonder, you'll find his bunk.'

Sands dismounted, and went with them to the rooms where he pointed out Bell's bed. Underneath there was a cheap carpetbag inside which was a rolled-up suit. Sam shook it out.

'Alfred Evelyn,' Dickens said. He stepped forward to look at the coat and the label inside the collar. He pointed. 'Nathan of Titchbourne Street – the theatrical costumier. That's where the dresses for *Money* came from.'

'No doubt now, then,' observed Sam. 'I'll need to take this as evidence. He looked inside the carpetbag. A shirt, a hair brush, a toothbrush, a pair of leather gloves, and in the pocket inside, a letter on yellowing paper. He unfolded it, scanned its contents and handed it to Dickens. 'Your story comes true, Charles.'

Dickens looked at the faded writing. The letter was from old Mr Bell written from Middleton House to Mrs Clarke, asking about the boy, Austin, and hoping all was well. It was dated 1832. Bell would have been about nine or ten years old then. So long ago. Had his tale really been true? Not that it mattered. The letter had brought Bell to England, to Dorset, to Manchester and London – and to murder.

'What can you tell us about him, Mr Sands? You knew him years back, you say, when he was a lad.'

They waited while Sands thought. 'Just a kid, really. Determined though. Wanted to get somewhere. Said his ma died when he was 'bout ten years old. His pa wasn't no good. Drank. Freddie left some little town, joined the circus. He had good hands on a horse – long and capable, hard hands. Left us when we got to New York. That's it. All I know, sir.'

Dickens pictured those long hands, so like the long, pale hand of Edwin Bell hanging down over the gun on the stage in Manchester. The hands that had held the knife that killed poor Oriel Greenwood, and the hands that had held the gun which killed Clement Bell in that dusty crypt. Perhaps the hands that had pushed Dora Bell down those stairs.

'Thank you, Mr Sands. You have been helpful. Now we must go.'

They went back into the stable yard. They could hear men calling to each other, and the horses whinnying. Some men sat on the mounting blocks or lounged, smoking, waiting to get into their quarters. Did any of them know Freddie Clarke from years back?

'Tell your men, Mr Sands, that if anyone knows anything about Frederick Clarke, he must tell me. The man is dangerous. And I will pursue him – to your country, if I must.'

'Surely will, Superintendent.' Sands held out his hand. Sam gave him his. They shook.

In the street outside two constables waited. The search was still going on down by Lambeth Palace and the riverside gardens, but nothing had been seen of the suspect. Sam was not surprised. He hadn't enough men to make a thorough job of it. But he must go to the Police Station in Lower Kennington Road. Strictly speaking, this was M Division's territory. Thankfully, he knew Superintendent Brannan very well, and Inspector Peters. If neither was there, he could leave a message, explaining the events of the night and asking that a lookout be kept for Bell. It wasn't far to the station – afterwards, they could walk over Vauxhall Bridge, take a cab up to

Devonshire Terrace and Norfolk Street. Neither Brannan nor Peters was there, but Sam met an old acquaintance, Inspector Wells, a stoutly built man with a listening face and a knowing eye who promised he would ensure that the beat constables would look out for Bell. He, Inspector Wells, was about to leave the station on some business of his own, and he would listen and look for the wanted man.

'It's a beautiful case, I'm about, Mr Jones, and pretty well complete – only a little wanting to complete it which I intend to find out this very night.' He looked at Dickens with a smile. 'A lady in the case. A missing lady.' He placed a fat forefinger to his nose. 'But I shall look out for your man just the same.'

'I am much obliged,' said Sam, but Inspector Wells was gazing at Dickens as if he might be thinking of taking his portrait. Wells's forefinger tapped at his nose then at his mouth after which he smiled his knowing smile.

'A lady in the case, as I said. I know you, sir, that I do, but no name tonight, I daresay.' With another tap of his nose, Inspector Wells went off into the dark in search of his lost lady.

'A rum cove,' murmured Dickens.

'Known for it – deep, they say, very deep.'

'As a well. Though not so wide as a church door – stout enough, though,'

'And sharp. No name, forsooth, but a subtle reference to *David Copperfield*, I noticed.' Sam was laughing.

They walked over Vauxhall Bridge, and stood for a moment looking at the black water of the Thames. Dickens remembered the night they had stood on Waterloo Bridge when they were searching for Mrs Hart, a woman whose only son had been murdered. He had thought then of the dreadful silence down there under the swell.

'Has he crossed over, do you think?' he asked Sam.

'I think so. Those clothes … what was missing?'

Dickens thought. 'The clergyman's collar, the false beard – some sort of greatcoat, surely. The greatcoat that Mrs Ginger said he wore when he left for the theatre.'

'He had that lodging in Cloth Fair …'

'But he would not go back there – he must know we have found Clement. The newspaper report said an unidentified man, but he will know.'

'He could have taken another room in another lodging, in another disguise, in an abandoned house … by God, Clement Bell's house is shut up! Mrs Stark has gone and taken the maid with her. He could be there – let's get a cab. Bow Street first. I'll need some men.'

They left the police wagon in Powell Street and entered King Square on foot, where the Bell house was in darkness. Sam deployed Constables Dacre and Semple under the command of Inspector Grove to go round the back. Grove was armed. He was to wait in the garden in case Bell tried to escape. Sam and Constable Rogers, also armed, and two other constables took the front. Another two stayed on the opposite side of the road where Dickens waited in a cab just outside the portico of the church of St Barnabas. Sam did not want to take any chances.

Rogers tried the front door – it was locked. Sam went down the area steps. The kitchen door had been forced. They crept in. Rogers shone his bull's-eye lamp to show where the door was that led into the hall. The house was silent and cold. They went into the corridor. Looking left, they saw the back door of the house. He hoped Grove would have the wit to stay where he was.

They crept into the hall, standing at the bottom of the staircase where poor Mrs Bell had fallen. The parlour door was open, but there was no light. Sam signalled to Rogers that they would go upstairs. Then he motioned him to stop. He had a sense someone was there. He heard the faintest sound – as if someone had paused in mid-step. Someone was listening.

The noise was deafening. A sudden flash of light. The smell of cordite. Rogers falling. The back door bursting open. Footsteps running. A door slamming shut. Sam charging upstairs. Into Mrs Bell's room. Too dark to see. The next room. A rush of feet on the stairs. Inspector Grove going up another flight followed by Dacres.

Sam rushed after them. Too many rooms. And then the open window. The fire escape. Grove fired into the garden, but the figure darted behind a tree. Impossible to see. Semple was coming through the garden door – unarmed.

'Semple! Get back!' Sam shouted. Semple vanished into the trees.

The figure ran. Someone else was after him. Rogers without his pot hat. Another shot, and another as Bell returned the fire. They saw him dart through the garden door and slam it shut. They heard running feet down the alley. Rogers ran after him, stumbled, righted himself, struggled with the door and was out.

Sam charged back down the stairs. Dickens was there with a pot hat in his hand. Sam ran out into the garden, the others following. They heard another shot. Whose? Bell had a revolver – six bullets – three left, perhaps. Rogers had a police issue flintlock – two bullets. If he had fired that last shot then he was now unprotected. Another shot – the revolver, thought Sam.

'Dacre, stay with Mr Dickens!' Sam shouted. 'Get into the parlour.'

Outside in the alley, Sam directed Grove to the right. 'Take Semple. Shoot Bell if you have to.' They had three shots to Bell's two. That gave them a chance. Sam had not fired – two left. He turned left, keeping close to the back walls of the garden.

A figure came back into the alley. Sam raised his gun. Rogers. 'Vanished, sir.'

Another shot rang out. Sam and Rogers ran back. A voice high and urgent. Dickens shouting.

'At the front! He's out there!'

Sam and Rogers dashed back through the garden, into the hall to the front door. One of the constables was lying on the opposite pavement. The other stood gaping at the disappearing cab. They stood frozen, watching it turn into Powell Street, hearing the rush of the hooves on stone – a cabman held at gunpoint, driving too fast down towards York Road.

Sam turned back to look at the constable lying on the ground. His eyes were closed and there was blood on the pavement, a black pool in the light of his lamp.

28

HIGHGATE CEMETERY

'He's alive,' Sam said wearily in answer to Dickens's question, 'no thanks to me.' They were in the office at Bow Street. The morning was a sullen grey. Rain threatened, and they had the funeral to attend.

The constable had been taken in the police wagon to the nearest hospital – St Luke's on Old Street. The bullet had grazed the young man's shoulder. Sam had waited until the constable was cleaned up and bandaged. The doctor had assured him that the wound was superficial – the constable would live.

But he might not have. That was the refrain sounding through Sam's head. He had gone home, but had hardly slept, tossing in the bed, getting up to doze on the sofa, then dreaming fitfully – dreams in which a man on horseback rode at him. He could hear the thunder of hooves, wild whoops from invisible riders, and then he was in a dark house, and a woman was lying at the bottom of some stairs that led up to a stage. Charles Dickens stood looking at him, his face livid in the gas light, and he held a gun. In the dream, Sam opened his mouth to shout, but no sound came. A terrible noise. A flash. Then he woke.

'No, Sam. Bell is responsible. You told me that in Manchester when I—'

'I was angry, Charles, and anger clouded my judgement.

I took you – you of all people – to a house where we knew there might have been an armed man. I took Rogers in …'

'But you took all precautions. Grove was meant to stay outside. You told him. If he had obeyed your order, he could have shot him as he came down the fire escape.'

'I know, but he heard the shot and thought Bell was downstairs – he thought he was helping. And I was the commanding officer. Questions will be asked.'

'But I am here, and, like Sam Weller, as lively as a live trout in a lime basket. Your constable will recover. This is not like you, Sam.'

Sam smiled at him. 'No, it is not. It's time I pulled myself together.'

'Did you find anything at the house?'

'The cavalryman's uniform, and a pair of boots, and that coat.'

'The coat he wore when Mrs Ginger saw him last,' nodded Dickens.

'Pity he wasn't in it. Grove looked in what he thought was Clement Bell's bedroom. Someone had been in the wardrobe. I bet Austin Bell took some of Clement's clothes. That's what he went to the house for.'

'Ironic. Impersonating his brother, again. What about the cab?'

'It came back, or, at least, one of my constables met it in York Road – Bell was gone. The cabman wasn't injured, apart from his feelings, that is – Wot woz the perlice abaht lettin' willuns loose on a cabman wot woz jest doin' 'is job? Someone owed 'im two fares – dint serpose 'e'd get paid, neither.'

'Rig'larly done over and robbed of me stumpy.'

Sam grinned. 'Something like that. Toby Tickit, his name was.'

'Tickit! Suited him – little clockwork sort of fellow. And he'll come for his money, no doubt.'

'They generally do. Pity Bell didn't ask for a ride to his lodgings.'

'Yes, and what lodgings, I wonder? He must have found somewhere to hide out. Would he go back to that house by St Bartholomew's Church?'

'He'd know we would look there – I've already sent two men in plain clothes.'

'There's still the post office.'

'True.' Sam looked at his watch. 'Time we were going to Crown Street. I will be very glad when this funeral is over.'

Robert Brim had wanted the simplest possible funeral. It was in the nature of that quiet, unassuming man. He wished to be buried with his wife in Highgate Cemetery, and from the shop in Crown Street, a hearse and two mourning carriages – no plumes, no professional mourners – went up Tottenham Court Road, away from the city at a smart trot up Hampstead Road to Highgate Hill where the carriages slowed to a dignified pace. In the first mourning carriage were Dickens and Sam with Mark Lemon, Constable Rogers and Scrap. Sam had not wanted him to come, but the boy had insisted.

'Wot am I ter tell Miss Nell? Am I ter say I dint go ter see 'er pa, ter say goodbye for 'er? Me wot's known 'em all – longer than you, Mr Jones. I'm their best friend, I am.'

Sam had seen the tears in his eyes. He had got it wrong, he had thought, so wrong, and he had apologised, trying to explain that he had wanted to protect him. Scrap had been implacable: 'It's them wot needs protection, wot needs me ter tell 'em it woz awright. Dint go to me ma's funeral. Don't even know where she is. 'Tain't right. No one told

me. Dint think I knowed, but I did – knowed she woz dead.'
He rubbed his eyes with his knuckles.

Sam wondered, not for the first time, what had been
Scrap's life before. He rarely spoke of his pa – only once
before of his ma. Scrap had his own secrets, dreadful memories, and no one in whom to confide them. The boy was
looking at him, his expression stern.

Put in his place, he had gone into the bedroom and
brought out a black armband which he had offered to Scrap,
who took it with a smile. 'Ta. Knew yer'd see I woz right.'

In the second carriage were Matthew Tape and Ambrose
Tiplady, and Mr Brim's neighbour, Daniel Mills, who once
played the violin for Mr Brim at the shop.

The carriages turned in through the grand Tudor style
entrance flanked by the mortuary chapels, the Anglican on
one side and the Dissenting Chapel on the other. Dickens
thought of his sister Fanny who had died of the same
dreadful disease as Mr Brim, and who was buried in the
Dissenters' ground. He would go to see her grave after the
burial.

The carriages turned into the south-west path, away
from the Egyptian Monument, winding through the tree-
lined lanes to the quiet place where Mrs Brim was buried.
The grave was ready.

They stood under the grey sky while the clergyman read
the burial service. Dickens could see the cloud-crowned
city in the distance below. It was quiet here, peaceful.
Mr Brim would sleep well, and his children would come
some day when they were old enough to look at the
grave. He looked at Sam, who had stood at the grave of his
only daughter. He thought of Fanny again, and the little
crippled boy who had pined for his mother, and who was
buried with her. Scrap looked determined, like one who

had steeled himself to courage. And little Ambrose Tiplady, his face was so unusually solemn that he looked suddenly older. He remembered Kettle in Manchester, and how he had seen that boy's face overlaid for a moment with the face that would be his in later life. That's what life did, he thought. It wrote its sorrows on the youthful face. The battle of life. Well, they would have to hide their hearts, he and Sam, and turn back to the city where Austin Bell waited, and must be found.

While Sam spoke to Matthew Tape, Dickens walked to the Dissenters' ground. He stood, thinking about Fanny and their childhood, the times when he had walked from his lodgings to fetch her from the Royal Academy of Music in Tenterden Street so that they could spend Sunday in the Marshalsea Prison with the rest of the family. He had envied her education when he had none, but he had loved her. She had been a good wife and mother. *Loving and loved, her bright example shone* – the words of Douglas Jerrold's poem came back to him suddenly. *Thoughts on Visiting Highgate Cemetery.* Time to go.

He walked away past the quiet graves. Jerrold was right. It was a place of pleasant walks, and grassy slopes, and girt about with trees, but he was right, too, when he had written of it as *the shrine of blighted hopes.* Blighted hopes – that was what Austin Bell had done, destroyed the hope and promise of innocent lives. His deeds had created ripples across the still water of quiet, unremarkable lives so that the survivors could never be the same again: Oriel Greenwood's mother, Edwin Bell's wife, Mrs Stark, Dora Bell's father, old Mr Richardson, all their lives cruelly rent. Even Marion Ginger – gone to Penrith, Sam had said, to be a widow's companion. Memories stained with the blood spilled by a man who thought only of himself, of his own desires, who nursed his own anger and resentment until they filled him with a poison so corrosive that he must sweep away everything in his path.

Sam was waiting by the entrance. Dickens would go to Wellington Street to immerse himself in the work that would take his mind off the case. Rogers was to take Scrap to meet Mollie Spoon at the shop so that he could show her around. It would be good for him – he would relish the responsibility, and then he was to go back to Sam's house in Norfolk Street. And Sam? He would go back to Bow Street and deal with his paperwork. He had already put another man at the post office.

'I am going to the *Punch* dinner tonight at the Crown in Vinegar Yard. Harry Wills is coming with me straight from Wellington Street, and I'll take a cab home.' Dickens wanted to reassure Sam that he would not be taking any chances. The Superintendant had enough to worry about.

'Still,' said Sam, 'I'll make sure one of my men watches your house – I need to be sure after last night's business.'

29

SCRAP

Mollie Spoon was becoming anxious. It was growing dark. There were candles, no doubt, in the parlour at the back of the shop, but it would be too dark to see her way. She went to the door which led to the parlour and the stairs. She looked up and thought of the man who had died up there. Poor man. It was creepy being alone here – his ghost upstairs.

Where was that dratted boy? A few minutes, Scrap had said. It would only take a few minutes. That was nearly an hour ago. Wandered off, she supposed. Met some other lads. Boys was like that. Didn't she know it. Walter, her brother – 'e'd been in trouble a thousand times for not comin' home when 'e should. Pa 'ad leathered 'im often enough, but it 'adn't done no good.

She couldn't understand it. A man had come to the shop. Clergyman with a bushy beard. He'd asked for directions to St Paul's. Said he was a stranger, had got lost. Scrap had explained, but the man had said he was late for an appointment. Could the boy go part of the way with him? Perhaps he knew some shortcuts. Scrap had gone willingly, but he ought to be back now.

She went to the door and looked up and down the street, but no sign of either Alf or Scrap. Time was getting on. She heard the church clock strike six. She went back in to stand at the counter. What a thing it was. Alf an' her, shopkeepin' – well, she'd be doin' the shopkeepin'. Alf wouldn't give up the police. Not he. Not while Superintendent Jones lived and breathed. Alf's hero. Sergeant soon, 'e'd promised.

There was a noise at the door and it opened to reveal Alf Rogers with his bull's-eye lantern. 'What you doin' in the dark, Mollie?'

'Scrap left me ages ago – it was too dark ter find the candles.'

'Scrap left?' Rogers frowned. 'Where'd 'e go? It musta bin important.' He could not imagine what would take Scrap away from his duties. 'What 'appened?'

'A man came askin' the way ter St Paul's. Scrap went with 'im ter show 'im the way. Said e'd be a few minutes – that were an hour ago.'

'What man? What was 'e like?' Rogers asked, his voice urgent.

'Clergyman – big bushy beard.' Mollie saw Alf's face change.

The constable thought quickly. Get back to Bow Street, get the Superintendent. Get a couple of beat constables to look along the alleys which snaked beyond Crown Street. Think. Where would Bell take the lad? King Square? His old lodgings in Cloth Fair? 'E'd take a cab – 'e'd 'ave ter. Couldn't drag the boy on foot – but Bell would 'ave a gun. Why'd 'e take Scrap? Never mind. Start the search – do somethin'.

'Mollie, someone's got 'im – stay 'ere while I get a couple of constables. Then we'll 'ave ter go to Bow Street.'

He went out and Mollie heard feet running up the street. Rogers did not have to go far before finding two policemen.

'Lad missin' – ter do with the shootin's last night. Want you ter go to the cab stand on St Martin's Lane. Find out if any of 'em's seen a boy and a clergyman with a black bushy beard. I need ter know where they went. And I want you ter look in the alleys behind 'ere – ask if anyone's seen 'em. Both of you come to Bow Street in thirty minutes. No later. Mr Jones'll be waitin'.'

At the Superintendent's name, the constables nodded and left without a word.

Rogers returned to the shop. He and Mollie ran, pushing their way across St Martin's Lane, dashing into Castle Street, down Cross Street, traversing Long Acre then into Bow Street.

Six o'clock struck. Dickens blotted his paper. He was satisfied: he had finished his introduction to *Household Words*:

> *The road is not so rough that it need daunt our feet: the way is not so steep that we need stop for breath, and, looking faintly down, be stricken motionless. Go on, is all we hear, Go on! In a glow already, with the air from yonder height upon us, and the inspiriting voices joining in this acclamation, we echo back the cry, and go on cheerily.*

Harry Wills came in. 'Ready?'

'I'll just wash my hands and face. I'm all ink. I'll just be a few minutes.'

'By the way, this came. The boy found it in the hall. Must have come by hand. Odd, though.' He held out a letter. 'It's addressed to Sir John Vesey.'

'What! Let me see it.' Dickens almost snatched it from his sub-editor. He looked at the envelope, and saw that the name was indeed Sir John Vesey, the part he had played in *Money* in Manchester. He opened it carefully, though his hands shook. Wills looked at him as he read the letter and saw how his face paled.

'What is it Charles?'

'Someone is ill – a friend.' He must not give anything away. 'Listen, Harry, I will have to go, but I will meet you at the Crown later, when I can get away.' He thought for a moment. 'If anyone asks, say I am gone to church.'

'Church?' Wills was puzzled.

'Yes, tell them that. I must go.' He took his hat and coat from the stand and hurried away from Wellington Street. Wills, standing at the bow window, watched him hesitate and then turn towards The Strand. He felt anxious. Well, he would go to the *Punch* dinner at about six-thirty and hope Dickens would be back. But, still, it was odd.

Dickens had paused, looking up towards Bow Street – but no, the letter was clear on that. He held it fast in his hand. Get a cab to Smithfield, then walk. He went towards the cab stand. Perhaps one of the drivers would have a lamp. Read the letter. Make sure.

There was a waterman seated on a tub near the kerbstone with a brass plate and number suspended round his neck. Dickens recognised him – Bill Barker. Bill obliged him with a lantern, and Dickens read the words again:

Sir John,

I have a little scrap of something belonging to you – you might be interested in getting it back. I do not want to keep it, and it certainly don't want to stay here. It is entirely up to you. If you do not wish to recover this scrap then I shall dispose of it. If you should care to collect it, then I will wait for you in the burial ground of St Bartholomew the Great. Seven o'clock will suit me. I should, of course, prefer that you come alone. Mr Jones can be so rash with his firearms. I should not wish for any harm to come to your scrap.

Your obliging friend,

Alfred Evelyn

'Awright, Mr Dickens, sir? Not bad news I 'opes?' asked Bill.

'No, Bill, but I need a cab to take me to Smithfield. Hob about?' He thought about getting a message to Sam.

'Fraid not, sir.'

Dickens sighed, well, he had left a message of sorts. Gone to church. When he was missed, Wills or someone would go to Sam, but not for hours perhaps. He got into the cab and directed the driver to Smithfield. Would he harm Scrap? Perhaps not. He wants me. To kill me? What else? Dickens found that he could hardly contemplate it. Here he was in a perfectly ordinary cab going, perhaps, to his death. He felt ice cold. Should he have gone for Sam? But then what about Scrap? Bell would kill him if the police turned up. Scrap would not matter to him. He might let him go if he sees me. Then it will be just him and me, and I must fight for my life. A gun would have been useful. I have only my stick – and my tongue. Words. Would words do it? Reason in the face of madness?

The cab stopped on Ludgate Hill. He heard Bill's voice shout 'Go on! Go on!' and the cab moved forward. There was no turning back.

30

GRAVE PERIL

Superintendent Jones listened to the account of Scrap's disappearance, the clergyman with the bushy beard, and of Rogers' instructions to the two constables. He felt the anger flare, but he controlled it, curling his hands tightly round the cool wooden arms of his chair, then he stood up.

Rogers explained, 'I told Wright to come back within thirty minutes – after 'e'd questioned the cab drivers. 'E should be back soon.'

'You did well. In the meantime, we need to think. Bell said St Paul's?'

'Yes, I thought it meant that 'e was near 'is old haunts – not far from Cloth Fair.'

'Could be. I doubt he'd take Scrap to King Square – he'll know we will watch the place.' Sam thought for a moment. Where to take a lad? Somewhere quiet. He looked at Rogers. 'The crypt in St Bartholomew's Church! He's used it before. It's a place to start, but we have to get in without his knowing.'

'Two entrances we know of – the door from the lodging house, and through the church.'

'Yes. When you and Stemp searched, did you notice any other possible ways in?'

'There was a gratin' outside – rusty, easy ter shift. Might be able ter get in that way.'

'Mmm.' Sam was silent. Thinking. Rogers waited. 'But why take Scrap? Bell could have got away last night – he did get away. What's his game now?'

'Wants to lure us there, p'raps?'

Sam looked at him, and Rogers saw his eyes harden suddenly. 'Or someone else?'

Before Rogers could speak there was a knock on the door. Inspector Grove came in. 'A Mr Wills to see you, sir, about Mr Dickens. Says it's urgent.'

Harry Wills came in. He had been walking up Bow Street to Drury Lane, intending to go to the Crown in Vinegar Yard. But he had felt such unease about Dickens that on impulse he went into the police station – he would ask to see the Superintendent.

'What's the matter, Mr Wills?' asked Sam. 'What about Mr Dickens?'

Harry told them about the letter addressed to Sir John Vesey, about the church, and about him saying if anyone asked.

Wills looked at Sam's anxious facce. 'What is it?'

'Mr Dickens is in grave peril, and we must act now.'

Another knock at the door brought in Constable Wright who had discovered a cabman who had seen the clergyman with a boy getting into a cab, and, better, the cabman thought he had heard the clergyman direct the driver to Smithfield.

'Now, Wright, I want you to go down to the cab stand just by Wellington Street on The Strand. You're to ask about Mr Dickens – they'll know him. Ask did he get in a cab, and, if so, where to. You need to be quick. Come back here. If we're gone, then follow us to St Bartholomew's Church, Smithfield. Take a cab. There'll be a man in plain clothes at the entrance at Cloth Fair – Semple. Get your instructions from him. Do not come in unless he tells you. Now go.'

'Mr Wills, I've no time to lose. You may wait here at the station, or go, as you please, but I must ask you to wait in the Inspector's room. Rogers, show Mr Wills to Grove's office and bring the Inspector back with you. Send in any constables who are waiting to go off duty.'

'Mollie, you should go to my ma's,' said Rogers.

They had forgotten all about Mollie Spoon who had sat quietly, her eyes following the conversation. She made no protest. 'I'll go now.'

Sam was left alone for a few minutes. Now, strategy. Plain clothes men in the churchyard and in Cloth Fair. Two armed men in the church, and one in the narrow passage which led to the lodging house from the crypt. Their orders would be to shoot him. He would like to take him alive, see him hang. He felt no pity for Bell.

Rogers came back with the Inspector. The constables were waiting outside, some in their own clothes as they were going off duty. Inspector Grove had told them they were needed and they were ready.

'Rogers has told me about the crypt – I'll go down through the grating. I'm thin enough.' Grove wanted to make up for last night. Sam knew it.

'He'll be armed. The boy will be there, and Mr Dickens.' He imagined them trussed up with Bell pointing his gun, seated amongst the debris that they had seen when they had discovered Clement Bell's body. 'Take no chances. Shoot him as soon as you see him. Don't shout. Don't warn him. And don't miss.'

To the two constables in uniform he said, 'I want you to make enquiries about —' he remembered Mrs Timmins's missing daughter, Polly – 'a missing child – a girl named Polly. You'll sound convincing because it is true – the child is missing.' The constables nodded. 'Don't mention the boy, and do not mention Mr Dickens – we don't want a hue and cry. If you find out anything, you come back to Semple and he will tell me. Keep it quiet.'

He turned to the other men. 'And that goes for all of us. Stemp —' he looked at Stemp, tough as leather, face like stone, he wouldn't falter, 'I want you in that passageway which leads to the crypt, you remember it?' Stemp inclined his head. 'Shoot him if he comes out.'

He told the others where they should be. He and Rogers would be armed as well as Stemp. They would enter the crypt from the church. Sam wanted to see for himself, and if he came their way, neither would hesitate.

'Go now and go separately, apart from Kent and Woods in uniform. Semple, you take your position at the Cloth Fair entrance. No one comes in. You two in the churchyard, flush out any loungers – get rid of them. Again, no one comes in. That's it.'

Wright came back just as they were about to leave; he had spoken to the waterman who had lent his lamp to Mr Dickens.

'Name o' Bill Barker – said Mr Dickens was readin' a paper – a letter 'e thought, an' that 'e looked worried. Got a cab ter Smithfield.

Rogers looked at Sam. They were right. Bell had lured Dickens to the church – and Scrap was the bait.

31

STRANGE MEETING

The cab laboured up Old Bailey Street past Newgate, dark and forbidding, louring over the crowded streets like a black cliff. Gloomy depository of guilt and misery, he had written once. He thought so still, watching the people passing to and fro, unmindful of the throng of wretched creatures pent up within. He had thought once of the bound and helpless creature whose miserable career would terminate in a violent and shameful death. But Bell did not deserve compassion.

The cab trundled on into Giltspur Street and stopped by the hospital. Go on, go on, the refrain went in his head. He got out and paid the driver, giving him a substantial tip. Something to remember me by, he thought. The cabman who took Charles Dickens on his last journey. He'll make his fortune. At least my last deed will be a generous one – he almost laughed, but the sight of the little pointed archway stopped him. The thought of going through into that narrow passage which led to the burial ground was very nearly insupportable. Those old graves, the rank, unweeded grasses, the shadows, the dark – and that great black cat which had stared at them with its unblinking yellow eyes. What a creature of the night that was. He felt terror then and his heart seemed ready to leap from his breast. This will not do, he told himself. My heart must be made hard as stone, and I must be blade-sharp when I meet him. He went into the narrow passage.

Mary Lyons was waiting just inside the church. She could see the burial ground – horrible place. She was waiting for Perce – the American. She'd seen him earlier going down through the entrance into Cloth Fair. What was he doing back 'ere? She'd thought he'd gone forever – and he owed her five bob.

A few weeks back, he was living in the lodgings by the church. She'd no money to pay for her room. He'd let her stay in his with the baby – kind, really, but he'd wanted somethin'. She hadn't minded. He was a gent – clean, not filthy and stinking like some she'd had. And he wasn't a brute. Did it as if it was not important. Plenty like that, though. Said he'd give her five bob, but she'd never got it cos he'd gone.

Funny that. That was the day she'd seen the man in the corridor. Looked like Perce, he did. Said he was looking for Mr Smalpace. She'd pointed out the room and then gone out with the baby. When she came back Perce had upped and gone. Not a sign of him, and she with nothin'. She'd had to sleep in the crypt. Dry but cold – she'd taken the blanket from Perce's bed. He owed her that, and so did that bitch who collected the rent, and had thrown her out when she couldn't pay.

It had been all right, except Catherine, the baby, had cried, and she'd been bothered that someone would hear. And then she'd heard scrabblin'. Rats, she thought. She'd gone to look. And she'd seen it – the dead body. She'd taken Cathy, and she'd run. She didn't know if it was the man who'd asked for Perce – it might have been. And Perce had gone. And no five bob. And the baby's shoe lost, and that ribbon she'd loved so – chewed to bits – the only toy she had.

Plenty of people had known about the police comin', but no one seemed to know who the dead man was. She'd asked Matthew Duddy who worked in the fringe factory, but he said he didn't know. He'd found the body. Gave him a turn, he'd said. She told him she'd seen it, too, but she didn't mention Perce – only that she'd slept down there. Matthew said he thought he'd heard a child cry. That's why he went to look. Perhaps she should tell the police. No fear, she'd said. It was up to them to do the job they were paid for.

Matthew Duddy liked her, she could tell. He was lookin' after the baby for her. He seemed quite taken with Cathy. Didn't seem to mind that she wouldn't say who the father was. Not that she knew – could have been any one of Mrs Cutler's clients at Bell Lane, and Mrs Cutler had told her to get rid of the child. But Mary couldn't do it, and she was glad, though her old job was gone. She loved Cathy. But it was hard, scrapin' a livin' – she'd stolen things, too. And she'd earned a few bob the same way as she had with Perce. That's why she wasn't keen on the police. But when she'd seen Perce, she'd thought about that five bob. He could bloody well pay up.

Then she saw him. He had a lantern. Waitin' for someone, most like. Should she go across? She started, but then she hesitated. Someone else was walkin' across the burial ground. A man. Best wait and see.

The newcomer came across to where Perce was standing. She saw Perce raise the lamp so that the man's face was illuminated. She'd seen him before. Who was he? A gent, for sure. Then she remembered. He'd been with the policeman when they'd come to Bell Lane searchin' for Louisa Mapp – over a year ago that was, before Cathy. But she hadn't known his name. She didn't think he was a policeman, but what was he doing here? She couldn't hear what was being said. Perce lowered the lantern, and then she saw the glint of metal in his hand. Bloody hell, Perce had got a gun. And that other poor bugger had been shot. She froze. What the hell to do? Then she almost leapt in the air. Something had touched her. She looked down. That bleedin' cat.

When she looked again, she saw that the two men were going towards the Cloth Fair. She followed them, keeping her distance. She hoped Perce wouldn't look round. He had his arm on the smaller man's shoulders, keepin' him close. She saw them cross the road into an alleyway. They were swallowed up in the darkness. She hurried across the road and saw them disappearing round a corner into a narrow, dirty little court. She heard a door closing. She edged her way into the court. There was a huddle of old buildings, what looked like a warehouse of some kind, and next to it an old stable, perhaps. She looked up. A faint light showed briefly through a crack in the wood of the upper storey. There, perhaps.

What now? Should she try to find a policeman? She ought to. Couldn't have that man on her conscience. That other man in the crypt had been dead already. This was different. Maybe she could tell someone else, someone in a nearby house. She stepped back into the shadows. What to do?

Bell's arm had felt like a lead weight on his shoulder and he had felt the gun in his side, the side which always pained him when he was overworked or under stress. It pained him now. Bell took him into the tangle of alleys off Cloth Fair, and then into a tiny yard where there was a collection of old wooden buildings – stables? A warehouse? Bell opened a door into a tumbledown building. There was a brick floor, empty boxes, and a rickety wooden staircase leading up to what looked like a hayloft. Bell shoved him up the dilapidated stairs. All was quiet. His heart sank. No one would find them here. The place seemed deserted – no use shouting then. In the hayloft someone had made a makeshift home. Scrap was on some sort of bed, fashioned from packing cases, a gag over his mouth, a rope tying him to a roof support. He looked at Dickens, his eyes wide. Dickens scanned the place. No way out. There was a cracked skylight in the roof through which he could see one cold star.

'Pray, Sir John, do be seated. I am quite at your service.' Bell's eyes shone with malice and he pointed to a battered stool, sitting himself on an old chair at the other end of a rough-hewn table.

Dickens noted the words from the play. 'I thought I was at yours,' he observed, keeping his tone as even as possible, though he wondered that Bell could not hear his heart knocking at his ribs. He sat down.

'Droll, Mr Dickens, always droll as I remember, except when crossed. Temper then.' His voice was mocking. He leant back in his chair.

'You do not need the boy now. Let him go.'

'Straight to our Mr Jones, the famous Superintendent whose name is legend for he finds out his man, does he not? But not this time, eh? He'll miss the mark this time.'

'Perhaps.'

'The death of Mr Dickens. Dear, dear – what a scandal. The greatest writer of our age found shot to death, and the murderer escaped. A nation in mourning, and poor Mr Jones, *the fixed figure for the time of scorn to point his slow, unmoving finger at.*'

Othello, Dickens thought. Iago, more like, but he merely said, 'The boy, then.'

'I have not quite made up my mind. Timing is all – I must not have the Superintendent here too soon. But I admire your concern for the boy. Mr Dickens, defender of the poor – his final act to sacrifice himself for the sake of an urchin. Almost worth dying for the fulsome obituaries – a pity you will not be around to read them.'

Uncanny, Dickens thought, how that speech echoed his own thoughts when he had given the tip to the cabman. It was as if the man could see right through him. He had thought before that Bell had a power of seeing into the weakness of other men.

There was a bottle of wine on the table and two tumblers. 'What shall we drink to, Mr Dickens – your health?'

He was tempted to decline, but it would buy time. Bell might let Scrap go. 'Thank you.'

Bell poured and pushed a glass over to Dickens. The gun never wavered.

Dickens raised his glass and waited for Bell. Then he said, '*Our duties and the pledge.*'

'Oh, ho, Macbeth – how apt.'

'*There's blood upon thy face.*' He'll shoot me for that.

Bell smiled sardonically. '*What, will these hands ne'er be clean?*' Bell could match him quotation for quotation. Where would this lead, thought Dickens. Risk it.

'*Will all great Neptune's ocean wash this blood clean from thy hand?*'

Bell opened his left hand and stretched it out, the long white hand that Dickens had thought was the hand of a dead man. He looked at the hand. He spoke again, something changed now, something inexpressibly weary in his voice. '*No, this my hand will rather the multitudinous seas incarnadine, making the green one red.*'

He is a good actor, better than I realised, thought Dickens.

Bell continued. '*Tomorrow, and tomorrow, and tomorrow.*' Dickens sat still, the pulse of his heart echoing the beat of the line. 'The boy can go.'

Keeping the gun trained on Dickens, Bell used his other hand to untie the rope which tied Scrap to the bed. Dickens looked at Scrap. Just go, don't try anything, his eyes said.

'You can take the gag off yourself when you are outside. Now, take your chance.'

Scrap kept his eyes on Dickens as he went to the stairs. Dickens nodded.

'And tell Mr Jones that it will all be over when he gets here,' Bell said.

Scrap went and they heard his feet on the stairs. The door banged shut. Bell sat down again. The silence settled between them. Cloud blotted out the star. *Out, out, brief candle.*

32

SKYLIGHT

Scrap fled from the yard, tugging at the gag. He felt himself choking, but he managed to pull it down over his chin. In the alley he stopped. Which way? He couldn't remember. He thought he would go through the churchyard, across the market and through the lanes and alleys to Bow Street as he had done before when the body had been found. Gawd, which way? He couldn't afford to go wrong. If he could get to Mr Jones in time. *Which way?*

Mary Lyons saw the boy in the alley. He'd come from the yard. Perhaps she could send him to find a policeman. 'E'd want a penny. They always did. Matthew Duddy had given her a shilling in coppers. The boy might do it, and then she could just disappear. She went across to him.

'Can you find a policeman for me?'

The boy looked at her in astonishment. He must know what a policeman is, she thought impatiently. 'A policeman! Somethin's goin' on in the stable – in there. I want to stop it. Give you a penny.'

'The church – I gotter get ter the church. Which way?' stammered the boy. He looked terrified. Tears were starting in his eyes.

'I gotter get the perlice,' Mary said again.

Neither understanding the other, they ran to the entrance to the church in Cloth Fair, where Semple was waiting.

'Yer can't come through 'ere,' Semple said roughly as the boy tried to push past. 'Get out of it.'

Scrap recognised him. Perhaps Mr Jones was near. 'Mr Semple, it's me, Scrap. I gotter see Mr Jones. I knows where Mr Dickens is.'

Semple dragged him through the entrance, leaving the woman behind.

Sam and Rogers were at the entrance to the crypt when they heard Semple's voice shouting.

'What the hell?' They turned and went towards the church door which flew open.

Scrap flung himself at Sam. 'Mr Dickens – 'e's got 'im in a stable. The man said ter tell yer it 'ud all be over when you got there. 'E's got a gun.' Scrap burst into tears. 'It'll be too late.'

'Rogers, get the men,' ordered Sam. 'Where Scrap? Where?'

'A woman showed me the way. She's at the passage.'

'Semple, get her – now!'

When Sam and Scrap reached the passage, Semple was there with Mary Lyons. No time for questions. 'Take us.'

Sam stopped them at the entrance to the yard. Mary Lyons pointed out the stable. They saw the chink of light upstairs. Bell had freed Scrap, knowing he would fetch the police, knowing Scrap would come for him at Bow Street. Bell did not know that they were only round the corner. There was no one about. If a shot had been heard, people would have come from the nearby cottages in the alleys, surely. Assume they are there and Charles is alive. Careful, be careful. He ushered the others away into the lee of the wall.

'Only one way in?' Sam asked Scrap.

'Dint see, but the stable's big – might be a way into another alley.'

Sam sent two men to get into the warehouse abutting the stable. 'See if there's any way in at the back. Take off your boots. No noise. Not a word. Only use your lamp when you get in. If the door is locked, one of you come back for me.' On tiptoe they went, dissolving into the shadows.

He saw that there was a narrow gap between the stable and the wall. A man could get down there. He told another constable to remove his boots. There must be no sound to alert Bell.

'Anything else you can remember about the place, Scrap, anything?'

'Skylight in the roof.'

Sam looked up. The roof was quite low, only two storeys to the stable. The warehouse was higher. It might be possible to get onto the roof. Risky. If Bell heard, he might shoot. If they got in a back way, they would have to go up the stairs – risky, too. He needed to know more.

'Scrap, I need you to remember the layout of the room. Where is Mr Dickens? Picture it in your mind.'

Scrap closed his eyes. 'They're sittin' at a table. Mr Dickens 'as 'is back to the stairs. Bell is sittin' opposite.'

Damn, thought Sam. If they went in up the stairs Bell would see them. He could shoot Dickens, and even if they got the first shot, Dickens was in the way.

'Where is Bell in relation to the skylight?'

Scrap thought again. ''Bout two feet in front.'

It might be possible to jump him. The breaking glass would make him look up. Dickens might have a chance. Might.

The constable came back from the warehouse. The door had no lock. The place was abandoned. It had been built against a wall. No way out.

Rogers spoke up. 'I'll get on the roof, sir. I'm light enough. I'll take off me boots and coat. If I jump through the skylight, it'll take 'im by surprise. Give Mr Dickens a chance.' Rogers had thought it out, too.

Sam hesitated, looking at that earnest face. 'He'll shoot.'

''E might miss.' Rogers grinned. 'We gotter try, sir. An', beggin' your pardon sir, you're too heavy.'

'Grove —' Grove was a single man – no Mollie Spoon waiting for him.

'Still in the crypt, sir. Thin enough, yes, but 'e ain't 'ere. Gotter try. Anyways, we don't know that Bell's still sittin' at that table. 'E might be on 'is feet – I might get a shot at 'im.'

'Right. We'll do it.' Sam did not have time to deliberate.

They stood in the entrance. Sam dared not risk his lamp, but he could see the buildings, two shadow shapes in the dark. He measured the distance between the warehouse roof and the roof of the stable. Too big. If Rogers jumped he might land heavily and alert Bell. He looked at the gap between the wall and the side of the stable where the constable had squeezed in. The wall continued in their direction, turning at a right angle to where they were standing. He saw that the wall stopped suddenly down the alleyway – a corner. There must be another alley. Down there, Rogers could climb the wall, and from the top he would be able to crawl onto the stable roof. They could use their lamps down there, and give him a leg up.

The constable squeezed out from the gap and crept back to them.

'Anything?'

'No, sir. Gap in the wooden wall, but not big enough to get in without makin' a racket. All quiet up there.'

What was happening? They might be dead – but they might not. Sam saw that Rogers was taking off his coat and heavy boots. Time to act.

'Stemp, come with me and Rogers,' he whispered. 'We'll get him onto the wall. Burgess and Dean, go back and hide yourselves in the shadows by the warehouse. You two,' he indicated the other two constables, 'stay here. Guard this entrance. And all of you, no shooting if two men come out. If one comes, make sure it is not Mr Dickens. If Bell tries to escape, stop him.'

'What if he brings out Mr Dickens?' Burgess asked quietly.

Sam's voice was firm. 'Fire your gun in the air to warn the others. Watch where they go. The gunshot will bring us back. Then we follow.' He caught sight of Scrap then, and the woman. He'd almost forgotten them.

'Scrap, and Miss …?'

'Lyons.'

'Mary? From Mrs Cutler's?'

Mary nodded. She looked frightened.

'You two come with us – you can hide in the alley. Not a sound.'

Scrap, Mary, Stemp, Rogers and Sam made their way into the alley. Sam motioned Scrap and Mary to conceal themselves in a broken-down doorway. He went on with Stemp and Rogers until they came to the point where they could see the stable roof.

Hefty Stemp bent down to take Rogers on his shoulders. The constable grasped the top of the wall and then hauled one leg over the wall, then the second. Leaning forward, he tried to lie flat on the slope of the roof. It felt flimsy and he hoped to God that the whole lot wouldn't collapse. He looked down to see the Superintendent's face looking up at him, and jerked his head to say that Stemp should come up.

Stemp used Sam's bent back so that he could get beside Rogers on the wall. They waited, listening. Not a sound. Rogers leant forward and put his hands on the roof, his feet still on the wall. He heard Stemp shift along to take his place. He felt Stemp's hands on his feet. Stemp lifted them and pushed slightly. Rogers used his hands, one, then the other to move up the roof towards the skylight. He stopped, inched again, inched again, stopped, lay still, hardly breathing, inched again. Then his face was on the edge of the skylight. He raised his head enough to take a look. In that second he saw them – Bell and Mr Dickens seated at the table. Now, he had to move to the side so that he could stand and jump down through the glass. He lay still again, waiting. Then he crawled sideways, and was able to use the ridge of the roof to haul himself up.

The cloud shifted. The star was back. That one shining star. *I see the star* – he and Fanny used to say that when they were children, haunting the graveyard near their house in Chatham. Well, she was there now, and he would join her soon, perhaps. He felt strangely calm. Bell had put the gun down on the table. He hadn't spoken for what seemed like ages. He was looking at his hands.

'*Life's but a walking shadow, a poor player that struts and frets his hour upon the stage, and then is heard no more.* Poor players, we, eh? Signifying nothing. Don't you think?'

His voice was slurred now. The bottle of wine was nearly empty.

'I never thought so,' Dickens said.

'No, you wouldn't. Cheerful soul, ain't you.' Bell looked down at his hands again, as if he were seeing them for the first time.

Dickens's fingers itched to seize the gun, but he was not near enough.

Dickens looked up at the skylight. Something moved. Gone in a second. Someone on the roof? He picked up his glass. When Bell looked up, he was drinking. Bell drained his own glass. The flame in the oil lamp flickered. Bell picked up the gun. Dickens heard the click of the hammer being drawn back.

An explosion of glass. Dickens flung himself off the stool. As he fell, gunshot. A hideous bang. The smell of sulphur. He lay still.

'Mr Dickens?' Rogers shouted out in the dark, his voice hoarse and high.

Dickens hauled himself up. He could make out the shape of the policeman in the dark.

'Rogers?'

'Are you all right Mr Dickens?'

'Yes. The gunshot? Who?'

'Bell, sir. Must 'ave shot himself.'

A light shone down through the skylight. They looked up. Stemp with his bull's-eye lantern. Ghostlight.

Dickens looked at the figure sprawled in the chair. Bell had shot himself in the mouth. His face had gone, the face of the brother, the actor, the murderer. We can never know who he was. And this is where it all started, he thought, with me looking down at a dead man in a chair. He saw the white hand hanging, and the gun on the floor where it had fallen. And he recognised with surprise the patent leather shoes worn by Alfred Evelyn. Blood on them. Frederick Clarke. Austin Bell. Clement Bell. Alfred Evelyn.

And one man in his time plays many parts … Last scene of all That ends this strange eventful history …

It was over.

33

WEIGHED IN THE BALANCE

'Rogers, how can I thank you?' Dickens, Sam and Rogers were sitting in Sam's office at Bow Street. Rogers had his hands bandaged. The cuts from the flying glass were superficial, but they had bled all over his shirt cuffs and he had twisted his ankle when he had landed in the hayloft.

'Doin' my duty, Mr Dickens. Never 'ad much of a head for heights, mind.'

'You didn't tell me that!' Sam exclaimed.

'Didn't think about it till I stood up on that roof. Glad ter get down, I was.'

'What a way to do it, I thought a bomb had gone off,' said Dickens. 'But duty or not, Rogers, you risked your life for me and I thank you.'

'Would he have shot you, do you think?' asked Sam. 'There was only one bullet in that gun – just the one.'

'I don't think he had decided,' answered Dickens. 'There we were sitting in silence over a bottle of wine – like two old friends. I just sat still when I thought I saw a shadow on the skylight. Then he picked up the gun and the lamp went out.'

'I oughter go, sir,' said Rogers. 'Mollie is at my ma's. She'll be …'

'Worried, I know,' said Sam. 'What will you tell her?'

'Some, not all. Gotter think about the weddin'.'

'Good. You get off, then. You did well, Sergeant.'

Rogers beamed. 'Cor, sir, Sergeant. Thanks, sir.'

'Thank you. Goodnight.'

'Goodnight, Sergeant Rogers,' Dickens added. Rogers went. They heard him whistling as he closed the door.

'What happened in there?' Sam asked Dickens when they were alone.

'Nothing much. He drank. I didn't. He quoted Shakespeare. I quoted Shakespeare. Shakespeare saved me.'

'What?'

'I quoted Macbeth's words. I said there was blood upon his face – wished I hadn't for a minute, too provocative.'

'Banquo's murderer.'

'Precisely. But then he said the part about the multitudinous seas incarnadine, and something altered in him. He let Scrap go. I thought perhaps he would let me go, too, but I was never sure. But now I think he had come to the end of something. I do not think he had the strength left in him to kill me.'

Sam was silent for a while. There was something he wanted to know. He looked at Dickens, who gave him a half smile and spoke, as if reading his thoughts. 'I thought about getting hold of that gun and then I thought what I might do with it. I suppose I would have fired if he had come at me, but I didn't want to kill him. I suppose something in me pitied him – he knew what he'd done and that it was all for nothing.'

'I'm glad you didn't have to … it's not a thing … Did he tell you why?'

'It was as I imagined – near enough, anyway. Austin showed Edwin Bell the letter. Edwin told him it would not stand up in court; in any case old Mr Bell's will was made, and he was too old and ill to change it. Clement, he said, was lazy and complacent. Austin thought about the life he'd led, and Clement's easy one. Worse, Clement laughed – nothing they could do, even if Austin were their brother.'

'And Oriel Greenwood?'

Charles looked sombrely at him. '*I am in blood stepped in so far that, should I wade no more, returning were as tedious as go o'er.*'

'No going back.'

'Quite.'

'And Dora Bell?'

'An accident, that's all.'

'I suppose it could be true. We can never know now, but what a waste it all was. All those lives thrown away because he felt cheated.' Too many had died, Sam thought, for nothing. He felt a kind of sick emptiness – murder did that. But Dickens was alive and looking at him anxiously.

'We did the best we could, did we not – we stopped him.' Dickens saw the tiredness in Sam's eyes.

'We did, Charles. Now it's time we went home.'

Someone was knocking at the door urgently. Sam raised his eyes. What now?

A uniformed constable came in, one of the two Sam had sent on enquiries in Cloth Fair. 'News for you, sir. Thought yer'd like ter know, sir, we found that kiddie.'

'Kiddie?'

'Polly Timmins, sir, the one as was missin'.'

'Good God! Where?'

'Comin' back from Smithfield, we went through them alleys back o' Cursitor Street and there she was. Just standin', cryin' 'er eyes out. Gawd knows where she'd bin. Asked 'er name – she said "Polly Timmins". Lost, she said. Wanted 'er mammy. That was a facer, sir. I remembered she lived in Parker Street so I took 'er.'

'You did right, Woods. You and Inspector Bax can question her tomorrow. I'd like to know what happened.'

'Right, sir, thank you, sir.' Woods went out.

Sam smiled at Dickens. 'Providence? That I should think of that child. The idea was that they should ask around Cloth Fair without mentioning you or Scrap. I thought someone might give us information unwittingly.'

'There's providence in it all.'

'I should like to think so.'

Dickens grinned. 'O'course there is. What'd become of the undertakers without it?'

Sam laughed.

They went out into the night. The carriageway and pavement of the station were crowded with the tattered sweepings of the night being brought in: the screeching harlots in their draggled satins and limp feathers, like a collection of shabby hens; the drunkards yelling and singing wild songs of revolution; a ragged urchin kicking out at his captor; a great hulk of a man with burning eyes and a broken nose stood a head taller than the rest, flanked by two constables who had him in handcuffs – he looked as though he might burst out of them at any minute. A one-eared dog looked up at the man. Then a constable kicked it away, and it fled, howling away down the street. The man looked after it, and then was led, unresisting, into the station.

Thieves, vagabonds, rogues, bruisers and bludgers, pimps and palmers, cutpurses and coiners, kidsmen, dragsmen, magsmen – all the vices of London and their representatives, heaving and cursing, sweating and stinking, alive and kicking.

And one little girl, safe at home. That was something, thought Sam. He smiled.

'Penny for 'em?' asked Dickens.

'Polly Timmins and that lot – weighed in an even balance?'

'Rogers and Mollie Spoon, Feak and his mother,' Dickens offered.

'Inspector Hardacre, Constable Peter Kettle …'

'Mrs Sweet and her good girl, Amy, Mrs Entwistle …'

'Stemp, Semple, Woods …'

'There you are then.'

34

AFTERWARDS

At St Giles's Church the sun had shone and Mollie Spoon, polished to a veritable glitter, had married Alfred Rogers, who'd limped up the aisle. He was all right and in fact it'd done 'em a favour: Sergeant, time off, three days in Ramsgate, an' Mr Dickens had bought 'em all champagne for the party, an' 'e'd given them a cheque. They'd 'ave to put it in the bank – fancy, a bank account!

And now here they were on the pier in Ramsgate under a sparkling sun, the sea dancing to its own tune, and the promenade full of people: nursemaids, old ladies in invalid carriages, young ladies giggling at young men with red faces, parties coming from the steamboat. Mollie loved it all. Rogers just loved her. He looked out at the glittering sea and gave his bride a squeeze.

On the quiet beach at Reculver on the Kent coast, the waves came in little curls, creeping up the sand, retreating, curling again, and the two children danced in and out. Their stockings were wet and the girl's pinafore was soaked. But it didn't matter. The little dog darted in and out, yapping at the water which would not stay still. Sam heard their delighted cries from where he stood with Scrap. Scrap was looking at the sea. Where did it go – and where did it come from?

'Big enough ain't it?' he observed after a few minutes of silent contemplation.

Sam saw Elizabeth coming towards him, a few tendrils of hair flying, walking with long, eager strides. She looked like a girl. Scrap ran to her, and then scrambled down the dunes to the beach where Poll saw him first and barked and barked.

Elizabeth and Sam went down, too. Eleanor smiled and ran to him. Later, when the children were in bed, he told Elizabeth all.

'And Charles?'

'Inimitable, of course.'

Along the coast at Brighton, where he had gone to write his next instalment of *David Copperfield*, Dickens had taken his usual lodgings at 148 King's Road, and now he was walking at his usual swift pace on the Downs. He walked and walked, feeling the fresh wind blowing away the London darkness. Out of darkness into the marvellous light, the air like glass. Somewhere, unseen, a lark was singing. He sat on the springing turf. The sun warmed his face as he looked out towards the hazy blue of the distant sea, that old image of eternity he loved so much.

Catherine was resting with Georgina to look after her. The new baby would arrive in August. A girl, he hoped. Too many boys clattering up and down staircases, each one seeming to be wearing out a hundred and fifty pairs of double-soled boots. Dora, he thought. That's what we'll call her – after Dora in *David Copperfield*.

He thought of Dora Bell and her unborn child. Accident, Austin Bell had said. Perhaps, but he had caused it, just as he had brought about the other deaths. And nearly his own. For whom had Bell intended that one bullet? No use thinking about that. Listen to that lark pouring out her melody.

In the quiet evening, Dickens sat at his desk where the blue slips waited and the goose quill was poised. He wrote the last words of his chapter. He wrote about David Copperfield watching the moon, or the stars, or the falling rain, or hearing the wind, and thinking of Mr Peggotty roaming the wide world in search of Little Em'ly, his solitary figure toiling on. He put down his pen, turned out the lamp. The moon silvered the room, making phantoms of the desk, his coat on the back of the door, the white scarf moving in the faint draught from the open window. Ghostlight.

HISTORICAL NOTE

The first edition of the periodical *Household Words* came out on Saturday, 30 March 1850. It was in this magazine that Dickens wrote his articles on the London Police, including the anecdote *On Duty with Inspector Field*. The character of Superintendent Sam Jones of Bow Street is fictional, though his character does owe something to Inspector Field, particularly his authority over the criminals he and Dickens encounter. There is no evidence that Dickens was ever involved in a murder case, but he was interested in crime, and went out with the police.

Dickens met Mrs Elizabeth Gaskell (1810–1865), author of *Mary Barton*, in May 1849 and he asked her to contribute to *Household Words*, to which she submitted the story *Lizzie Leigh*. Mrs Gaskell wrote to Dickens in January 1850 about a young girl imprisoned for theft in Salford's New Bailey Prison. Mrs Gaskell wanted to help her on her release, and Dickens promptly gave his assistance. The girl emigrated to the Cape in March 1850. Dickens offered to visit Mrs Gaskell in Manchester to discuss her contribution to *Household Words*. He did not go, but I have imagined his visit to her.

Geraldine Jewsbury (1812–1880) also wrote for *Household Words*. Her first contribution was a story entitled *The Young*

Jew of Tunis which appeared in April 1850. I have imagined Dickens's encounter with this novelist whose work is now largely forgotten.

Dickens did act in Manchester with his company of friends, including Mark Lemon, John Leech and Dudley Costello, in 1845 and 1848, but not in 1850. Dickens acted in Bulwer-Lytton's play *Not So Bad as We Seem* in 1851. He admired Bulwer-Lytton's play, *Money*, but did not take a production to Manchester.

Dickens's sister, Fanny Burnett, lived in Manchester and he visited her there. She died of consumption in 1848 and is buried in Highgate Cemetery. Dickens wrote to John Forster about her death: '*She showed me how thin and worn she was; spoke about an invention she had heard of that she would like to have tried, for the deformed child's back.*'

The little crippled boy, Fanny's son, on whom Dickens drew for Tiny Tim and Paul Dombey, died just four months after his mother, two weeks after Dickens's sixth son, Henry Fielding Dickens, was born on 15 January 1849. The fragile baby, Dora, died on 14 April 1850.

In July 1844, Dickens, his wife, four children and assorted servants set off for a prolonged stay in Italy. Dickens visited all the major cities and sights, putting his experiences together in a volume of essays entitled *Pictures from Italy* (1846). One of the most vivid excursions was his ascent of Vesuvius in which he was accompanied by his wife, Catherine, and her sister Georgina, who were carried part of the way in litters. Near the summit the party stopped, but Dickens was determined to see inside the crater. He went on up to the very edge with two others so that he could look into 'the Hell of boiling fire below.' They came down rolling in the ashes, their faces blackened, everywhere singed and their clothes 'half-alight.' The descent from the mountain afterwards was just as hazardous and one guide was killed.

In January 1842, Dickens and his wife Catherine visited America for the first time. They went to Boston, New York, Philadelphia, Washington, Baltimore, Cincinnati, St Louis, and Niagara Falls, travelling by train, ferry, canal boat, steamboat and stagecoach. It was on the *Pike* steamboat, taking them from Cincinnati to Louisville, that Dickens met Pitchlynn, a chief of the Choctaw tribe. They spoke of the poetry of Sir Walter Scott and politics and the future of the tribes. Dickens was rather disappointed not to see Pitchlynn in his native dress, at which remark Pitchlynn 'threw up his right arm for a moment, as though he were brandishing some heavy weapon.' Dickens recorded his 'long black hair' and 'very bright, keen, dark and piercing eyes', and he kept the lithographic portrait that Pitchlynn sent him. *American Notes* (1842) is the volume which records Dickens's first American visit.

ABOUT THE AUTHOR

J.C. Briggs taught English for many years in Hong Kong and Lancashire. Now retired, she lives in Cumbria.

ALSO IN THE CHARLES DICKENS & SUPERINTENDENT JONES SERIES

The Murder of Patience Brooke
Death at Hungerford Stairs

Also from The History Press

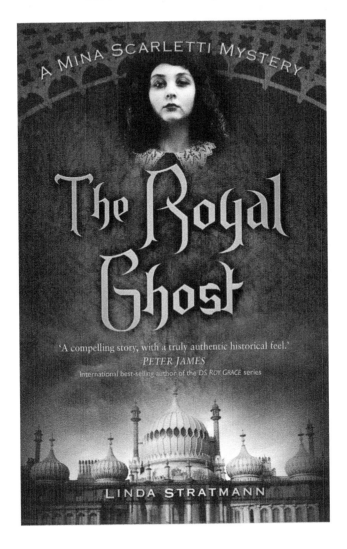

A MINA SCARLETTI MYSTERY

The Royal Ghost

'A compelling story, with a truly authentic historical feel.'
PETER JAMES
International best-selling author of the *DS ROY GRACE* series

LINDA STRATMANN

Lightning Source UK Ltd.
Milton Keynes UK
UKOW05f1104100916

282668UK00002B/5/P

9 780750 969802